MASK

OF THE

DEER

WOMAN

MASK
OF THE
DEER
WOMAN

✴

Laurie L. Dove

BERKLEY

NEW YORK

BERKLEY
An imprint of Penguin Random House LLC
penguinrandomhouse.com

Book design by Nancy Resnick
Title page illustration by gomolach/Shutterstock.com

Library of Congress Cataloging-in-Publication Data
Names: Dove, Laurie L., author.
Title: Mask of the Deer Woman / Laurie L. Dove.
Description: New York : Berkley, 2025.
Identifiers: LCCN 2024016556 (print) | LCCN 2024016557 (ebook) |
ISBN 9780593816103 (hardcover) | ISBN 9780593816127 (ebook)
Subjects: LCGFT: Thrillers (Fiction) | Detective and mystery fiction. | Novels.
Classification: LCC PS3604.O93646 M37 2025 (print) | LCC PS3604.O93646 (ebook) |
DDC 813/.6--dc23/eng/20240415
LC record available at https://lccn.loc.gov/2024016556
LC ebook record available at https://lccn.loc.gov/2024016557

Printed in the United States of America
1st Printing

MASK
OF THE
DEER
WOMAN

PROLOGUE

MONDAY

The beetles could help her disappear, but not in the same way the others had disappeared. She would do it for a better life.

This was why, even though someone had trashed her van, even though her cell phone was now one big, useless glitch and even though her mother was probably sick with worry, Chenoa Cloud had hiked for days to reach this ravine in the dark.

If the beetles were nocturnal, so was she.

The November wind whirred into the chasm and up the sleeves of her jacket like a threat, carrying with it loamy soil laced with the scent of decay. Chenoa tried to clear her head, to think instead of the waist-high switchgrass that had been gentle company as she walked across Oklahoma's eroded plains, but the memories of missing friends were too intrusive. The moment her mind went quiet, or she felt hopeful, or—and this was especially annoying—she was alone in the dark, they were there with her, the ones who left and never came back, or who couldn't come back.

How many girls had she known who'd never been heard from again? Rez girls gone. Families that searched. Or didn't. Fleeting news coverage, the missing girls' faces flashing on glowing screens before vanishing once more.

A shiver crawled across Chenoa's scalp as she took careful steps through the lonely cut that ran along the edge of the reservation. *Forget the switchgrass. Think of the beetles.* She trailed her hand along the ragged sandstone wall on one side of the narrow path and knew she must be close. The smell of death, that harbinger of an American burying beetle colony, grew stronger. Maybe she would come upon them feeding on a carcass right in front of her. Or maybe they would be tucked into a cave, an expanse suddenly opening under her fingertips in the dark.

The image of a black and red beetle on a screen at the front of a lecture hall flashed in her mind. Any graduate student who could find and document an endangered species, or better yet, a species long feared extinct, would be awarded grant money and a Smithsonian job at the end of the rainbow. It was the moment that had changed the trajectory of her future.

That was when she'd realized she had a secret, hard and smooth as a seed, its electric shock singing through her body. In an instant she knew why the American burying beetle looked so familiar, and she knew exactly how to win.

She was going home.

Every weekend since, Chenoa had driven her Volkswagen from campus to the rez—a risky endeavor in the unreliable van— to conduct a search that had started to feel pointless. Until she found a single crumbling carapace in this, the last place on Saliquaw land where she knew to look. The crimson markings on the dried-out shell were enough to drive her onward. No matter the weather, no matter the hell she'd catch from her mother, no matter what she was afraid to find.

Chenoa stumbled to the floor of the ravine, the sound of gnarled branches overhead, her visibility doused by the inky night. A pungent odor filled her nose, her mouth, like fetid fermenting fruit, and something fleshier, rotten, underneath. Here was the source of the smell at last: a raccoon, its ribs picked clean, its tail still thick with fur.

Chenoa moved carefully, using her headlamp to illuminate the decay from every angle, and found her future: a pair of American burying beetles in a clash of antennae and pincers, the victor to gain a mate. To gain it all. A place where it could survive, even on this land that made people fight for all they had.

A thrill began to work its way up from her belly. It spread through her chest and into her throat, which she exposed, grateful, to the hidden moon. She'd found them. They were her ticket to a different life.

The American burying beetle would be a triumph for the reservation, thanks to the recent passage of a Recovering America's Wildlife Act that would dedicate annually nearly 100 million dollars in federal funds directly to tribal nations for on-the-ground conservation projects. Or it would spell disaster, bring the reservation's development plans to a screeching halt with punitive fines for habitat damage. Either way, nothing would stop her from proving the beetle's existence. It was her way out.

"Rez life isn't for everyone," Chenoa whispered over the battling beetles.

The night sounds closed in.

Chenoa began to recite their names. The girls, gone. Kimberley. Tayen. Loxie. Aileen. She needed to tame her thoughts, put memories into a manageable order, ignore the warning that pulsed inside her like an organ.

Chenoa stood and tried to scan the night, but her headlamp made her blind to anything outside its range of light.

If she heard the sound, it registered only as a feeling. The snap of an instinct breaking open inside.

There was someone else. Out here in the ravine. Where only she should be.

Where she should be alone.

"Hey, hey, it's okay."

A man, hands outstretched in front of him, fingers wide.

"Sorry. Didn't mean to spook you. I just . . ."

He was close now, talking fast, and Chenoa was standing, rooted. Her mind was trying to make sense of it, of someone out here, with her. In the dark.

Then he lunged.

CHAPTER ONE

✳

FIVE DAYS EARLIER

Carrie Starr stepped out of the Ford Bronco held up by mismatched tires that she'd just cajoled into lumbering across the Saliquaw Nation. It was her official service vehicle, and apparently the one perk afforded her by the Bureau of Indian Affairs, because the cinder-block building that served as her office sure didn't qualify.

It was Wednesday, her third day as tribal marshal, the result of a new federal statute meant to stem the tide of missing Indigenous women, and already she had the junkyard truck and an office that doubled as a storeroom. There were no deputies or dispatch, no crime-scene techs or ballistics experts—none of the human capital she'd had access to in Chicago. There was a working landline, which was a bit of a surprise, but it rang to a heavy seventies-era handset that reassured her that low expectations could always sink a bit more. The one call she'd gotten on the avocado green throwback had been from a woman screaming down the line. At first she'd thought it was a prank but had decided not to take any chances and kept the receiver to her ear instead of slamming it down.

The woman eventually began to make sense, and from what Starr had been able to gather, was demanding an audience with the new tribal marshal.

So here she was. Day three. Standing in front of a rickety mobile home on a dusty reservation where she didn't belong, working a job she didn't really want, sure she wasn't ready to face a fuming mother convinced her daughter was missing.

A wary brown dog trotted by like it was late for an appointment, sidestepping three men wearing different versions of the same flannel jacket and stoking a fire in a fifty-gallon drum. Behind them was a gray mobile home almost identical to the one she was about to approach. Rectangles of warped plywood staked to long handles listed against the faded siding. The messages were more of the same she'd already seen fastened to buildings, fences and telephone poles around the reservation.

NO PIPELINE was a popular one, but there were a few DON'T FRACK THE FUTURE signs, and even an outlier that made one side of her mouth lift a little: HIDE YO KIDS HIDE YO WIFE THEY FRACKIN EVRYBDY.

The men watched her read the signs. The fire smelled good, made her think of better things. She was just about to dip back into the driver's side of the Bronco and take a pull from the bottle under the seat when a door slapped open behind her.

"Odeina Cloud," the woman announced, sandwiched behind a sagging screen door. "You Carrie Starr? I called about my girl, my daughter, Chenoa."

Starr cringed. The only thing worse than being on the reservation where her father had been raised was being called by her first name. He'd been looking through the bottom of a bottle when he'd plucked Carrie's name from history, but it had been the wrong kind. Named her after Carrie Nation, a white woman who preached in an Oklahoma church and filled her wagon with bricks so she could smash saloon windows for selling the devil's drink. He'd made sure Starr carried a stranger's history instead of knowing her own. She made sure no one called her Carrie anymore.

"Marshal." Starr tapped the badge on her chest. "Marshal Starr," she said, turning to look at the men behind her.

"Well, isn't that fancy?" said the woman in the doorway. She looked Starr over. "You're a tall one. Just gonna stand there?"

Odeina Cloud had glasses perched on the bridge of her nose, and even from a distance Starr could see that her long hair had once been the color of coal but was now shot through with silver that framed her round face. She looked more like a middle school principal than anything, even though she was wearing a mustard yellow waitress uniform with wide orange lapels and matching apron.

Starr wondered whether the woman would be able to smell the alcohol on her breath, and reached into a side pocket of her uniform pants, which were the same unfortunate brown as her jacket and shirt, to retrieve a mint. *No sense getting detention today,* she thought, and shook her head. She hadn't come this far only to tell the same stupid jokes.

Starr shifted her weight, feeling the pinch of her new BIA-issued boots, as a blustery wind kicked up the trailer's loose skirting, creating an open maw that felt like an omen. The thought of being inside this tin can created a trail of goose bumps under her sleeves.

There was something about the rez, even with its expansive spaces, that made her feel claustrophobic. The unease had set in almost immediately, from her first patrol over acres of dust and prairie grass.

Quinn would have laughed at her reluctance, at how she planted her feet on a square of red dirt between the busted-up Bronco and the woman beckoning her into the trailer. Her daughter had been a force of nature, not afraid of anything.

Stop it, Starr thought. *This is not the time.*

"Good grief," Odeina said, "you need me to hold your hand and lead you over here?"

Starr heard laughter erupt from the men feeding the drum fire and glanced back at the Bronco. She could picture the whiskey stowed under the torn upholstery of the driver's seat but willed herself to walk away from it. *Incentivize yourself,* she thought. *It will be here when you're done.*

Starr's boots kicked up puffs of dust that the wind whisked away. They made a hollow sound on a trio of metal steps that ascended to the trailer door. The afternoon light filtered through a cover of low clouds that turned it flat and cagey; in the trailer's dim interior it was nearly impossible to make out any details. The woman had already retreated from the doorway to somewhere inside and was talking too fast, her sentences running together like a stream Starr wasn't ready to dip a toe into—much less leap.

Starr's right hand settled on her sidearm as she let her eyes adjust, taking in the open stretch of kitchen and living room. There were slim hallways at each end, which she presumed led to bedrooms. She liked to know where she was and what kind of space she was dealing with before she turned her attention to anything else. She'd been in too many off-kilter situations with agitated people not to get the lay of the land.

Odeina, still talking, closed the door behind her. Starr caught bits and pieces of Odeina's diatribe, but her mind was a sieve.

Something about college and a van, but now there was a cell phone that rang and rang. "Rang and rang," Odeina said again. Starr's head felt thick and her mouth dry. She needed water. Or something stronger.

Starr was an inch above six feet, and the boots made her six two. She towered over Odeina, who for some inexplicable reason had started whispering through clenched teeth.

"Okay, first of all, let's get this straight. And I'll say it real slow for you. My. Daughter. Is. Missing." She took a deep breath. "I have already talked to the sheriff's office, but according to his deputy, the rez is out of their jurisdiction. So I called the police department over in Dexter Springs. Same runaround. Then I hear from my neighbor over there"—she motioned toward the trailer across the road—"that we have some kind of new . . ." She searched the ceiling for a word.

"Tribal marshal?"

Odeina snapped her fingers and pointed at Starr. "Yes. Tribal marshal. You, apparently. Some kind of BIA nonsense, but good grief, I hope it helps. And it's about time, since our daughters are . . ." She pulled a name tag from her shirt pocket and fastened it over her heart. "Okay, here's the thing. You're not here to learn about anyone else but my daughter. So listen."

A buzzing started in Starr's head, far away and getting closer. She looked at Odeina in her uniform with the carrot-colored apron. She took in the orderly kitchen. The entire place was deliberate. Spare. The only thing that stood out was a large flatscreen taking up one wall of the living room, which explained the satellite dish on the roof. Opposite the television was a drab couch under a display of carefully spaced artwork. Some kind of Indigenous thing, she guessed. In the far corner, near the TV, was a rocking chair covered in blankets.

"You been doing some cleaning?" Starr said. It wouldn't be the first time a frantic caller was the person she liked for a crime.

Odeina tossed her head back, exasperated, her hair splaying behind her, eyes shut tight.

"Chenoa goes out sometimes, like every kid her age. I get that. What I am trying to get across to you people is that there are certain things she would not miss." Odeina exhaled slowly, speaking so quietly Starr had to lean in to hear her. "For one, Chenoa said she was going to be here for her grandmother's birthday last weekend. She would not miss it, no matter what. But here it is, Wednesday. No Chenoa. She also wouldn't be gone for days without telling me where she was. And she would not ignore my calls. Not for days ignore them."

Starr was taking in the words at last, but there was something off about this scene. She could feel it. Some threat that hadn't yet materialized.

A few days was nothing out here. *It took twenty-four hours just to figure out where you were on the rez*, she thought, glancing out a dust-pocked window to the open horizon. *Or why.*

From the corner of her eye, Starr caught movement.

"Who else is here?" Starr asked, and scanned the living room. She quietly unsnapped the holster on her belt and curled her fingers around the grip of her sidearm. She could drop someone if she had to, but *fuck*, not her first week on the job. The rez was supposed to be a place to do penance, to limp along until she could get her career shored up, get her shit together. She couldn't afford to repeat what happened in Chicago.

The blankets on the rocking chair in the corner of the living room shifted, and Starr reflexively pulled her weapon.

Odeina screamed.

Starr ignored Odeina and trained her gun on the blankets, but

Odeina wouldn't stop making noise. She turned the barrel toward Odeina instead, then oscillated between her and the blankets, unsure which target held the biggest threat.

"Are you crazy?" Odeina yelled. She motioned with both hands to the blankets, which had now gone quite still.

"Move," Starr said. "Over there."

Starr signaled a direction with her gun and Odeina sidestepped closer to the blankets, her hands still raised. *Consolidate the targets,* Starr thought.

Odeina gestured at the mass of coverings, as if to show that she would remove them from the chair.

Starr nodded affirmatively.

Odeina tugged a velvety-looking blanket, then a downy comforter, a crocheted coverlet and finally a heavy bearskin. Only the chair's occupant remained.

CHAPTER TWO

✦

Starr realized she was looking at a very old woman and lowered her weapon. There wasn't a threat. Not now, never had been.

Until this moment, she hadn't really thought she was a danger to anyone other than herself. Well, and that one guy she gunned down in Chicago. And probably her daughter.

Shut up, she told herself. The room went still. The only sound was a gale that swept over the prairie, persistently trying to buffet the trailer onto its side. She could feel the sway as if she were on a dinghy in Lake Michigan, right off Lake Shore Drive, cold spray stinging her face and icicles forming on her hair. It had been shorter then; she couldn't remember the last time she'd had a haircut. There were a lot of things she'd stopped doing after she was suspended.

"What is wrong with you? This is Lucy Cloud, my mother-in-law. Didn't you wonder why I was whispering? She was sleeping."

The fury in Odeina's voice brought Starr back to the present like an ice bath. There hadn't been a buzzing in her head after all; it had just been Odeina speaking low.

"Grandmother," Starr said. It was one of the few things she knew about this place from her father, that this was the respectful way to address a tribal elder. Even though he had never returned to his extended family, her father had carried that reverence with him the rest of his life.

Starr tried to slow her breathing. She hid the trembling of her hands by returning her sidearm to its holster and hooking each thumb into a side of her service belt. *Fucking adrenaline,* Starr thought.

"Right," she said, all business. "Anybody else in here?"

"I saw this already," interrupted the old woman, who began to make a terrible sound, pulling air into her lungs and then wheezing it out like leaky bellows. Starr realized it was laughter.

"Yes, yes. I'm sure you did." Odeina's eyes rolled toward the water-stained ceiling, but she cooed soothingly as she heaved the bearskin back onto the old woman's lap and tucked in the fallen blankets, returning her to her cocoon.

Helplessness made Starr uncomfortable, so she half turned to the living room's opposite wall, where she pretended to study the arrangement. She'd seen it as a mass of folksy art when she'd first scanned the living room, but now realized the display was composed of individual masks. Carved, mostly out of wood, she supposed. Maybe they were what had set her off—creepy enough—but there was something different about them now.

After she finished settling her mother-in-law, Odeina marched past Starr and into the kitchen, where she pulled a snapshot from under a magnet on the refrigerator.

"Here's a picture of my girl," Odeina said, "not that the tribal council is doing anything. Not that you're doing anything either. I'd go tell them you're an idiot, but knowing them, it wouldn't matter a bit."

Odeina drew in a deep breath, held it, let it out slowly.

Starr's senses were coming back to her, and she could smell the contents of a large pot on the stovetop, steam escaping from the lid. When was the last time she'd eaten?

"I took this picture at her college graduation, right before she started classes for a master's degree." Odeina looked at the photograph. "Her hair is different now."

Starr walked toward the battered kitchen table as Odeina slid into one of the chairs around it, still holding the picture. Starr said nothing; she figured the least she could do was zip it long enough for Odeina to spill her guts, and in return maybe Odeina wouldn't report to the tribal council that Starr had pulled a gun on her. Starr lowered herself into a chair opposite Odeina but wished for a shot of whiskey or to light the joint she'd tucked into her shirt pocket. It was all too much. These women, this place. Girls who went missing.

"I thought she had gone back to the university for the weekend or that she was staying with friends, that maybe she'd forgotten about her grandmother's birthday. There could have been some explanation," Odeina said. "But this morning one of her professors, called himself her research adviser, rang to find out why she missed class and then a meeting with him. Had my number as her emergency contact. I don't know, I tell him, but I do know she's not here. So where is she these last"—she stuck up her fingers one at a time for effect—"one, two, three, four . . . now five days?"

Starr already knew what Odeina had yelled into the phone earlier. It was as if Chenoa had vanished into the night. Packed a few things into her van, prayed it would start and waved goodbye when it did. *Find her,* Odeina had said, over and over. *Find her.*

"That's unusual, for her to be gone that long? She's never done anything like that before?"

Odeina glared at her.

"She has a phone?"

"Been calling it," Odeina said. "At first it rang and rang, wouldn't stop ringing. Called it just before you got here, and it went straight to voice mail, like the battery's dead."

Starr didn't blame Chenoa for not answering the call. She could imagine Chenoa seeing her mother's number pop up and hitting DECLINE. It was a good sign that it rang at all. She'd probably had car trouble. Or stayed with a friend—maybe a boyfriend, maybe a girlfriend—longer than she'd meant to. Maybe she'd left the area entirely, not gone back to school. Kids dropped out of college all the time.

Starr figured that on the outside chance some harm had actually come to Chenoa, the phone would have lost its charge by now. Or maybe Chenoa was just hiding out at a friend's house. Starr had been warned that this happened on the rez, young adults roving from place to place. Or gathering in packs at abandoned homes, turning up on their own days later.

It was part of what made tracing the disappearances of Indigenous women so difficult; it could be days, even weeks, before they were truly missed. Then a quandary: where to report them missing? Until Starr's arrival, there hadn't been a tribal police presence for years. As tribal numbers had dwindled on this reservation, the lack of on-site law enforcement created a gap that local agencies couldn't fill, and they were quick to blame alcohol or drugs, runaways, sometimes prostitution. Even when a missing woman from the rez had last been seen in the county, the sheriff's office simply countered that the reservation was not their jurisdiction and did nothing at all. Sounded like that was exactly what Odeina had heard from them.

Starr didn't plan to waste her time looking for Chenoa either. She had her marching orders, which were to sift through dusty boxes of BIA cold-case files that had been sealed since who knew when. She guessed Odeina just didn't want to admit the truth: Chenoa had taken off, and at twenty-two she had every right to do so—without telling anyone where she was going or how long she'd be gone.

An ad for a truck-driving school blared from the big TV in the living room, which Odeina had just turned on to keep the grandmother entertained. The old woman, tucked under a mountain of blankets and fur, stared off into space instead. She was surprisingly unruffled, Starr thought, considering she'd recently stared down the barrel of a loaded gun.

Why don't I drive a semi? Starr watched the commercial, a manic announcer pointing to a number that flashed across the screen. *Be my own boss, make decent money. Nobody screaming at me.* Starr made a mental note to look up driving schools when she got home. Search for any other profession, actually.

She'd taken this job on the rez because it was the only offer she'd gotten, and that was only because she had Indigenous blood running through her veins. It was the one time something her father passed down to her had become useful.

"I don't want to upset her," Odeina said, returning to the kitchen. She and Starr watched in silence as the old woman pulled her bony hands from under the blankets and patted one with the other as if, after a lifetime of keeping them busy, they refused to rest. "The county sheriff was useless," Odeina said. "He told me that because Chenoa vanished from the rez, he couldn't set foot here without permission from the tribal council. So I went down to Byrd's house—he's chief of the tribal council—and he refused. Flat out refused. I could have strangled him." She looked up at Starr. "I've been searching for her myself, but if I miss one more shift at the Trading Post I'm toast. I've asked everyone I can think of, and none of us know where she is."

Odeina's voice wavered. She slapped the glossy snapshot down on the table in front of Starr. Even with the TV blaring, it made a sharp sound that ricocheted off the thin walls.

"Who else do I tell? You?" Odeina said. "What are you going to do? You don't even know the rez or know where to look, and now you're sitting there, saying nothing, looking like you don't even believe me. What good are you? Do you even know how many of our young women have disappeared over the years?"

Starr knew she should be paying attention. She could hear the fear swelling in Odeina's voice, knew fear made people unpredictable, but she couldn't take her eyes off the masks. She had learned to ignore the way reality had begun to shift sometimes, but still she could see something burning, alive, behind the ocher finish of a wooden face. The frozen curve of its mouth was turned up like a kept secret. Had it been that way before?

Atop the mask—*no, not a mask anymore*, she thought, *real*—the tines of velvet antlers began to sprout and grow. She felt the room tilt. Not in the way a thick blunt swirled her thoughts, but in a disorienting two-step that waved her mind one back, two forward, one back, two forward. A sickly bile climbed her throat. For one wild moment Starr believed she would vomit violently on her standard-issue boots. Her instinct was to get up, to run for the door, but her feet wouldn't move, were fused to the thin linoleum that separated living from dining. *Or living from dying.*

The idea was suddenly in her head, pushing itself into every nook, filling empty spaces, dulling other sounds.

Starr looked at the picture on the table between them. Chenoa wearing a graduation cap and gown, smiling out at her. Chenoa holding a college diploma in front of her heart, behind her a tree heavy with white blossoms.

"There is something you have to understand," Odeina said. "When Chenoa started coming back on weekends, it was for a reason. To finish her research project. She wouldn't say much about it, except that it was some kind of bug she wanted to find. I only know that much because she asked if I'd ever seen one"— she pointed her chin toward the old woman—"and especially if she had. All Chen did was drive her van into the wilderness area and go on these long walks. Then she'd hole up in her room to write everything down. A few weeks ago, she started staying out longer and longer."

Starr raised an eyebrow, not sure she understood. Or cared.

"I am telling you, when she came home she wouldn't stop talking about what she was looking for. She was obsessed with those bugs or beetles or whatever, and all she wanted was to talk about her research, wouldn't let me get a word in edgewise, asked me if anyone else had ever seen these particular bugs. She wouldn't admit it—she didn't talk much about what she was going to do after graduation—but I had the feeling she was . . ." Odeina turned her head and looked out the tiny window above the kitchen's shallow steel sink for several seconds. "It was like maybe she'd figured out her future, like she found some answers out there." She shook her head. "I don't know. The only thing I know for sure is that she is not here and she did not run off."

"Or maybe she did," Starr said. "Got in with a bad crowd. Maybe drugs."

Odeina's shoulders stiffened.

"Possibilities," Starr said, and shrugged. "Look. She's an adult. She came home for the weekend after living on her own. It's an adjustment. I get that. Maybe she forgets about the meeting with her adviser. Maybe she misses a day or two of class. Hell, maybe she's here after all, with somebody you just don't know. Or maybe she needed a change of scenery. Happens all the time. She's twenty-two, so she has the right to go missing if she wants to."

For a second Starr thought Odeina was going to leap over the table and attack her, but the woman kept her balled-up fists to herself, clenching and unclenching them on the table like she was furiously waiting for a meal. Starr could sense the old woman eavesdropping on their conversation, and glanced toward her, but the old woman remained motionless.

"Chenoa is missing," Odeina said. "Do something about it."

CHAPTER THREE

✳

Miles away, Horace-Wayne Holder stood on the edge of reservation land and surveyed the scrabbly open space before him. He pulled the brim of his cowboy hat down as the wind picked up. Water was low, and there would be a hard winter before spring rains.

Holder was on private ground that bordered a good stretch of the rez. Land now owned by a one-member LLC set up by an anonymous trust Holder had formed to keep his own name off the deed. Land he had purchased quietly from a ranching family whose next generation had moved away for life in some faraway city. Holder had, in fact, been buying up land that spanned the eighteen miles between Dexter Springs and the rez for some time, making sure to scoop up the mineral rights along with it. This was yet another acreage he'd secured along the Kansas-Oklahoma border, not for its surface potential—it was dotted with scrub cedar and pitted with hollows—but for what lay underneath.

If he narrowed his eyes, Holder could practically see the drilling sites, the man camps—what Blackstream Oil called the instant housing for fieldworkers—and the tank farms the company
would need. As long as Blackstream could reach an agreement
with the tribal council, Holder would get a life-changing payout.
Not only from the city of Dexter Springs, for the right to build
curb-and-gutter access roads through his land to the oil field in
the reservation's wilderness area; Holder also expected a payout
directly from Blackstream in the future, when it inevitably ran
the rez dry and set its sights on his land. Sure, everyone in Dexter
Springs who kept tabs on city business thought the curb-and-
gutter roads were overkill, but why not roll out the red carpet for
a company that was going to make them all rich?

Holder smiled.

Of all the obstacles he had met and overcome to get to this
point, trouble with a college girl on the rez was not one he had
anticipated. He'd suffered through so many lukewarm mugs of
tea in stale kitchens while he patted the hands of widows or old
farmers considering what to do with their family land. Juggling
financing. And refinancing. Running a shell game to make the
numbers work. Convincing oil company scouts to at least get
permission to drill test wells. Impassioned plans shared behind
the mayor's closed office door. Carefully orchestrated meetings
with a reservation official who understood dollar signs.

And now it all came down to this one hitch in his giddyup.

Holder lifted the brim of his Stetson and scratched at his forehead with a thumb.

His stop at Rita's Roast in Dexter Springs that morning had
paid off once again. The old men at their permanent roost under
the WILL TRADE GOSSIP FOR COFFEE sign spent their mornings

talking about weather, politics and, when the place started to clear out, everybody's business. What they didn't know, they guessed. They spun stories based off ties that ran deep and memories that ran long. There'd been an Indian woman in there, they told him, looking for her daughter, who was doing some environmental do-gooder nonsense on the rez. The next time the woman came in, Holder was there to ask her questions: Might even be an endangered species out there? Now, wouldn't that be something?

He hitched up his Wranglers by his belt, HOLDER tooled into the leather, and reached through the open window of the truck for his binoculars. He thought of the road access—not just a dirt track, but one of those million-dollar-a-mile projects—that would create a path to a future he'd once thought impossible. It was going to happen on the very spot where he stood, and soon transport trucks would be ferrying oil out of the reservation's wasteland. That's how he thought of it, wasteland, not worth the effort it took to walk across it, unless the mineral rights were considered.

Somehow, even after the oil boom of the 1980s, when Oklahoma's most prosperous decade of both the twentieth and twenty-first centuries was recorded in numbers—wells drilled, crude pumped—this rich cache had been overlooked. While banks burgeoned and oil companies built towering gold-windowed office buildings in which men in sport coats and polished cowboy boots measured time on Rolex watches, and success in savings and loan assets, the real fortune was yet to be had. It had been right under their feet all along, a lurking marvel hidden on reservation land.

In the eighties it had been impossible to pump oil through ledges of substrate, and it hadn't even seemed necessary, with the richness of the oil fields the riggers had easily tapped into. But by 1989 Oklahoma's fortunes had changed. The state's per capita income fell to eighty percent of the national average, oil rigs were sold for scrap, the few banks that didn't fail went through a painful recapitalization, and business and personal bankruptcies reached new heights.

Now fracking made it not only possible but extremely feasible to reclaim stubborn crude and lift a man's circumstances right out of the ashes. Holder was a phoenix, and he'd come to claim what was owed.

As he looked out at the rangy space before him, which he knew abutted the reservation's wilderness area, he felt something miraculous. A curious joy was taking hold behind the silver of his belt buckle and wrapping around his middle like the worn leather of his belt. It rose effervescent like poured champagne—of which he'd only once had a taste, in Oklahoma City, over a final transfer of deeds—then bubbled up through his chest and into his throat, where it burst forth with a force that surprised him. Holder wasn't accustomed to laughing. It was as if he'd discovered a copper mine in the Congo: nothing but profit, assuming you could reach a deal with the natives.

The victory, although he shared it with Antell—Blackstream Oil's man on the ground—and the mayor, who wanted her own piece of the pie, felt like his alone. It would be a reward for the years he'd spent with his grandparents, who had bet and lost the family farm, only to take up life in a Dexter Springs brick duplex with a view of a vacant lot through a meager kitchen window. It was a half life in a half home. His grandmother could stand for hours, spinning a sponge over a sudsy plate. Was she looking at the open horizon and remembering what she'd lost? Or considering his father, who, no longer tied to the land, had left for the city? His mother had been gone already.

Holder's adolescence was measured in loss: a father scattered, a mother flown, a grandmother curled so far inward she vibrated with anger. A grandfather, freed from hours in the field, working a coffee cup with gossipy old men at the gas station. That was where Holder first heard rumors of an untapped fortune. He spent hours poring over geological records like treasure maps, tracing the oil-filled strata of Paleozoic islands once covered by deep Cambrian ocean. Spent hours in sticky bars to catch geographical rumors from ancient oil-field workers who were now other things: welders, factory men, broken.

Holder had, in some ways, a lot more than when he'd started. He'd learned to make a living. But here lay before him a fortune, the kind that would put his finances in a venerated orbit for generations. Things he'd wanted once—a wife, children, a meager life on his own assemblage of farmland—were no match for this feeling. And he was so close to the finish line.

He lifted the binoculars. This remote edge of the reservation was inhabited primarily by partying teenagers on summer nights and by the occasional lone pickup with its windows fogged. He was taking his shot, and to borrow a phrase from his high school basketball days, he knew it would be nothing but net.

But there *was* a hitch, wasn't there? Something that shouldn't have been a problem at all but over the past few days had become yet one more thing to eliminate.

Horace-Wayne Holder narrowed his eyes and studied the topography through the binoculars. Nothing—no one—would stand in his way, not when he was so close. He glassed the distance, making adjustments until he could clearly see a ridge above a line of trees crowding a dry creek.

The only thing that stood between Holder and his finish line was now hiking across a patchy stretch of land bordering the reservation's wilderness area.

So, there she was, the final obstacle. Now he just needed to figure out how to make her go away.

CHAPTER FOUR

✴

Starr knew she'd have to go through the motions, look like she was doing all the right things, gathering all the necessary information. Problem was, the BIA sent her to the rez to figure out some answers for all the girls and women who were actually missing. The faster she cleared a few cold cases, the faster she could get out of here. She needed a drink.

Odeina led Starr through the living room, past the old woman and down a short hallway to the doorway of Chenoa's small, square room, the walls an eggshell color that shifted with the sun. There was a twin bed, a dresser, a closet with mirrored sliding doors. One of the mirrors had a crack that ran diagonally from top to bottom, forming peaks and valleys like a ridgeline.

"I'll just take a look around," Starr said. "Anything gone? Something that might have been important to your daughter?" She'd never been the studious type, but decided to hazard a guess. "Books, laptop, anything?"

Starr noted clothes slung over the bed frame, as if waiting for Chenoa to wear them. A stack of unpacked boxes towered against one wall, labeled in loopy cursive marker: textbooks, kitchen stuff, summer clothes.

"Everything's still here, far as I can tell," Odeina said.

A three-ring binder lay open on the bed, a serious contrast against the pink and green gingham of the coverlet. Starr could see that it contained a stack of reports. She drew a pen from her shirt pocket, careful not to disturb the joint she was saving for the ride back to the office, and flipped a few pages. Some charts. Printouts of news stories.

Beside the binder there were photographs, taken from several angles, of a black bug with four fiery red patches on its back. Starr turned to the desk and skimmed a cut-out newspaper article that detailed a new agreement between the US Fish and Wildlife Service and the Oklahoma Department of Transportation requiring developers to purchase credits to offset disruptions to protected habitats. In the margin Starr could see a handwritten note, presumably made by Chenoa: *Manitou*. Was that a person? A place? Hell, for all she knew, it was the name of a beetle.

The research materials stood out against the room's remnants of childhood: a music box on the dresser, movie posters of alabaster-skinned vampires taped to the walls. A tiny circle of wildflowers braided together that was disintegrating next to a collection of interesting rocks on a shelf. A handful of science fair ribbons awarded by a local school. Starr sifted through sketches that had drifted across Chenoa's desk, taking in the delicate muzzle of a paint pony, a likeness of the old woman, a rez dog sleeping half in and half out of shadows. Tacked to a corkboard was an invitation, faded construction paper strung with tissue-paper ghosts over a crooked scrawl: *Hey Boo-tiful! It would be spectertacular if you would go to HOCO with me.*

Chenoa's interests had outgrown the room, but it didn't look like she'd made big changes since coming back every weekend. *Temporary digs,* Starr thought, picking up a framed photograph of a younger Chenoa and a couple of friends, their arms around one another's shoulders, each of them wearing a necklace of cobalt, white and coral beads. The girls knew nothing of what lay before them, the large and small heartbreaks they'd face in the years ahead.

Starr placed the picture frame face down on the dresser. So many youthful possibilities in their smiles. Too much hope, so much life. She thought of Quinn and quelled a rising panic that threatened to set her adrift. The question that had been riding her all week popped again into her mind: How was she supposed to save these girls when she hadn't even been able to save her own?

Starr searched dresser drawers, the back of the closet, between the thin mattress and the box spring, and felt her way under every stationary surface.

No drug stash, no hidden bottles. No laptop. No diary filled with entries about lovers or escape plans.

The only clue was the girl's research, serious and reflective, laid out on the bed as if it were a detective's desk. *I'll probably have to treat this like a missing person case just so this lady leaves me alone,* thought Starr. If Chenoa was missing, like Odeina believed, Starr knew the crucial forty-eight-hour clock had already run out; leads had dried up; evidence had been wiped away by weather.

"Is there a place called Manitou on here?" Starr said, leaning toward Chenoa's bed and pointing at the kind of map you can still find at travel centers.

Odeina nodded, opened the map and smoothed the stiff paper across part of the bed that wasn't taken up with the three-ring binder. She followed trails with her finger until Starr understood the most direct route to Manitou, a series of naturally occurring caves at the far edge of the reservation's vast wilderness area. Odeina gave Starr the names of the other girls in the framed photograph she had found, listed a few other friends the girl might have visited, suggested other areas on the reservation to search and showed Starr the parts she'd already covered.

Talk about pissing into the wind, Starr thought. Even with the recent push to investigate a rash of disappearances on tribal land, the BIA had only budgeted for two marshals to patrol a nearly fifty-eight-thousand-acre reservation—most of it wilderness— when there should have been twenty, maybe more. Starr was tasked with hiring a deputy marshal, but there'd been no time yet to look at the résumés that had come in.

Starr was the entirety of the tribe's law enforcement.

She tried to refold the map as she thought about what to say to the girl's mother. She had to strike the right balance. Not too concerned, but not negligent either. By the time Starr had walked from Chenoa's room and down the short hallway carrying a backpack of her research, she'd wrangled the map and decided her next move. One deftly handled wrap-up was all she needed. She could feel the old woman watching her, and she nodded an acknowledgment, eager to be out the door.

"Deer Woman," said the elder, pointing to a carved wooden mask on the wall. Starr eyed its oblong ears and long face slit horizontally by sharp carved teeth. How had she not seen those teeth earlier? "She can shift from one world to another, from a woman to a deer. Alert and cautious, delicate and deadly, she tramples people to death. Vengeance."

Starr walked closer to the mask, and turned to face it so neither Odeina nor Lucy Cloud could see her expression. She knew Deer Woman all right. It was one of the strange names her father spoke in the dark as if he watched home movies through the bottom of a whiskey bottle.

"Deer Woman is a protector known to many tribes," said the old woman. She looked out the window for a long moment. "Not so many years ago I knew a young man who was hunting alone in our woods. It was bitterly cold and he was discouraged, not having seen any game. All at once he came upon a clearing, and before him stood a beautiful woman in traditional dress. Farther still was a cabin, warmly lit from inside, the smoke of a fire billowing from the chimney. The cabin looked inviting in the cold dawn, and the woman motioned to him. *Come to the cabin with me,* she seemed to say. Her eyes, he later told me, were the most beautiful eyes he'd ever seen, and when she looked at him it was as though they pierced right through him, clear to his spirit, to the secret part of him he shared with no one. He started to follow her. Until he remembered a warning from his grandmother: *Never go with Deer Woman. She will take your spirit.* Could this be Deer Woman? he wondered. He began to walk away, but he could not resist turning back for one last look. When he did, there was no cabin and no woman. Just a deer standing in the wood."

Bullshit, Starr thought. Fairy tales. They were no more real to her now than they had been as a child, but a shiver still ran up her arms.

"You see, don't you? Deer Woman can judge a man by not only his actions but his secret thoughts. If he would have been lured to her, she would have killed him. Trampled him with her hooves. Gored him with her antlers." The old woman wheezed with laughter. "Deer Woman is a solution or a trap. Whether she takes a life depends on the man. He respected his grandmother, so he survived."

Starr turned toward the door, toward a way out.

Odeina rushed to Starr and held out the commencement photograph. "Take this picture of Chenoa. Memorize it. Find her."

Starr watched as the old woman withdrew her hands from under the mound of coverings and, like the thin talons of a prey bird, ran them through her hair to the top of her head until they were, fingers outstretched, like antlers.

It was as wild a thing as Starr had ever seen. Not in the way wilderness is untamed—sentient or not, moving toward survival—but a wildness all the same.

The truth of this filled the space as clearly as the scent of venison simmering in a stew pot not three feet away. Surrounded to the east by prairie and to the west by ravines choked with trees, the reservation resisted progress.

Why wouldn't Chenoa want to get away? she thought. Maybe permanently. It was what Starr wanted to do, and she'd only just arrived.

"Chenoa's not going to hurt herself, not her," said the old woman, as if she could read Starr's thoughts. "Not run off either. But you? What are you going to do?" Her rheumy eyes took Starr in. "Only one of us wants life, and that's the girl."

Starr took the photograph, corners bent and curling, from Odeina's outstretched hand. She meant to give it a cursory glance to satisfy Odeina; instead, it drew her in. The white cap and gown were a contrast to Chenoa's sun-kissed skin, but her smile made her face come alive. Starr studied Chenoa's features and noticed two eyeteeth curving into her bottom lip. The effect was both endearing and disturbing.

"She's the one missing," said the old woman, "but they're all twice gone. Once in real life and once in the news." The caw of her laughter filled the trailer until it reverberated. Then, as quickly as she'd become animated, her face went stone still.

Starr's eyes settled on Odeina, who held her elbows in her hands as if doing so was the only thing standing between her and assaulting a marshal. Then, as the old woman started flapping her arms, Odeina turned away from Starr.

"She gets confused sometimes," Odeina said. She went to the old woman and made soft noises as she settled her arms back under the blankets. Like a starling tucking in its reticulated wings, thought Starr.

"Chenoa?" the old woman said suddenly, looking around. "Chenoa?" Her gaze roosted on Odeina's face, who shook her head no. It was something the old woman seemed to understand in an instant, her head slumping forward, heavy on her thin neck.

"We're all one moment away. One." Lucy Cloud held up a thin crooked finger and directed it at Starr. "You would trample someone who came after your child."

"Yeah, well . . ." Starr said, tapping Chenoa's graduation photo against the palm of her hand. "I'd better go."

The women's faces turned toward her, and the sharp angle of their necks made Starr take an involuntary step backward toward the door.

"I'll borrow this and see what I can do," she said, holding up the picture. The light outside the mobile home's cramped windows had the peculiar glow of late afternoon. Starr had been there much longer than she'd realized.

Odeina clamped her lips together. "She would not just leave us. She would not."

Starr slipped over one arm the backpack she'd borrowed from the girl's room. She could feel the weight of Chenoa's notebooks and papers and hoped Odeina would feel like Starr was taking some sort of action. The old woman raised her voice in Starr's direction.

"Deer Woman walks between worlds. She has caught your scent," she said. "The blood of our people runs through your veins, and it is not something that can be hidden the way you hide it from yourself, Carrie Starr. You will see."

Starr nodded to the women, and stepped through the open door and down the steps, eager for firm ground. She felt a disorientation that she could compare only to the constant shifting of waves.

One look at the old Bronco, still where she'd parked it on the dirt track that ran between the mobile homes, and her senses righted themselves. "Damn it," she cursed under her breath. The Bronco wore a fresh stain of red spray paint, still dripping down the exterior of the driver's-side door. *Colonizer* was crudely graffitied over the vehicle's faded MARSHAL decal. Starr walked to the passenger side and found fresh paint there too.

The message was clear: No one wanted her here. Except the BIA, which had appointed her with little direction and even less oversight. But the tribal members, the tribal council, no one— except maybe Odeina—thought they needed her help.

Starr looked down the road one way, then the other, searching for any kind of movement. She saw no one. Not the men she'd seen earlier by the signs protesting fracking. Not even a rez dog. There was only a fire slowly burning itself out in a fifty-gallon drum in the cold, dry Oklahoma twilight.

So much for a warm welcome.

CHAPTER FIVE

✳

Starr leaned against the open doorway that separated the marshal's office from the community center in the same cinderblock longhouse. It was nearly six p.m., and she was ready to call it a day.

Two volunteers were setting up an optimistic number of chairs in the community-center half of the building, leaving a wide central aisle that stretched toward a white plastic table at the front of the room where she presumed tribal council members would sit.

Another volunteer handed her a flyer outlining the distribution of commodities, and Starr studied the pictures of rectangular orange cheese and tins of Spam as the room began to fill. There were bursts of noise from outside—loose mufflers, the slam of car doors—that entered with the people who came in from the parking lot.

It was about two weeks before Thanksgiving, and Starr gathered from snatches of conversation that it had been a dry fall, with people who planted crops or worked cattle looking skyward, worried about the weather and wondering when it would rain. Already Starr had seen the intense black smoke of a pasture fire while volunteer firefighters struggled to get the blaze under control.

Tonight wasn't Chicago cold, but Starr felt the temperature drop as the sun went down. People kept their coats on inside, waiting for the heat of bodies and opinions to burn the chill from the air. Starr hooked the fingers of one hand on the lip of the doorframe overhead.

She kept turning to check the old jail cell, which long ago had been baked into one corner of her office. A thin, question-mark-shaped man had wandered in about twenty minutes ago and passed out on the cot, muttering about old times, so she'd shrugged and gently slid the cell door closed. He probably wouldn't stir for hours, but she kept turning to check anyway. Habit, she told herself, but knew it was something else entirely, a reflex born of suspicion, honed on Chicago streets. There was something in the air.

"This meeting of the tribal council is called to order," said Chief Elmore Byrd, a man with thick shoulders and a big belly, who was seated at the center of the council table. There were two people on each side of him, also seated. The room was still filling with attendees, and Starr marveled at the size of the crowd. Until this moment she'd seen only a handful of people on the rez, and would not have expected such a turnout. Over the noise, council members answered *here* to their names in the roll call. Byrd flipped his long, loose hair over one shoulder and looked around the room before he spoke.

"Good to see so many of you here. We don't usually have such attendance. Except Bob's wife, who is our most regular—and usually our only—audience member." The crowd laughed and beside Byrd a scarecrow-like man wearing a long-sleeved Western shirt, who Starr figured must be Bob, turned crimson. "I hope you'll all come back when we discuss something that's not this exciting, like putting sand on the roads," Byrd continued.

"Junior volunteers," someone yelled from the back of the room, and the crowd erupted in laughter. People craned their necks to spot Junior Echo, a big man who wore his hair the old way, in two thin braids down his back.

"Get to the pipeline," Junior said, but kept his eyes to the floor. He hulked over the sides of a folding chair, which Starr admired for its tenacity. Her eyebrows rose when she noticed a six-pack near his boots. He looked remarkably like a bear as he used one big paw to feel for a bottle. He lifted it to his lap and twisted the top, then tipped it to his lips.

Whatever gets you through, she thought.

"At this time, I will open the first order of new business," Byrd said. "Item one, pipeline access."

A hush fell over the room.

"What has been proposed to us, and what we believe is in the tribe's best interest, is a partnership with Blackstream Oil. They have offered a ten percent share of profit from any oil pulled from our reserve, and an annual fee to us in exchange for the right to construct the necessary infrastructure, including pipelines . . . and for working in partnership with the city of Dexter Springs to build a road system that will allow full access to the site. This could be a changing moment for us, a way to benefit our tribal members of all ages in ways we've been unable to before."

A swell of small noises was audible throughout the room, a tide Starr couldn't be sure was favorable. Byrd continued. "As an added way to pay their respect to our land, and to us who inhabit it, Blackstream Oil has agreed to build a health clinic on the reserve and pay a stipend to our tribal government so that we may hire staff for it. Full-time."

Chaos shot through the community center, everyone talking at once. A few people at the back of the standing-room crowd lifted hand-lettered signs and began to protest. DEATH TO BIG OIL and KEEP IT IN THE GROUND rose and fell in time with stamping feet, while people in favor of the clinic, and thus Blackstream Oil, clapped loudly.

"Order." A gavel banged against a wood block, but the plastic table ate the sound. "Order!" said Byrd. He stood, raising both arms for silence.

"Bring the good drugs when you build it," someone yelled. Several people laughed. A few others made loud shushing sounds. The signs still waved.

"We have, tonight," said Byrd, "representatives of Blackstream Oil and the city of Dexter Springs. Blackstream and the city have already reached an agreement about the pipeline."

Starr watched as a wiry young man stood and faced the council members, his button-down shirt crisply tucked into black suit pants atop polished black dress shoes.

"Bernard Gilfoil," he said by way of introduction, and held a stack of note cards.

Byrd put his palms up to quiet the raucous meeting attendees.

The young man cleared his throat, introduced himself again and motioned for the tall Norwegian on his left to take the floor. "And this is Johan Antell, who is here from Blackstream Oil."

"We respectfully request access to eighteen thousand acres of land," Antell said, his clipped accent chopping through air that was becoming thick with heat.

A wood-burning stove in a tiled corner ticked as heat expanded its cast iron body, and Starr could see flames lashing through its iron grate as logs shifted inside. It was the loudest sound in the room.

Then the man from Dexter Springs stepped forward.

"From the approximate geographical boundary," Bernard said, "of Turkey Creek, in Crawl Canyon, to the north, bordered by privately owned real property to the south and east and by open reserve to the west, we propose a surface lease, along with mineral and oil rights for the parcel, for an initial period of ninety-nine years, with an option for extension, should all parties agree. In return, Blackstream Oil's generous terms are as Chief Byrd described."

There was a jeer from the back. "Should be more," said a man, who was quickly hushed by a woman sitting under a row of construction-paper pumpkins tacked to the wall. Twice a week the tribe's elders met in the community center for a hot lunch and, from what Starr could see, arts and crafts.

"I believe most people are familiar with the area in the proposal, as we've heard talk of little else lately," said Byrd. "Council, questions for our guests?"

The council was silent.

"At this time, I will open the meeting to public comment," said Byrd. Then, noticing a scruffy man rising from his seat in the audience, Byrd hastily added, "Limited to those who signed up last week, and *only* related to the item at hand. Scurvy, this doesn't mean you."

The man plopped down, defeated. Starr got a whiff of weed when he did.

"Anyone else?" Byrd said.

People lined the central aisle to address the council individually.

"We need this, for our children, for our elders. If Blackstream thinks there's oil out there, then I say we do it. And we'll benefit from it," said a woman at the front of the line. There were nods all around, including from the next attendee to address the council, a man who felt the agreement would pave the way for something else entirely.

"We are the only nation in this region without a casino," he said, arms outstretched to the left and right to make a point. "The only one. There are thirteen tribal casinos in the tri-county area already. You might not think there's room for another one, but there is. I hear tell they're all raking it in. Just not us, 'cause we don't have a tourist attraction or anything like that."

"Trading Post," someone hollered, and laughter lit up the crowd. Even Byrd smiled before he banged the gavel.

"What about the land? What about the damage the fracking will do?" said a young woman who'd set her sign down long enough to go up to the front of the room and speak. "Think about our water, about all the contamination that happened with the mining. Have we all forgotten?" She turned to face the crowd. "A company like this, they could turn it all into poison again."

There were more people, Starr began to realize, who favored the project than it had appeared. They were the quiet ones. The council members were quiet too, their faces blank as the emotions of each new speaker seemed to seesaw the crowd. Starr watched the man who'd spoken on behalf of the city. She could see his thick blond hair neatly parted on one side and wondered what he was thinking. She wished she could see his face.

Starr scanned the crowd for Odeina Cloud, but Chenoa's mother appeared to be absent. Several people had taken off their coats, and someone had used a brick to prop open an exit door, allowing cigarette smoke to waft inside. Starr inhaled and tasted the sweet bite of tobacco at the back of her throat. She overheard two young women whispering nearby. The one who'd begged the council to look for other ways to fill their coffers was convinced ruin would come to the reservation's living creatures, small and large, tribal members included.

Starr wondered how the Saliquaw Nation would balance the benefits and risks of an oil operation, and thought of Chenoa's notebooks. Did they hold any answers in the descriptions, the charts and graphs? She remembered the newspaper article about reparations paid for disturbing endangered species. Why had the article been worth saving? It had been an article about a road project, hadn't it? No, Starr thought. She wasn't asking the right question. Not why Chenoa believed the information was worth saving, but whether it applied to the rez.

"If you go forward with the oil deal, it will show us you don't care about our people." It was Junior's turn to speak to the council. "There is more to life than money. We have what we need—"

"Oh, for crying out loud," rang out a woman's voice. "Aren't you tired of being poor?"

"Not having a pot to piss in?" said a man from the other side of the room.

"We are protecting the future of our nation by working with the oil company," Byrd interrupted.

"I'm not done talking," Junior shouted over him.

It took just four words to turn the meeting into a screaming match.

"Out of order," Byrd said, banging his gavel again and again.

Starr's casual lean against the doorjamb evaporated. She could see where this was going. Things were about to get weird.

Byrd eyed each council member in turn, and then called the vote. As he tallied the yeas and nays, a shoving match broke out between a middle-aged man and the two young women, both gesticulating wildly with their signs. Junior entered the fray with a haymaker intended for the man, but knocked a different guy flat.

"Outside," Starr yelled over the din. "Everybody outside."

She rolled her eyes as she started ushering people toward the door. *Sure, this job is easy. Just like they said. Nothing ever happens on the rez.*

CHAPTER SIX

Bernard Gilfoil, caught up in the crush of bodies surging from the community center into the chill night air, had a front-row view of the big man they called Junior. He watched him take a swing at a lean, scrappy man. And miss.

The smaller man moved in fast, shoved his shoulder into Junior's gut and jabbed at his kidneys. Junior swayed on his feet and blinked at his balled hand like he couldn't understand why it hadn't connected with bone.

"You gonna give disrespect to me?" Junior slurred.

Bernard couldn't take his eyes off their strange dance.

The woman next to him, the sheen of her blue-black hair catching in the community building's lone floodlight, pulled fake lashes off one eyelid, then the other, and grinned at him as she rushed into the fray. Several other people followed her, Junior and the small man now the center of a whirring, angry wheel of bodies.

Bernard scrambled backward, scanning the faces of strangers around him. A woman across the circle looked at him, unblinking, a smile playing at the corner of her mouth. Dark hair dropped lushly over her shoulders and spilled across the long suede coat she wore.

The man beside him noticed and elbowed him.

"Nice, eh?"

When Bernard nodded, the man laughed. "Don't mess with those rez women. Might be Deer Woman in disguise."

Bernard caught sight of Antell, that Norwegian iceberg, standing in the open doorway of the community center, shaking hands with Byrd. When he turned his attention back to the fight, the woman was gone.

Bernard shoved his way out of the crowd. When he reached the refuge of his car, and soon after heard the dull crunch of rocks under its moving tires, he allowed himself to smile. The fight was of no consequence. Chief Byrd would get his people in line. The Band-Aid had been ripped off; the tribal council meeting had been a necessary evil to move the oil deal forward. Give the people their say and all that.

The meeting had ended in disaster, but not before the tribal council voted in favor of the project. He'd played his part to perfection. Outlined the legalities and cost projections in broad strokes. Carefully skirted the troublesome specifics. He built his entire presentation around the positives offered to the Saliquaw Nation by the partnership between Blackstream Oil and the city of Dexter Springs.

Damn, he was good at this. He was so keyed up, riding such a high. He slammed his palms against the steering wheel, then punched the padded ceiling above the driver's seat.

"Hell yeah!" Bernard screamed. He was a god.

Then he patted the headliner nervously, made sure he hadn't worked it loose. His mother would know if he tore up her

Chrysler. She'd know if he cussed in it. Sense it, though she rarely drove anymore, and give him a talking to. He apologized to the heavens for swearing. He laughed out loud. It was a nervous sound rich with adrenaline.

Bernard pushed the black frames of his thick glasses higher on the bridge of his nose and turned the car not toward Dexter Springs but toward the meager glow of scattered yard lights that signaled the presence of rez housing. He needed time to think.

Had Junior recognized him? Junior had been occupied, maybe even drunk, during the fight. But what about earlier, when Bernard had stood in front of the council and made a case for fracking on the rez? He thought about those late nights when, as a teenager, he'd hung out with hot rez girls and passed bottles of UV Blue around the shack Junior called home. He'd loved to party on the rez back then, loved the cloak it pulled over the self-consciousness he wore everywhere else. It was like another country, where he could pretend to be someone he wasn't.

He'd been surprised to see Junior at the meeting, surprised too by how he looked just the same more than a decade later. Bernard had the impression that Junior kept to himself, didn't get involved. Oh, but he'd gotten involved tonight. More than involved. He'd tried to turn the tide, to pit everyone against Bernard.

The sudden glare of headlights caught Bernard by surprise. He lifted a hand from the steering wheel to shield his eyes and veered to the side of the road to let the high beams pass, a MARSHAL decal bouncing past his window, the service vehicle nearly scraping his mother's car. He wrestled the Chrysler as it hit the narrow road's rough shoulder. When he glanced at the dash clock, Bernard realized the meeting had ended more than an hour ago. How long had he been driving around the rez?

He steered off Saliquaw land, honked at the shotgun-blasted

NOW LEAVING OKLAHOMA sign and, taking comfort in the certainty of his immediate future, gave two quick beeps to the WELCOME TO KANSAS marker that followed.

In another twenty minutes he would pull into the driveway on Ash Street. He knew exactly how the headlights would look as they swept the shorn lawn and the white railing of the porch to drop shadows across the stuffy living room where the floral fabrics and scented potpourri made him want to scream.

CHAPTER SEVEN

✦

Forty-five minutes after the meeting ended, the community building's parking lot had finally cleared out. Junior had been holding a man in cowboy boots over his head, but when Chief Byrd caught Starr's attention she'd set aside her amusement and moved through the crowd to stand eye to eye with Junior until he lowered the man to his feet.

Starr knew where her bread was buttered.

If the BIA got one whiff of dissatisfaction from Byrd they could pull her from the post. She wasn't so invested in the reservation that she was loath to leave it, but she was dedicated to staying out from under the BIA's microscope. She'd gotten the job. Now all she had to do was keep it. Until she could figure out what to do next.

The crowd was already starting to lose interest when she braced Junior against the back of the Bronco and pulled a pair of cuffs from her belt. She could feel him go still all at once, strength building like a gator right before it launches into a death roll, that tense split second between fight or forfeit.

Once she'd gotten his meaty wrists into the cuffs and packed him into the old Ford, Starr used both arms to wave the last lookie-loos along, like she'd seen cattle ranchers do with a reluctant herd.

"Go on," she said, walking around to the driver's side of the Bronco, feeling for all the world like she'd fallen down some Wild West version of Alice's rabbit hole. One man was pointing at the spray paint and laughing.

Starr yanked on the door several times before its hinges whined open, then got behind the wheel and wiggled the keys in the ignition until the engine grumbled to life. Junior was taking up half the bench seat; she hadn't felt the need to put him in the back. She'd seen plenty of mean drunks, but she didn't think Junior Echo was one of them. He was just big. And she knew what that was like. Assumptions were made. She'd heard the comments her whole life. *Big-boned. Tall drink of water.* She'd gotten her dad's height, his tawny skin, his thick dark hair, and none of her mother's daintiness. The fine-tuning had missed her, all except her mother's green Irish eyes.

"Okay, let's get you home," Starr said, "but you'll have to tell me where to turn as we get closer."

She put the Bronco in gear and glanced at Junior, who was leaning his head on the passenger window. He nodded and she drove ahead and to the right, where the road curved away from the community center and the rows of houses surrounding it. Junior began working the cuffs on his wrists.

"I'll take off the cuffs when we get there," Starr said.

She had briefly considered putting Junior in the cell overnight, but she didn't want to keep an eye on him. Besides, she had one drunk in there already, and she'd just have to deal with him in the morning. She'd rather roll a fat one, slip into her ratty bathrobe and smoke up the garage of her rental than worry about getting this big lug some food and water while he sobered up behind bars.

Although Junior had looked to be only five beers in while the meeting wore on, closer proximity had revealed the familiar smell of whiskey on his breath. Maybe the beer had been to keep the buzz going, but the whiskey . . . well, that's what had tipped the scales in his favor. The way she saw it, he'd be more work if he slept it off in the box. This wasn't her fight anyway. What did she care whether these people sold oil from under their land? They could sell organic cow shit to tourists and call it art for all she cared.

All she had to do was give the appearance that she could do her job. Keep the peace. Hang on until she knew what to do next, if there was a next. It didn't feel like it most days. She thought sometimes about putting the barrel of the Glock in her mouth, feeling the cold steel and only a moment of doubt before blanking into sweet oblivion. But she wasn't ready to see her daughter, assuming there was an afterlife.

Starr couldn't shake the feeling that she'd let Quinn down, deeply disappointed her in some cruel way she couldn't identify. It was like catching fog with a butterfly net, this feeling.

And now there was Chenoa, who was old enough to go where she pleased without her mother's permission. When Starr had entered the marshal's office after leaving Odeina's trailer, the phone was already trilling. Odeina hadn't even given her time to search for Chenoa—if she was going to search at all. Starr thought of the picture taken of Chenoa at her graduation last year. Starr was starting to see Chenoa around the edges of her mind when her thoughts should be focused only on Quinn. That damn Odeina was getting in her head.

"Shut up," Starr muttered.

"What?" Junior glared at her.

"Not about you." But she did wonder. What made Junior Echo tick? For someone who carried amber bottles around like pacifiers, he seemed overly invested in fighting the pipeline.

Junior was built like a linebacker who'd gone soft in the gut and jowls. He had looked settled but now seemed like he could fly into a rage at any moment. This wasn't Chicago, she reminded herself. Things were different here. After she put Junior in cuffs, Byrd had pulled her aside to say that the big man had tried to start another fight last week; three men had pulled him off a local at the Trading Post. *Watch him,* Byrd had warned.

Junior said nothing as the wheels bumped along the road. Then he made a dismissive sound, *pshh,* so quietly that Starr wondered at first if it had been her imagination. "You don't belong here," he said.

Starr looked him over and shrugged. She couldn't really argue. She felt the same way. She didn't give a shit about this place or the people here, and she sure didn't give a shit about this guy. He could say whatever he wanted. It couldn't be worse than the things she told herself.

"Left here?" She wasn't exactly sure where he lived, not in the dark, even after Byrd's general directions.

Junior grunted and then motioned with his head, and she steered the Bronco onto a lane that didn't look much like a road. Prairie grass that grew tall between the dusty tracks rustled against the undercarriage of the old Ford as cool November air drifted through the open windows and into the cab. Starr had rolled her window down to keep Junior's sourness at bay. It was as if the stench of anger and alcohol came straight out of his pores. If she and Junior didn't both hate themselves so much, they might have been comforted by their commonality.

"Your dad was a real son of a bitch, ya know that?"

"I know it," she said. "Were you acquainted? Back then?"

Junior laughed, a deep, hoarse sound. She heard the cuffs rattle in his lap.

"Hell, we grew up together. He shaved the eyebrows off one of the Annuas brothers at powwow one year," he said. "They woke up mad as wet hens, all of 'em." He stared out the open window, remembering. "All because they'd chased him through the fairgrounds for having that stupid look on his face, same one he always had."

As a kid, her dad's left eye hadn't tracked with his right. Lazy eye, he'd called it, and said he'd worn a patch to correct it.

"He thought he looked like a pirate, but he looked like a fist magnet," Junior said, shaking his head. His shoulders vibrated with laughter. "What an idiot."

This wasn't one of the stories her dad had told while peering at his past through the bottom of a bottle. Starr was quiet as the Bronco rattled down the lane, carrying them deep into the reserve and toward Junior's place.

"You there when he died?" Junior asked, serious now.

"Yep," she said. She'd been loyal to the end, even though her old man surely hadn't deserved it. All those years of drinking. All those years she'd taken care of everything. She'd been a kid. "You knew him pretty well, sounds like."

What in the . . . Starr pumped the brake as a deer leapt across the road, coming within inches of the Bronco's hood. She and Junior both looked to the ditches, watching for more. She thought of her old man, dead and gone; of the ache and relief and shame that he'd been six feet under before Quinn was born, a grandfather her child would never have. Then later, the pain of it all that kept pushing its way to the surface. Pain Starr held on her own. No one to carry an ounce of it, not anyone but her.

"He was my best friend," Junior said. "Once." Silence filled the space, whatever molecules weren't already crowded with the scents of sweat and leather and beer and whiskey—and something else, underneath. "Then he took up with a white bitch and I never saw him again."

"Fuck you," she said, just as headlights came over a rise and a car nearly hit them head-on. She floored the gas pedal to avoid a collision, jerking the wheel right and then back, enough to bang the side of Junior's head against the doorframe, fast and hard.

Junior growled, a guttural sound from deep in his chest, but she didn't care. She'd fight him right here if she had to, take the cuffs off and go at it, take the big, drunk man to the ground. She should have put him in the box until morning. Next time she would. This wasn't a mistake she would make again.

As Junior suspected, it was true that her mother hadn't exactly approved of her dad's side of the family. Starr didn't remember much of her mother, except being punished when she ran through the house with her dad whooping and dancing. That was in the *before*, when her dad's joking and laughing filled the family's Chicago apartment with sunlight.

"There," Junior said, pointing, as they came to the top of a rise. Starr couldn't see anything new as she turned onto a narrow lane, but when the Bronco veered right and down, the headlights revealed a tiny cabin, its exterior a mismatch of plywood and its yard a weedy cemetery for transmissions and tires.

"You think you're gonna come in and save us," Junior said when Starr cut the engine and opened her door. There was a slur to his speech. "What do you know about us, anyway? What did he tell you? He was gone, never came back. Never wanted to come back, I'll bet. Think you're better, like your old man . . ."

"Sit tight," she said, and slammed the door, which sent the old Ford rocking on its tired shocks. Then she walked around to the passenger side to let him out. His words were like a watery stream: on and on they went, no end in sight from where she stood.

". . . didn't need him here, but not once . . . did he . . ." Junior was still rambling, spittle flying, as she reached for the handle, wrenched the door open and pulled him out of the truck, all three-hundred-some pounds of him, thick as a side of beef and about as elegant.

"Come on," she said. "Let's go."

"Colonizer, huh?" Junior said once he'd slid from the seat, gained his balance and noticed the spray paint.

The MARSHAL decals had been the only new things on her service vehicle, and now both were ruined with graffiti. The tagged door reflected how Junior saw her—white. How everyone here saw her. As an outsider who didn't belong. But to her mother's side of the family she'd been too Native. She wasn't enough for anyone.

"Dad said I was half."

Junior smiled at her, a great lopsided expression, and shook the cuffs in front of him to remind her to remove them. He watched as she worked through one pocket, then another, to find the key.

"He taught you that much, at least," he said, "that you're an Indian too."

"Native American," she said, then corrected herself. "Indigenous. That's what it is now."

"That why you're here? Wanna fulfill your dream to be a real Indian?"

"Well," she said, "that's awful sweet of you."

"Or you wanna cash in, figure you can get oil money, get that per cap?" he said. "Maybe you think your daddy's some kind of magic Indian, called you back to this place from the great beyond? Gotta be one or the other."

Starr stepped back and took a deep breath, still searching her pockets, one by one, for the key. She took her time. If she let him out of the cuffs too soon, she'd be tempted to say he took a swing at her so she could get in a few punches.

Around them the night was as dark as she'd ever seen it. Without the glow of city lights, the Bronco was a spotlight aimed at the worn cabin, everything around it sinking into night. Junior took a few rolling steps toward her and then settled into another tirade, shaking the cuffs on his wrists. The more impatient he became, the slower she looked for the key.

The dry prairie grass behind her rattled with hidden movement. She looked again at the cabin, the glare of headlights bleeding into it through a front window. The light cast long shadows against an interior wall, the glow yellow and shifting like a broken yolk. A buzzing began in her head.

"Hey, you got company?"

"Just my Yella dog." Junior craned his neck to look over the roof of the Bronco at the cabin. "He oughta be out here barking. I keep him chained to the front steps when I'm gone so he don't go off with the coyotes. Did that once, gone for two weeks. Thought he'd never come back—"

Junior interrupted himself by sending a long, loud whistle into the dark. Then he tilted his ear to the silence.

"Get these off of me." He stepped toward her, wrists outstretched.

Starr couldn't tear her eyes away from the headlights' play

against the bare window, the wall, the shadows inside the cabin. Had she seen something move?

"You keep it unlocked?"

"Yeah, nobody's coming out here, messing with me." He nodded, then seemed to have a new thought. "Hey, don't go in there, man. You don't need to go in there. C'mon."

Starr stared intently now, cataloging the shadows inside the cabin. This one a bare-bulb lamp. That one a piece of low-slung furniture. Now something new.

Against the beam of light shooting through the cabin's window and onto the interior wall, a shadow grew larger. Starr tried to blink it away. Closed her eyes. Opened them. Yet there it was. She could make out a new shape, separate from its shadow, in profile: breasts, slim shoulders, a delicate face. And above it all, antlers, striving upward from a soft mass of fawn-colored hair.

She felt strangely out of time, the buzzing louder now.

Starr thought suddenly of the old woman at Odeina's. The image of Lucy Cloud's wizened fingers stretched out like antlers turned words loose in Starr's head. *Deer Woman; spirit animal; once a victim, now a victor; a cautionary tale with hooves.* Starr could feel the story come alive within her.

Her father had talked of Deer Woman long before Starr saw the mask on Odeina's wall, long before the old woman and her tall tale. But maybe—maybe for the first time—Starr wondered whether she'd known Deer Woman from the moment she'd clung to one last hope that her daughter would be found alive.

She wanted nothing more than to draw close, run her fingertips over Deer Woman's face, curl her fingers in her soft hair. Touch her.

A solution or a trap. Wasn't that what the old woman had said? Starr tried not to think about the old woman's story, but it kept rising through her consciousness and now there was no stopping it. Deer Woman felt to Starr like the embodiment of the one thing Starr believed: that enforcing the law and carrying out justice were very different. People would always find a way around the law—she'd seen it herself many times in Chicago as defendants she'd collared walked away from court proceedings without consequence—but justice was a different matter. Justice could still be served when external laws fell short, and she was a woman willing to make things right, as long as she could live with the sacrifice.

"Stay here," she told Junior, keeping her eyes on the house. "Don't move. I mean it. You move, you even breathe, I'll shoot your fucking head off."

Starr didn't listen for a response, just moved to the driver's side of the Bronco and switched off the lights, then slipped toward the cabin with her service weapon held low and balanced by her flashlight. Insects whirred in stereo, momentarily stopping as she passed them. At the rickety stairs leading to the front door she could see the chrome glint of a chain around one end of a post. Her eyes followed the chain under the wobbly stairs to where a yellow Lab lay, its legs drawn protectively around its soft belly. A blank eye stared up at her, a dark puddle of blood like an obscene moat around its head.

Starr clicked off the flashlight and set it on a step, wiping her wet palm on her jeans. She moved toward the door and turned the knob, the click too loud for her liking. She reached for her shoulder, where a mic should have been clipped, to call for backup. No radio. Right, she was on the fucking rez. Why hadn't she hired a deputy? She thought of the thin stack of résumés on her desk and wanted to kick her own ass.

"Tribal marshal," she called, and pushed the door, which

swung inward with a stutter, its awkward angle caused by a now-broken hinge. It was quiet in the house, except for the sound of Junior outside, who had taken to calling his dog at regular intervals.

"Yella!" he bellowed. "Yella!"

Starr let out a long breath. *Just clear the house and get out,* she told herself, then reached back to grab her flashlight off the step so she could move fully into the room. A single lamp, its shade missing, near the one front window. *Check.*

Starr scanned the room, hoping she'd find a mounted buck on the wall. Hadn't she seen antlers?

Do you see a deer in this house? she asked herself. *Focus. Stupid questions get you killed.*

Junior's cabin turned out to be one long room. Beside the lamp, a sagging couch listed against the far wall. In a dark corner an upholstered armchair vomited stuffing from its cushions. There were amber bottles everywhere: on the floor, the couch, even stacked on top of a television crowned with rabbit ears, an aluminum-foil flag affixed to one rod in a crooked salute. She'd seen Chicago crack houses in better shape.

Nothing moved, save some small thing scurrying along the wall toward an alcove that was the shack's kitchen. There were no other sounds in the place, except those coming from Junior outside, threatening to move from where she'd left him.

Starr stepped onto a loose carpet remnant that covered most of the living room floor and felt a crunch under her boots. It sounded like stepping on soda crackers but smelled of stale air and something not unpleasantly gamy. Like roast pheasant. Maybe duck. But starting to go bad, as though it had been last night's dinner. Or the night before's.

Starr moved forward to take cover behind a floor-to-ceiling

structural beam situated in the center of the room. *Deep breath, deep breath.*

She swung around and stepped wide, pointing her Glock into the kitchen alcove she'd spotted. It was empty except for a few sparse shelves and a counter set against the back wall of the cabin. She had to breathe through her mouth now, working to identify the smells that assaulted her nose. WD-40. Sweetgrass. Metal shavings. Stale grease. *Something wicked this way comes,* she thought, and wondered where that line was from. Strange thoughts popped into her head at the worst moments. Wrong. It was all wrong.

Beyond the stench of a congealed mass that had been left to sit in a pot on the stove, Starr could feel a heavy presence, dangerous and just out of reach.

There was one more place to search. Starr came out of the kitchen alcove and moved to her right, heading again toward the back of the cabin. With her foot she prodded open the only interior door. She'd presumed it led to a bathroom, and she was right. But it too was empty.

Starr shook her head, hoping to rattle her brain back into place. It wasn't possible, was it? Deer Woman was a myth, and she knew better than to get tangled in the stories her father had told. But Odeina's mother-in-law . . .

Don't fall for it, she told herself. It was late and she was exhausted. She hadn't eaten yet; she wanted to fuel up with the weed waiting for her at home, work her way through a bag of Cheetos when she was done. Chase it with Jameson. Tall. Neat.

At the back of the cabin there was a door that probably opened right into the wilderness. Trees. Grass. Creatures. It was getting more difficult to tell what was truly wild.

What had she seen in the shadows? The place was empty. No

deer. No woman. She holstered her gun and, with a shaky sigh, leaned against a wall. She'd take a breather, then make her way out the back door, but she couldn't stop thinking about the mess outside.

She'd have to be the one to tell Junior about the dog.

Above the back door Starr noticed a wooden rack holding a rifle, and walked closer. The rack was covered in a coat of dust, nothing disturbed. There had not been a recent reach and removal.

The tines of an antler curled around one of the wooden hooks of the gun rack, the tip of each tine painted red. Was this new? Impossible to know. She lifted her flashlight, the antler's minute grooves making canyon upon canyon of shadow, except where blocked by something else. Flowers in miniature, like little white daisies on slender green stems, had been braided into a loop and tossed over an antler tine.

Starr reached up and pushed a finger through the dust. She opened the back door to the thick night and stood shivering with leftover adrenaline in the cold Oklahoma wind. Somewhere in the inky woods beyond was the rustle of movement.

For one wild moment she saw a deer, impossibly dark against the pitch, its antlers beckoning her to come forth, come forth.

CHAPTER EIGHT

Starr had been sitting behind the steering wheel of the old Bronco for at least thirty minutes in the dark, watching the dashboard clock inch closer to ten p.m. She'd left the shack without answers, paused to take a closer look at the yellow Lab lying in blood under the front steps, and now was waiting for Junior to finish working a shovel into prairie earth as hard as stone. Before she'd even decided whether she was going to stick around, he'd started digging in the arc of the amber headlights. So she stayed.

None of this made sense.

Showing Junior the dog had been the worst of it. She'd walked back to him, his questions bouncing off her chest, and she'd silently removed the cuffs from his wrists. By then he knew. The answers she was about to deliver, they were bad. She'd wanted to remain wary of him, but the bloody scene had taken all the fight out of him. The dog's death had closed him off like a slammed door.

Through the bug-splattered windshield she studied the cabin's rickety front steps and let out a heavy sigh, drumming the bottom of the steering wheel with her thumbs.

It had been a colossal mistake to take this job, to try to keep hold of her career, but what were her choices? Being a cop, then a detective, was the only real job she'd ever known, and it had, until recently, worked well as an antidote to her father. He never worked regular hours, but she often woke up in the night to find him missing. He drove a nice car, but raised her in a run-down apartment. He kept a shoebox filled with cash in his closet, but never seemed to have a dime.

Everything he was, she made a point to push against. She would do something respectable. But he was gone, six feet under since Quinn was an egg. Who had she really been fighting all those years? Who was she fighting now?

The antlered figure she'd seen through the cabin window replayed on a loop. What she'd witnessed—and she didn't know if she could possibly reconcile it—had been the graceful tines of antlers on a human body whose curves and valleys could only be described as female. How was that even possible? *It isn't,* she told herself. It wasn't at all possible. Still, the image was working its way deep into the gray folds of her brain. *Damn it.*

And the dog. When she left the shack, Starr had stopped to inspect the damage, hoping she was wrong about its injuries. After taking in as many details as she could in the gleam of the flashlight, she'd used a nearby board to lever the heavy Lab's deadweight and roll it over. What she hadn't been able to see from the way it had curled up to die was the beating it must have endured. *Fuck.* The other side of it had all the damage—all the visible damage, anyway. Something had taken a hard whack at its head, and it had died under the porch in its own blood, its paws sweeping convulsive arcs of earth.

What had killed the dog? Could another animal have done this damage? She scoured the ground around it, couldn't stop herself from expecting hoofprints. She found only the dog's own scratches in the bloody soil, its mouth scraping into the dirt.

Junior was on the move, pulling Starr back to the present. He dropped the shovel he'd been methodically pushing into soil that had probably never been turned, and she could see he had sweat through his shirt. His insulated Carhartt coat lay beside the hole, which was now a dark pit deep enough to make her skin crawl. She shouldn't be here for this.

Junior retrieved the dog and carried it like a sleeping child to the open hole, its tail drooping and unnaturally still. Starr moved from behind the steering wheel and through the open driver's door to lower the vehicle's wide back gate. She tugged a cooler toward her, glad she had beer on ice. She'd been saving it until after the council meeting.

And here it was, after.

She drank the first one without Junior. He was shoveling clumps of heavy earth back into the hole, covering the dog like he was tucking it into bed one last time.

Starr was halfway through the second beer when Junior approached, leaned on the scarred tailgate and stared out at nothing, one big hand rubbing the back of his neck.

"Beer?" she said.

Junior pulled on his coat, then took a bottle and cracked it open. He and Starr were both propped against the back of the Bronco, facing the two-track that had led them here. Starr looked at her watch. Ten fifteen p.m. Would this day ever come to an end?

"It's not natural, the way he died," he said. "Coyotes, they're a problem, but they didn't do that. Not a snake bite, too much damage." She heard his voice catch and waited. "I thought maybe it could be a mountain lion, but it looks . . . it just looks . . ."

"Like he was beaten over the head?"

"That's what I'm saying."

Starr waited a few minutes, then said, "You ever see a woman . . ." She hesitated. She couldn't stop thinking about the shadow she'd seen in the cabin: the sculpted chest, shoulders and head of a woman, but with antlers. And what she hadn't been able to see. Did her soft belly lead to human legs or to knees bent the wrong way? Was her body covered in the fine, downy hair of a fawn? And where her feet should have been, were there hooves? "This is going to sound crazy, so I'll just say it. You ever see a woman with antlers?"

The dank earthiness was still on him. She could smell it on Junior's clothes like a mist that enveloped them both, and she worked hard to keep her mind from veering into thoughts of graves and girls and tight spaces void of escape.

"He was a good dog," Junior said, wiping his nose on the rough twill of his jacket. "You wouldn't know. Forget it."

"I want to. Believe me. But that's not happening," she said, and then paused. "I'm sorry."

He tossed his empty bottle to the ground near his feet. Starr handed him another beer.

"A woman with antlers," he said. "You mean Deer Woman? I saw her once."

Starr waited, then drew a long and frothy swallow from a new bottle, condensation dripping down her wrist and running along the underside of her arm.

"Your dad and I, we started out one afternoon with my old man," Junior continued, "and tailed a buck through the woods on fresh powder, his prints easy to see as a full moon—they were that big and obvious. My old man, he kept on, mile after mile. I still remember the sound of our snowshoes, *shush shush, shush shush*. The heavy snow had made the woods so quiet that the silence roared in my ears. But there we went, nothing but *shush shush, shush shush* for hours, until I thought we might never . . ."

Starr tried to remember if this memory of Junior's was among the hunting stories her father must have told her. If her brain had locked away some image of her father with Junior and his dad working their way across a frozen landscape as the snowy surface shimmered with reflected light. She hadn't always been able to make sense of her dad's stories. Or maybe she hadn't really wanted to. She thought of her mother wrinkling her nose in disgust when her dad talked about *that place*. And after her mom was gone, well . . . anything more had felt . . . disloyal.

Junior paused and looked around, as if his vision could cut through the indigo blanket above them and sweep the scattered points of light away.

"It was like being in another world. Then we come over this rise where the tree cover thins. And there he was, the buck. Right there, in a clearing no bigger than . . ." He trailed off, glow from the taillights casting deep vertical lines across his face. "No bigger than my cabin, maybe. And he was close. Two truck lengths from us, maybe three. We could see the buck plain as day. Just in time too. The sun was starting to set. Maybe you don't know this, but at that time of day, if the shot didn't drop him we would end up trailing the deer in the dark. The coyotes would catch him long before we did. And we needed the meat that winter."

He turned to look at Starr, his bloodshot eyes two deep wells, then continued.

"We planned to butcher the deer and take the elders their share. It had been hard going for months. So, when we came upon the deer, my old man lined up the shot while it stood there like a statue. I mean, it just stood there, broadside like a target, waiting, nose lifted, nostrils flaring like it had picked up our scent. But instead of running, it stayed."

"What happened?"

Junior swiped the bottle across his forehead as if the cold could seep in, cool his fevered brain.

"It was a heart shot," he said. "Dropped the buck dead. We knew we'd have to work fast to field dress him, and packing him out would be a long, slow walk in the dark. But I didn't care. I wanted my dad to take the head; I'd seen an antlered skull mount in a hunting magazine, and I'd always thought about it, how cool it would be to have a bare skull and antlers on the wall. And this deer had a trophy rack, probably fourteen points. Biggest one I'd ever seen. But when my old man turned the deer over to gut it—"

He stopped so abruptly that Starr looked around to see why, sure there was something out in the night. A bobcat or coyote. Maybe a silent, swooping owl.

"It had antlers," he said. "Big antlers. Monster rack."

"No kidding. You said that already."

"And when he cut it open? Female. It was a doe, not a buck."

"Huh. A doe doesn't have antlers?"

"It wasn't just that," he said. "I heard later that it happens sometimes, that maybe one in one thousand female deer grow antlers. And female caribou have antlers, but not our deer, not what we have here. These deer aren't supposed to have them."

"So, what else? I mean, the antlers, sure. Freak of nature, but—"

"She had a fawn. Inside," Junior said. "Fully developed, ready for birth, like it could kick its way clean out of her. It wasn't just that this buck—what we'd thought was a buck—had turned out to be a doe with antlers. It was that she had a fawn to care for, and it was still alive, inside her. What were we supposed to do? It wouldn't have lived much longer. So I sat there, on my knees, watching it move inside the caul while my old man skinned and parted the doe. Your dad didn't want any part of it, so I cut through the caul and sawed clear through the fawn's throat."

What could Starr say to that? She'd done her share of terrible things. She thought of all the times she'd upheld justice instead of meting it out. Until she had crossed that line. Until she'd pulled the trigger again and again. There was no coming back from that.

"You put it out of its misery," she offered. "Not so bad." She laid a hand on his shoulder.

"No," he said, turning to look at her directly. "You don't get it. It was bad medicine." He shuddered, looked over his shoulder. "Thing is," he said, turning back to look her in the eyes, "any-thing . . . anyone . . . I've loved has been taken from me. Ever since that day. Every single time. It's a curse."

"Who's taken them from you?"

"Deer Woman," he said.

Then Junior walked to the cabin, and through the crooked door. Didn't even bother to turn on a light.

Starr could hear what sounded like a party—music, voices, laughter—carried faintly on the wind. After a long while Starr started the Bronco's engine and watched as its headlights illuminated Junior's bent frame through the window where he was sitting in the dark.

Starr put distance between herself and the shack as fast as she was able to, the Bronco bumping over the two-track cut through tall grass, to a dirt road and finally back past the rows of mobile and cinder-block homes of the reservation, past the tribal office and toward the state line, toward home. *My day in reverse,* she thought, and could already feel herself drifting into a stupor. She reached across the seat and felt for a beer, then used one hand to open it. She drank half and pressed it between her legs, the cold seeping through her uniform pants.

No way in hell she was making a report on the dog. Or on Junior, for that matter. Or what she thought she'd seen in the house. But there had been something. Starr couldn't make sense of it, the way the deer, or the woman—had it been a woman?—must have lit out the back and into the woods that rose into the hills, dark as a bloody wound.

CHAPTER NINE

There was the bonfire, of course, just as she'd expected. But near it were a half dozen or so tree limbs stuck into the shore, canted at angles where the sand wasn't deep enough to keep them straight.

Sherry Ann Awiakta wondered why they remained unlit, a strange play of shadow and light passing over them. The bonfire roared from a spray of lighter fluid, the onlookers stepping back to avoid the heat that reached for them in momentary greed. Then the flames settled down, went back to the work they were meant for, burrowing deeply into the pile of driftwood.

It wasn't the usual crowd. She'd expected a few high school friends she hadn't seen in a long time, maybe some rez friends she'd grown up with, but instead she saw townies with girls who wore too much perfume and who flipped long hair over their shoulders when they laughed. Time had moved on without her.

She'd caught a ride back to the rez from a trucker, who had let her off at the highway so she could walk the rest of the way in. She'd meant to go home but had stopped at the Trading Post and spent the last of her money on a dry sandwich and an iced coffee, a final splurge to keep her head clear. Clear. That's what she was now, and she planned to stay that way. Make it right with her pops, maybe even stay awhile this time.

Sherry Ann walked by the keg, and a hand moved out of the shadows to offer a plastic cup with a foamy head that she carried toward the light and set down without taking a drink. She'd always loved a fire, the way it kept the cold at bay. She weaved through the limbs, pulled one up, heavier than she'd expected, and wrapped both hands around the rough surface like it was a throat. There was wadding bound around one end, and she could smell the bite of fuel that soaked it.

She touched the unlit torch to the bonfire. The blaze blossomed close and warm and spread a bright circle around her, and when she waved the torch through the air it whooshed playfully.

This was the moment she realized something good was happening. She looked past the edge of flame. Around her, men in denim jackets clapped one another on the back while a group of high school girls jumped up and squealed at some comment. A couple with their arms around each other shared a long, slow kiss.

Her mother had died the previous year, and Sherry Ann, without being sure exactly why, left. And then, with certainty, she'd known it was time to return. She was a bird on a migratory route, looping back to a homeland mapped in some hidden memory. This time would be different. Better. She smiled and sank onto a tree stump. She held the torch as it burst and crackled. Then she tossed it into the bonfire, where it sank into bright, hot flame.

When the man sat down next to her, Sherry Ann smiled. She'd seen him moving from group to group, searching faces. He'd stopped a few people as they were leaving, the evening air growing too cold to be fun. Or maybe their curfews were calling them home.

"Didn't find who you were looking for?" she said, watching the fire.

"No luck." He shifted his body toward her. She could feel his eyes on her profile. "That's probably a good thing, though. I was looking for somebody who didn't need to be here."

Sherry Ann nodded. "Sounds familiar. The reverse, I mean. I don't really need to be here either. It's all so different now."

They watched as a big man walked out of the tall grass and closer to the fire, where he patrolled the sand, shuffling his feet. When his shoes hit a discarded beer bottle, he bent unsteadily and grasped the bottle so that it glinted in the light of the bonfire. Then he took a few steps and stumbled to his knees.

A couple of girls holding White Claws giggled and Sherry Ann heard one say, "Who is that?"

"No idea," said the other.

Sherry Ann knew it was Junior. He was still a bear of a man, and she wondered if he was still running beer for high schoolers.

Junior got to his feet, sniffled into the sleeve of his coat and then stopped to retrieve another bottle. He added it to the sack he carried and made his way along the thin stretch of sand and out of the light as a spattering of raindrops hissed on the sand, sending people on the long walk back to the shelter of their unseen cars. The party was breaking up.

The stranger next to Sherry Ann didn't seem to notice the White Claw girls or the rain, or anything but the fire. He snapped a twig into smaller and smaller lengths and tossed them into the flames. When his hands were empty, he brushed them on his thighs and turned to her.

"Minkey," he said, holding out a hand. "I'm not from around here. You?"

CHAPTER TEN

THURSDAY

The sun came up too early the next morning. Starr rolled over and squeezed her eyes tight against the light, hoping to lasso the last possibility of sleep before Thursday arrived in earnest. She rarely got hangovers anymore, thanks to the balance of weed and liquor she'd learned to calibrate as if it were her career, but waking up was still the worst part. She felt vacated—milled out, only a husk. She had to pull herself up and out of the well of despair, tendrils of grief curling around her ankles as her fingers searched for handhold after slippery handhold.

Some days it worked better than others.

Starr groaned and kicked her legs under the sheet, slowly getting feeling back. The long hours of her job on the rez stretched before her like a desert, but this despair was better than feeling nothing, she supposed. Better. She wasn't better at all. If anything, she was worse.

Not even the sharp morning sunlight could burn from her

mind the image of a woman with antlers. It was seared into her thoughts, branded with a hot iron. Junior Echo—what had he called Deer Woman? A curse? And Lucy Cloud with her weird stories. Couldn't anyone tell it to her straight? They all talked in circles.

Starr pulled the sheet around her shoulders and over her head. Beneath her she could feel the scratch of the bare mattress, set directly on the floor. She wanted sleep.

There had been antlers, along with a flower crown, hanging on the gun rack above the back door of the cabin, but it was impossible to see them from the front of the cabin. It would have been impossible for those antlers to make the silhouette she'd seen in the window. She had seen it clearly, so clearly. Maybe she was going mad; maybe the rez was making her crazy.

Starr's cell phone began to buzz, vibrating the moving box that was her bedside table. Sure it was Odeina Cloud again, she grabbed for the phone, but it clattered to the floor. She waited for the room to stop moving, rolled onto her belly and felt for it over the side of the bed.

"What?" she said into the phone.

"Hey . . . um, Marshal?" Winnie's voice squeaked through the static, evidence of the one administrative duty Starr had managed to take care of yesterday: hiring a jill-of-all-trades for the marshal's office. Winnie had driven a school bus route for the last couple of decades but was newly retired. And, she said, bored. Now she was Starr's new dispatch, filing clerk, reservation expert. Everything.

"Yeah," Starr said, trying to sound like she'd been awake for hours.

"Elmore—uh, Chief Byrd—thought I oughta give you a call. Sorry about the hour."

Starr could hear the deep rumble of a voice in the background, and pictured Byrd standing over Winnie's shoulder, adding to what she had to say, or correcting it, as she tried to talk into the heavy avocado green handset on her desk.

"Yes. I know. I know." Starr could hear Winnie whispering, with what seemed like her palm muffling the receiver; then the line cleared. "Okay, yes, well . . . Marshal, seems the Spicer boy went down to run his hunting dog this morning, up by Crawl Canyon, and he, uh . . ."

"What?" said Starr, rubbing her temple with her left thumb. Birds had just taken flight in her chest, bashing into her ribs at breakneck speed. "What is it?"

Starr tried to picture a traffic accident, a burgled home, anything but . . .

"A body. The Spicer boy saw a woman, and at first he thought it was a joke, like a mannequin some kids had brought to a party."

Starr dropped the phone onto the mattress and grabbed for a packing box, hoping it was empty as she vomited bile and foam, retching as quietly as she could. When she'd finished, she wiped her mouth and chin with the back of one hand and put the phone on speaker. Winnie was still talking, doling out details. How much had she missed? It didn't matter.

She should have known.

Death was a dog that had caught her scent.

"The kids like to hang out there," Winnie said. "But, anyway, it wasn't a fake doll or anything, because when he looked closer, well, she was dead."

"Got the witness?" Starr said. She pushed the barf box into a corner and ignored the sloshing of its contents while she sat on the edge of the mattress. Something rattled inside. *Fuck*. It hadn't been empty after all. She'd have to deal with that later.

She listened as Winnie launched into a long-winded explanation of how the Spicer boy was related to her.

"Who's your cousin-uncle?" Starr asked as she walked out of the bedroom to grab her uniform from where it hung on the back of the bathroom door. There was so much her father never explained to her.

"And then, after he got that welding job—"

"Winnie," Starr interrupted. "You still have the witness there with you? Good. Keep him. I'll stop at the marshal's office and pick him up on my way out to the site."

Because I need him to show me how to get there, she thought.

She didn't know her way around the rez. Didn't know where to find, or even where to look for, Odeina's daughter. Good Lord, she hoped Chenoa Cloud hadn't been killed on her watch, when she hadn't really listened at all.

CHAPTER ELEVEN

Starr parked in front of the marshal's office and glanced at the time on the dash. Eight a.m. She pushed a piece of gum into her mouth, chewed for thirty seconds, then spit it into her hand, got out and flung it into the dried weeds that clung to the side of the building. A liver-spotted dog was tied to a steel boot scraper that stood sentinel by the entrance. The dog leapt back and forth, straining the rope and barking like it had treed a bear.

Starr watched the dog absently as her mind moved through next steps. *A dead girl. What a fantastic start to my fourth day on the job.* It was just her luck to catch a bad case, although there had been a time in her career when she'd longed to take the lead in a murder investigation. Once she had the opportunity, she started racking up solves before others could even make the homicide squad. But that was *before*. Some things, she knew now, you didn't come back from.

Starr didn't know yet whether this dead girl matched Chenoa Cloud's description. She wondered if later that day she'd be delivering news that would turn Odeina's life into a *before* and *after* too.

The lights were on in the office when Starr entered. Winnie pointed to a boy, who looked to be twelve or maybe thirteen, sitting in a chair. Chief Byrd was there, rubbing the kid's shoulder. Winnie looked stricken.

"This him?" Starr said. "C'mon, kid."

The boy looked at Byrd as if for permission, then rose and went toward her.

"We'll talk on the way. Can you show me what you found?"

"This is Achak," said Byrd, stepping between them, pronouncing it *Ay-shack*. "I've spoken with his father, and he agreed to let the boy go with you." He turned to the boy. "We'll make this quick as we can."

"Just him," Starr said. "You wait here if you want."

The last thing she needed was for Byrd to interfere. He'd already been chatting up the boy when she came in, she could tell. Now the kid's story would be different. The mind starts filling in blanks, adding or subtracting until everything seems to fit. She'd learned long ago to get to the witness first, and to go slowly before she put together a narrative. Avoid making assumptions.

Assembling the narrative was the most important part of working a case, crafting a story to figure out how pieces of evidence fit within the whole. She'd had only a couple of truly complex cases in Chicago. Motives—and their outcomes—were much simpler than people thought, and Chicago was a two-interviews-and-you're-done kind of place. Drugs. Abuse. Infidelity. Same song, different verse.

Byrd started to protest, but Starr offered a "we'll be back" wave as she opened the door for Achak. Outside, the boy moved to untie the dog, which bounded happily toward him, its entire body wiggling.

"Leave the dog," Starr said, "and get in."

"But Chief Byrd said I could take him with me," he said. "He promised."

"Fine. But you keep him on a leash. He doesn't touch anything near the scene. Got it?"

On the way, Achak—"Call me Chak," he said—took some prompting to talk. He haltingly explained that he sometimes took his dog, Bandit, out to Crawl Canyon to train. Turkey Creek, which ran the length of the divide, was wide and shallow, perfect for throwing and retrieving bait ducks. And, it turned out, he was only eleven. Tall for his age.

"That why you go by Chak, like Shaquille O'Neal?" Starr asked, and the boy grinned.

"You play basketball?"

"Used to. I had the height for it, but it was like my arms and legs grew too fast." She waved her arms. "No coordination."

Chak laughed, and pulled his dog away by the collar as it tried to lick his face.

Not doing too bad for what he saw this morning, Starr thought. But she'd seen kids recover remarkably quickly from some pretty terrible things.

"Hey, don't you have school today?" Starr realized.

"Meant to go," he said, then shrugged. "But it's duck season."

It took more than thirty minutes to reach the Crawl Canyon area by car, and like the whole of the reservation's wilderness area, it wasn't accessible by road. They'd have to hike in.

"Do me a favor and keep your dog on a short leash, okay?" Starr said. "We can't have him making tracks anywhere we might have evidence. And if I tell you to wait, you stop. Don't take another step until I give the go-ahead. Now, what direction are we headed?"

Chak pointed, and then curled a length of the dog's rope

around his hand. He'd already said the body was a few miles in, maybe three or four. Starr was almost glad for the company. By the time they'd walked for at least an hour, she'd had time to think about jurisdiction. It was strange to be first on the scene. No paramedics, no fire, no police cars, no coroner team ribboning off the evidence. This was reservation territory. She was it.

"She—or, I mean . . ." Chak said, then changed his mind. Simplified, started over. "I walked down this bank here."

Starr looked to where he pointed. They were right at a change in the landscape, from acres of prairie grass bowing in the wind to a riparian area with trees, and below that, to a wide and sandy bank.

Starr stared down at the water glinting diamonds in the crisp morning air. Here, the canyon wall was little more than a steep incline on the far side of the creek bank. Around them, the grass was a sea of russet and gold. She noticed the dark bodies of large birds making sweeping ovals overhead. The boy followed her gaze.

"Buzzards," he said.

"All right, show me where you walked and how you found the . . . her."

Without another word, Chak started down the incline to the creek. Starr watched him for a moment, wondering what it would have been like to spend her childhood on the rez, where even finding a body didn't rattle a boy's nerves.

The bank was bordered on both sides by scattered loblolly pines and scrub cedar, trees that stayed thick with green needles throughout the fall and winter. Around Starr and Chak, thorny trees sent branches into a shared space so tangled that the boy steered wide, kicking one of the trees' fallen hedge apples in an arc.

"Wait there," Starr called out as Chak and his dog reached the creek. He stopped, and the dog sat obediently at his side. About two hundred yards away there was a pile of burnt limbs and other debris beside the creek, just as the boy had said there would be. Teens from the rez—and townies, for that matter—partied here, he'd said. But not him, he'd added quickly. Not his thing.

Starr was imagining a crew putting up crime-scene tape as she reached Chak, who explained where he'd been with the dog and how it had put its nose to the ground and snuffled around before taking off like a shot. He then pointed to a stand of bushes.

"Okay, sit tight. I'll take a look," Starr said. "I may be over there awhile, so get comfortable. Just don't let this guy wander around." Starr ruffled the dog's ears and left for a better look.

From her vantage point, the stand of currant bushes looked like everything else. Natural. But once Starr walked around to the creek side she saw two bare feet, heels up and visible beneath the rangy branches whose purple fruit was spent and fallen. There were trails of ants using the fruit as highway markers, and even with the morbid addition, a half dozen cardinals flocked noisily to the fruit. They burst into flight as Starr came within reach.

Starr stood near the body for a long time, taking in every visible detail, then glanced back to make sure the boy was still where she'd left him. She bent closer.

The kid had been right. Young. Female. Dead.

Starr removed a pen from her pocket and used it to lift the woman's fingers, still pliable and soft. *Damn it.* Another girl who, only a few hours before, had been alive.

Starr had come here to get away from this. Why had it followed her? With a sinking feeling, she knew why.

She deserved it.

She wasn't going to escape from it. She couldn't run far enough or long enough or to the right place, where it wouldn't be part of everything she did.

Quinn.

The air shimmered and Starr could feel—actually feel—how she'd pulled Quinn's small frame into a hug, how she'd inhaled the smell of her daughter's thick blond hair. Lavender and mint. When she said it smelled good, Quinn laughed at her. But what Starr couldn't explain was that her own reaction was about more than that smell, no matter how much she loved it. It was the way she could press her face into Quinn's thick hair and feel it on her skin while they hugged. It gave Starr a moment, her expression unseen, to drink her daughter in. It happened less often as Quinn bounded into adolescence and, increasingly, away from her, but it was the last thing they had shared. *Weirdo,* Quinn had said, and she held Starr at arm's length before collapsing into another hug.

She'd seen Quinn's feet that day too. Seen them first, before her mind would allow her to take in anything else. They were two points under a white sheet on stainless steel. She couldn't bear to see her daughter's sweet face, wasn't ready to confirm something she wasn't ready to comprehend. Still, this was a formality she'd been compelled to undertake.

Starr had kept her eyes low, didn't look at the attendant standing near the head of the morgue table, ready to pull the sheet back. Instead, Starr lifted a corner of the sheet covering her daughter's feet, took in the painted toenails—on all but one; the tiniest little piggy without a nail. It was something that happened to them both, the little toe rubbing on shoes and the friction releasing the nail. It didn't even hurt; the nail just dangled there until it was pulled off. It was their own weird joke, their shared history, their strange genetic connection. Theirs.

Starr was outside her body now, watching herself hold the

corner of the sheet, watching herself put her hand on Quinn's foot, too cold to the touch. *She needs socks,* Starr thought wildly. She should have brought socks with her. *Quinn must be freezing in here.*

"Are you done now?" said a voice from behind her. Starr looked around. When had she left the scene, moved up the bank, returned to the boy? The currant bushes, the body, were yards away.

There was a deer antler at his feet.

"You see that?" Starr said, too quietly. "Do you see that?" Too loudly this time. Chak retreated a few steps and looked at her like she had grown antlers. "Those. Those antlers there. Did you touch those? Maybe find those antlers somewhere else and bring them here? Like a prank, maybe?"

"No," he said. "No way."

"They weren't there before, were they?"

Chak eyed her warily and shrugged.

"All right, let's go." Starr motioned back toward the way they'd come. This place was making her crazy. "You didn't touch anything when you saw . . . when you noticed the feet?"

Chak shook his head. No.

"Anyone you might recognize?"

Also no.

"Oh, hey, there's sometimes a truck parked by that ridge." Chak pointed into the distance, beyond the creek. "Tall guy. Glassing for deer, looks like. Sometimes we get poachers out here."

Starr handed him her notepad.

"Hike back to the Bronco. Should be an extra pen in the glove compartment. Draw me what you saw. Everything. I'll meet you there in a while."

Maybe she should deputize him, she thought, as he and the dog ran ahead. At least he'd known better than to wander around touching things. She hoped to hell she hadn't trampled on any evidence, with the way she'd walked away from the crime scene and come to her senses right in front of him—with no memory of how she'd gotten there.

She thought fondly of Chicago, of lab attendants in white suits, of sterile kits, of stacks of evidence markers, of herself ordering, *Send it to the crime lab.*

Starr retraced her steps and returned to the body, her eyes tracking the distance from the burned-out campfire to the scorch marks on the victim's skin. Some of her skin had blistered. There was a circle of burnt earth around the girl's legs, but the fire had put itself out before the currant bush covering her body could catch. Too green. There were a few half-charred logs nearby— the kind someone would have intentionally cut to an arm's length for a campfire—but the soft rain that had fallen in the night had wiped the sand of footprints and kept the logs from burning all the way down.

"Who did this to you?" Starr asked.

She knelt and gingerly leaned under the branches. There was something else too. She took the pen from her pocket again and lifted the girl's dark hair from where it had fallen across her face.

What was wrong with her mouth? It was open at an unnatural angle, and filled with . . . something. Dirt?

Starr leaned back. The victim's mouth was jammed with what Starr guessed amounted to handfuls of silt. Only it was lighter in color than the sand that lined the creek bed. And finer. She pressed into it with her pen. Packed tight.

Starr felt her scalp shrink with the horror of it. Had this happened before or after the victim died?

81

Starr stood and rubbed her palms against her thighs. She wanted a shot of whiskey, but she needed coffee. She dialed the county medical examiner's office on her cell phone; it took three tries to get the call to go through.

"Yeah, Dr. Moore? This is Marshal Starr from the Saliquaw Nation, and we're going to need your crew over here."

She paused to listen, waving a hand at the flies that had begun to gather.

"One victim. Female. Mid to late twenties. Recent, by the looks of it . . . Yeah, I'm putting markers out and will stick around until they get here. I'll send someone to show the way, but let them know they'll have to walk in. Road only goes so far."

Starr pulled a large evidence bag from her pocket and settled it around a charred log near the girl's head that had a suspicious smear that could be blood. After she collected the wood, she took a few pictures with her cell phone even though she'd instructed the ME to send out a photographer for crime-scene images.

"Bag the antlers too," she said to a blue jay, which disregarded her instructions from its perch on a nearby evergreen branch.

Starr looked again at the victim's feet and noted a series of stars tattooed on one ankle. Chenoa didn't have a tattoo.

She needed to reach Odeina before word of a dead girl got around.

CHAPTER TWELVE

✳

Helen Taylor, the mayor of Dexter Springs, stepped out of a freshly washed Lincoln Navigator at a city park few remembered and even fewer frequented.

The linear park was formed along a decommissioned railway that led to a timber bridge with privately owned land on the other side. During the summer, the shaded rails-to-trails recreation area shielded Helen's daily sprints from the glaring Oklahoma sun, the same sun that faded awnings and shopkeeper advertisements in downtown windows and gave her the type of natural tan that came only from hours on the golf course.

Now, though, Oklahoma was deep into fall on a Thursday morning, and there was no need to hide from the sunlight that shone weakly as Helen pushed the key fob and heard the familiar beep that let her know the Lincoln was secure. Not that anyone was out here to steal anything, but still, the prospect of secretly meeting Horace-Wayne Holder without the benefit of a crowd made her nervous, more than anything she'd set out to do so far.

If she pulled this off, they'd all be rich. It was going to plan. And she was going to keep it that way.

Running the trail had become a priority, in part because mornings were now uncomfortably cold for golf. There was another reason too, and it was one of her best ideas yet. And, oh, she had ideas.

She tucked the keys into an interior pocket of the windbreaker she wore with black Lululemon tights and red Brooks running shoes. Red not because she loved the color, but because it showed school spirit in Dexter Springs. She would signal her support of anything that would bring her goodwill come election time.

Helen pulled her hair back and felt the ponytail swing pleasantly across her back as she ran, her feet falling on a soft layer of damp leaves and, beneath that, the pea-sized gravel she'd insisted the city council have installed two years ago. She could smell the fecund odor of decay, but it was a welcome and earthy change from the carefully conditioned air of her office in city hall.

When a deer crashed out of the trees just as Helen reached the wooden slats of the old bridge she startled sideways, then clutched her knees to draw a few deep recovery breaths.

The deer stood frozen, a living and breathing barrier to her path. At fifteen yards, she saw the points of its antlers and the twitch of its ebony nose.

When she'd moved to Dexter Springs nine years ago, she'd had toddler twins, and a husband, Dan, who had convinced her that running the family's historic gas station was not only a job but a calling. She hadn't been fully on board with their move to Dan's hometown on the Kansas-Oklahoma border, but he'd been happy enough—and she'd been exhausted enough—that she left her corporate job in Kansas City.

At first she was content to spend more time with her children,

Rayne and Ryan, as Dan whistled off to the area's only operational filling station still standing on Route 66, that iconic highway that in 1926 realized the American initiative of connecting rural and urban areas. Her housewife era didn't last long. The ceaseless rounds of crackers and juice, the Cocomelon videos and a hundred other quasi-educational cartoons, the inanity of "Baby Shark" on repeat . . . the loneliness . . .

Six months after moving to Dexter Springs, she was volunteering at the local animal shelter, then the chamber of commerce. Then she volunteered to head a fundraising campaign for the public library, and finally . . . finally . . . she'd found her place among her husband's people when she ran for city council. It was a natural leap to a mayoral campaign, and here she was, days from a vote that would secure her second four-year term as mayor.

"Shoo," she said, waving her arms at the deer. "Go on."

The deer leapt into the trees and the birds resumed their raucous twittering. The sound of Helen's feet striking the worn slats of the bridge produced a rhythmic echo. Spring River, from which the town took inspiration for its name, was placid below. The current shifted slowly, the water tired after millennia cutting through stone.

She knew Holder was waiting a quarter of a mile past the bridge, where the trail took a right-of-way turn through a corner of his land.

During the time she'd known him, he'd become not only her most generous campaign donor but also underfoot, and this proximity engendered a familiarity that served both their agendas. While Holder had been chivalrously aiding the widows of area farmers so he could buy their land in private deals, Helen had been steadily expanding her domain too.

The town charter, which had not been updated in any serious fashion since its 1889 adoption, offered considerable influence to anyone who held the elected position of mayor, and Helen had little by little exercised this right of office. Her power grab had been accomplished steadily and without need of formal action, which meant that now she could largely act on her own. She could make decisions that she felt benefited the town without being hamstrung by the city council. City council members, for their part, didn't mind relinquishing the heavy lifting. They were elected volunteers, after all, and between their careers and a full slate of games at the baseball diamonds, most were happy enough to leave the budget up to her. She'd put an end to review sessions, and everyone was a bit grateful to learn they'd suddenly been freed of several long days' worth of decision-making every quarter.

Her strategic plan had all fallen into place since then, with a lauded expansion of city hall and public safety, and with several new housing developments and even plans for a new multimillion-dollar industrial complex. The trick, she'd learned, was to toe the tax line.

If she could prevent any tax increase that took money directly from residents' pockets, she found that those residents would, by and large, support any project that appeared to benefit the community. That's how she'd managed to railroad the funding, along with all the right motions and approvals, to construct a new city hall, a project the whiny amateurs on city council hadn't even been able to get out of committee in the last two decades. She got things done. Good things. Community things.

And what she had in the works would be her biggest accomplishment yet. But she had a few funding discrepancies to eliminate.

That's where Blackstream Oil came in. The deal between the rez and the drilling company wouldn't work without the access roads she was building via the city's coffers. Antell at Blackstream Oil knew this, so much so that he was willing to grease the wheels. It meant she'd be able to replenish the 350 thousand dollars in tax funds she'd siphoned off over the last four years. Once she'd deeply buried any financial wrongdoing—*embezzlement* was such a dirty word—she could seek higher office. Currently she was manifesting a US Senate seat, but she might be willing to consider the statehouse. If the kickbacks were right.

But she'd never get to phase two if the Blackstream Oil deal fell through with the rez. And that's why she had Holder. It was his job to manage any of the behind-the-scenes matters that might gum up the works, so to speak. In return, the city would pay a hefty easement fee to construct the new access roads through his land bordering the reservation so that Blackstream could ferry its workers, equipment and, most importantly, its gains. Holder was a frustrated, land-hungry rancher willing to do just about anything to amass a fortune. She was counting on his greed.

The terrain changed as she returned to the cushion of the trail. She felt the pulse in her neck. *Barely elevated,* she thought, and smiled to herself.

She was in the best shape of her life. Nothing was going to stop her now, especially not whatever problem Holder was clucking about this morning. He was like an old hen sometimes, ruffled by rumor or supposition, and he came to her with complaints so frequently that for the last few weeks they had been meeting out of sight on this little-used trail.

This morning Holder had called to report that he'd spent the last few days surveying the proposed oil field and access points, all the boundaries where the land he owned butted up against the reservation. Nothing but jackrabbits and Russian thistle blowing past, he'd said, and then laughed at his own joke: *You know, tumbleweeds?*

She'd been willing to go along with his *Hee Haw* sense of humor because she suspected she needed a true local, a Dexter Springs lifer, with his nose to the ground like a bloodhound, ferreting out any holdouts or complications, either in town or on the rez.

Then he'd said the words she'd never wanted to hear. *There might be a threat to the reservation's side of the deal.*

Now she knew she'd been right about Holder. He was going to prove his usefulness.

"Hola," he said when she spotted him up ahead, leaning on a fence post and using his pocketknife to scrape under the fingernails of one hand. "We got a little girl out there, could be a problem. Could be a real monkey wrench."

CHAPTER THIRTEEN

✳

S tarr had dropped off the boy at the marshal's office so Winnie could take him home; he'd seemed no worse for wear despite his discovery. Then she'd sat at her desk to jot down everything she knew about the case so far. She'd studied the sketch Chak had drawn, an outline of a pickup truck. Above it, he'd written *black* and penned an arrow pointing to the truck. Alongside the truck, he'd drawn a tall, thin stickman holding what she guessed were binoculars. Not much to go on.

"Heading to lunch," Starr said when Winnie returned. Time had slipped away from her. She planned to swing by Odeina's before she took a break, get in front of the news of a suspicious death, which was sure to spread like wildfire, and assure her that the body that had been discovered wasn't Chenoa's. But now it was noon and her belly was caving in on itself. The Cheetos she'd eaten in bed the night before were long gone. *No,* she thought, *they're in the bottom of a packing box, with everything else I threw up this morning.*

She braked hard as she reached Odeina's battered trailer, the buzzing there again in her head. Deer. Grazing near Odeina's front door. Lying down in the shade of the trailer. Standing alert, watching Starr. They were everywhere.

"Tell me someone else sees them too," Starr said, loudly enough that anyone with an open window might have heard her. She blinked. Again and again. She could blink them away, right? They couldn't be real.

Several of the deer closest to her lifted their heads in unison, watching her through the windshield. A few had budding antlers. The image in Junior's window last night flashed in Starr's mind.

In the light of day the events at Junior's shack seemed like a fever dream. Now her nightmares were multiplying.

"You ain't never seen that, huh?"

At the shock of a voice in her ear, Starr's body lifted off the Bronco's seat. The top of her head tapped the ceiling of the cab and she involuntarily hit the horn, sending dogs barking. The deer scattered, bounding in all directions.

It was Chak. Starr could see him outside her window as she clutched at her heart. He was doubled over with laughter.

She rolled her window down.

"Go to school."

"Eh." He shrugged, trying to control his laughter. "Trauma and all. I got the day off, for real now. But seriously, you scared of deers or what?"

"Not scared."

"Could've fooled me," Chak said, walking off.

"Wait." She called him back to her. "You mean to tell me you have this . . . this herd of deer just, you know, in your front yards like this?"

"Yeah, like no big. Pretty normal."

Starr got out and slammed the door, hoping it would keep them spooked. But she could already see them starting to return. Some of the deer had settled down to graze a few houses away, and a large doe peered from around the corner of Odeina's trailer.

"Should it be looking at me like that?"

But Chak had already walked away. She could tell by the shake of his shoulders that he was laughing again.

So, there was a herd of deer that grazed in the overgrown, open yards of the reservation's houses? It went against nature. When had these wild animals, in their collective wisdom, thrown over their fear? Starr looked around. Even the half-feral rez dogs didn't bat an eye at the deer.

Starr shook her head to break the spell and walked up the steps to knock on Odeina's front door. Maybe she could get ahead of Odeina by making an in-person visit. Maybe it would give her some breathing room, save her from the phone calls Odeina had continued to make since their visit yesterday.

Starr didn't need that kind of oversight, especially when she didn't have anything to tell Odeina. Not yet. Maybe not ever. Chenoa seemed to have a lot going for her, things that were bigger than anything she could cook up on the rez. She'd probably left for a while, maybe left for good. Still, Starr pictured Odeina sarcastically counting out the days on her fingers; this was the sixth day without word from Chenoa.

If Chenoa was actually in danger, as Odeina believed, any missing person investigation Starr started would be well into its *not likely to be found alive* stretch. Starr couldn't shake the very real possibility that the girl was a runner, even though Odeina insisted Chenoa would never take that route, was too invested in her family and in her research on the rez to disappear. But there were always secrets and lies. She knew that all too well.

Starr gave the door three more hard raps with her fist. Nothing. Then a curtain moved, and she could see the old woman motioning for her to enter. Still a little jumpy, Starr went in slowly, listening to the soft tick of her soles on the linoleum of the kitchen. To the left, in the living room, there was Lucy Cloud, covered up to her neck in a bearskin, fur side down.

"Grandmother." Starr nodded.

"Come. Sit."

Starr took the couch opposite the old woman, making sure to position herself directly under the masks so she couldn't see them change. She didn't need any of that weird shit today.

"Odeina's not here?"

The old woman shook her head.

"Know when she'll be back?"

A shrug.

"Okay, well," said Starr, "I can't stay, but I wanted to stop by and let her know what we've been working on in terms of finding Chenoa."

She always broke into formal speech when she delivered news like this. Non-news. Or bad news. It was best to do it quickly and get out. Best when she stayed standing.

Best when she kept her eyes from the masks.

"You come to tell us of Chenoa, but you don't have anything to say?" said the old woman.

They were both silent for a moment, Starr ready to make her exit.

"I remember a time when you had other things to say, when you were small and fresh as a fawn."

Great, Starr thought, *she's picked today to pull me into her dementia.*

"I just stopped here to offer an update," Starr said. *And now I need to get out,* she thought. Find Odeina before the old woman went nuts and made everything worse.

"Your father was here."

"That's true," Starr said. "Maybe you remember him, but look—that was a long time ago, and I've got to—"

"So were you."

"What did you say?" Starr felt a tingle run down her spine, and she looked—really looked—at the old woman. It wasn't a secret that her father had grown up on the reservation. His tie to this place was one of the things she'd exploited to get the rez job.

That was as far as his help went, though. Her father had left the reserve and never returned, least of all with her. His life on the rez was something he carried like a burden. Being here and not.

"Here?" Her voice sounded tinny. Why was there a ringing in her ears? She'd had enough bullshit for one day. For a lifetime. Reflexively, Starr shifted so she could keep an eye on the Deer Woman mask hanging above and behind her.

"He came back with you—don't you know? Just the two of you. Your mother, she wouldn't come along, but he brought you to us, proud as a mother hen. You were learning to walk, clumsy and curious. Junior and I helped care for you."

"Junior?"

"My son."

"Wait, wait, hold on. Junior's your son? He was married to"— Starr looked around wildly—"Odeina?"

A cackle rose high in the old woman's throat.

"No, no, not Odeina. She married my other son, Lon, Junior's brother. He's here and gone. Come, let me tell you a story."

"Whoa, whoa, whoa," Starr said, holding out both hands. "First of all, what do you mean, 'here and gone'? And why didn't you tell me you'd been my . . . my . . . babysitter, that I lived with you . . . and Junior?"

"Settle, settle." The old woman considered the wall of masks for several seconds. "This we've never discussed."

The buzzing resumed deep in Starr's brain, and she looked around as if the walls might have answers. What was this strange history? She stayed as if planted, a peculiar carpet-grown flower.

"Deer grazed on long grass," said the old woman, "but it listened always for danger. It could hear with all the parts of its body."

Starr pinched the bridge of her nose with two fingers. She could feel the painful prickle of frustration.

"Not only its ears, but the delicate whiskers by its narrow mouth, the hairs on its hide, the hard cleft of its hooves. When it sensed danger, it was off like an arrow, running, leaping. One morning it came to the river for a drink, quickstepping to the water, then halting for a tale on the wind that might say: *Danger. Danger is here.* But there was only a beaver, stout and lined thick with greasy fur, sunning on top of a mound of branches in the water, the rest of its home underneath. Deer eyed it warily. Beaver flipped onto his back. Deer took a drink. Beaver shivered water off his tail. 'You should worry more,' said Deer. 'Listen for wolves.' Beaver dove under the water instead, rolling and arching until he popped up in front of Deer. 'Wolves won't reach me in the water.' Beaver laughed. And at that moment, Alligator snapped Beaver into his throat. Only Beaver's tail stuck out of

Alligator's grinning mouth. But Deer wasn't there to see it; already Deer was running through the tall grass. Away. Away. Deer knew danger didn't always look like a wolf."

Starr pinched the bridge of her nose harder. She could feel the ache of tears constricting her throat.

This was the same kind of story that had driven her away from her father. Strange, without explanation. She wanted a straight answer for once in her life. Black or white. That was why she'd gone into law enforcement. She didn't want to deal in gray. Either it was wrong or it was right, and there was a law or a statute or a code to enforce it. It had been that simple. This clear line between good and bad was what made her a great cop and an even better detective. But that was *before*.

"And Lon? How is he here *and* gone?"

"You have forgotten it all," the old woman said, sighing. "The spirit world is the real world. Off the reserve, they might say he's dead ten years, but here we know there is no divide; we can walk in the spirit world and it's as real as the sun on our skin."

"Grandmother, what are you telling her?"

Starr hadn't heard Odeina come in through the door behind her.

Starr wanted to know the *why*. And she was damn sure going to find out. Maybe Junior was the answer. But first she had a dead girl on her hands.

Starr was out of the trailer before the old woman could say another word, with Odeina hot on her heels.

"She doesn't always know what she's saying," Odeina called after her. "She honors the old ways—and so do I, as much as I can—but if she told you not to look for Chenoa . . . if she told you . . ."

"I came to tell you not to panic," Starr said over her shoulder. "The body of a young woman was found on the reservation this morning, but it was not Chenoa."

Odeina clamped her hands over her mouth. Hope and shock, rage and disappointment, at once. Around her, spooked deer bounded away and into the wilderness.

CHAPTER FOURTEEN

✳

Instead of grabbing something to eat from the Trading Post, Starr drained what was left of the fifth of whiskey under the seat of the old Bronco before she returned to the community center—and what awaited her there.

The marshal's office, such as it was, had file boxes stacked around its entire inner perimeter. A bathroom jutted off the back of the rectangular building like an afterthought. Someone had recently equipped the space with three metal desks that looked like they'd been salvaged from a midcentury banking institution, along with a trio of swivel chairs and a drip coffee maker with hard-water stains rimming the carafe. There was a CB radio that was probably meant to serve as the official dispatch, but both Starr and Winnie had decided to rely on the landline and their cell phones, since neither of them had the expertise to get the antiquity up and running.

The BIA might have been so eager to bring in a tribal marshal that they would've hired anyone *who was warm and could hear thunder*, as Starr's dad used to say, but the bureau's sense of urgency didn't extend much past that point. Chief Byrd, aside from his response to the morning's immediate matter of a homicide victim, seemed content to remain in the background with everyone else. Winnie was Starr's best channel for rez information.

"Just missed Odeina," Winnie said from the desk she'd scooted under one of the two windows in the long wall opposite the jail cell. Winnie's height barely reached the badge on Starr's chest, and so far she'd worn an assortment of bright housedresses to work, accompanied by Crocs of different and equally loud colors. Almost every inch of her desk was covered in plants; they'd multiplied since yesterday.

"Was just at her house, so I've talked to her."

"Ooh," Winnie said, and went back to her sudoku puzzle. Without looking over her shoulder, she pointed the eraser of her pencil at the box. "He's hungry."

Inside the cell, the thin man lying on the cot, with his feet propped on the wall, revived himself.

". . . and then dip it in grease," he muttered up at the ceiling, as if he'd woken in the middle of a conversation.

"Fry bread," Winnie said. She shrugged at Starr and went back to the dog-eared puzzle book in front of her. "Joseph must have been dreaming about it."

She'd forgotten all about him.

Winnie said as far as she knew, they'd always kept the marshal's office unlocked, so Joseph could put himself to bed in the box once in a while. Starr had closed the cell during the meeting last night, and in all the ruckus had failed to open it again.

"Gets confused," Winnie said.

"I'll bet." Starr could see a wrinkled paper bag shaped like a forty-ounce lying beside the cot.

Joseph was standing now, pressing his face between two bars, chanting, "Eggs and bacon, eggs and bacon," keeping time like he was watching powwow dancers.

"Joseph, let's see what we can do about that," said Starr as she unlocked the door. There was a ripe odor of rising heat mixed with stale beer and sweat. Maybe she could get Winnie to run to the Trading Post and grab a sandwich for him. Breakfast had come and gone hours ago, but it didn't seem like he cared.

Starr, holding her breath, was guiding Joseph to the exit when a man she'd never seen before popped up from a perp chair beside her desk, knocking over a big ficus Winnie must have dragged in from somewhere. He immediately assumed the fig-leaf position, hands clasped over his crotch like he'd just taken a bite of forbidden fruit. He was young. Wet behind the ears. Fresh. Maybe thirty, thirty-two.

He started toward her, his face alive with questions, but Starr reached casually for the handle of her service weapon. This seemed to immediately dissuade the man from approaching, although he didn't seem alarmed.

"Haven't had nothin' all night," Joseph complained. "It's not right, shutting me in here. It's abuse. I got rights. At least get me an egg sandwich. I'd even take a . . ."

Starr ignored him, looking instead to the shiny young man.

As if she'd asked him a question, the man rolled up onto the balls of his feet.

"Shane," he said, pumping her hand. His touch was clammy, and Starr wiped her palm on her pants when he'd finally released his catch. "Shane Minkle."

When she didn't reply, he kept going. "They sent me over from town. Mayor heard about the . . . uh"—he leaned in close—"incident. Said you could use a little help over here, so I'm on loan." He saw her expression and tumbled onward. "What I mean is, uh, I'm sure you've got it under control, but, yeah, I'm your new right-hand man," he trailed off doubtfully.

"C'mon," she said, heading to the door and herding Joseph along with her. "Get your own breakfast, buddy. Lunch, dinner, whatever. Go to the Trading Post; get whatever you want." She pulled a twenty from her pocket, and Joseph snatched it before leaving without a backward glance.

Starr kept moving. Winnie tailed her out the door. Minkle followed.

"Look, Winnie, I need you to do something for me, about the"—she looked Minkle over, unsure whether she wanted to loop him in—"someone we found this morning. Can you put out some feelers, see if there's any rumors going around that might be helpful for me to know about . . . well, about anything? Call me if you hear something interesting. Anything at all."

"About Chenoa?"

"About anyone," Starr said. Why not let Minkle hear? Might as well sprinkle some factual information into the rumor mill. "The woman Chak found was not Chenoa. There's still no clear evidence that Chenoa didn't just leave for a few days, stay with friends, whatever. Maybe she went back to the university and just didn't feel like checking in. It's a little early to panic."

"So who was it?" Winnie said.

"We aren't sure whose body was found this morning."

The search for Chenoa would have to wait. Starr would have to sort this thing with Minkle later. She had a dead girl to meet at the morgue.

CHAPTER FIFTEEN

✳

Thirty minutes later, Starr and Minkle rattled through the pitted back lot of Dexter Springs' tiny hospital. A placard, the "E" missing, was affixed to an exterior wall near a plain gray door with a keypad. MORGU, it said.

Minkle was tense beside her and seemed eager to fulfill whatever nebulous duties he'd been assigned as a loaned officer. "Call me Minkey," he'd said to fill the silence. "No one calls me Minkle except when I'm late for dinner." He laughed nervously at his own joke.

Starr didn't have a plan, except to camp out in the medical examiner's office in the hope that her presence would make the autopsy go faster. Then she would send Minkey back where he'd come from. She didn't need Dexter Springs' mayor to send over a fresh recruit, even one on loan, until she made a new hire. *Out of bounds,* she thought, a phrase her father used to say. He was with her all the time here, a new wrinkle she didn't have time to even consider.

Starr punched in the passcode she'd received in a text. Nothing happened. She looked at the text again, this time keying in each digit with a long, hard press. There was a slow, ancient-sounding click, and she pulled on the door until its tired hydraulics mustered an opening wide enough for her and Minkey to slip through. The medical examiner's office probably used the bay more often, she thought, eyeing the coroner van behind the overhead door to their right.

They entered a long, sporadically lit corridor, the bank of fluorescents issuing a high-pitched whine. Minkey looked like a feral cat in a live trap, his wide eyes roving for escape.

"You ever seen one of these?" she asked.

"Me? Oh yeah. At the academy we toured—"

"No, not the morgue. A body. An autopsy."

"Oh . . ." He trailed off.

Starr pushed through a swinging double door. There was a woman at a counter, her lab coat a crisp white, who turned and extended a pleasant greeting.

"Marshal Starr?" She was wearing disposable shoe covers and a thin blue surgical cap. She had a clear face shield propped up onto her forehead like a welder's helmet.

Seeing Starr's nod, she directed them through another door, then down a corridor that was shorter than the first one they'd been in, and finally into an autopsy room.

"Doctor Tess Moore," she said, stopping near the door they'd just entered through. "I was working on the details of your report right as you walked in. Perfect timing." Her voice was so measured she might have been meeting Starr and Minkey at a cocktail party.

Dr. Moore stretched a pair of blue latex gloves, and then pulled them precisely over each slim finger. She handed a pair to Starr and she did the same, although with less grace. When Dr. Moore offered a pair to Minkey, he looked to Starr for approval and she shrugged, then caught Dr. Moore's gaze. Starr liked her already.

Minkey plastered an attentive look on his face and stood well behind them as they approached the body on the steel table. When he caught sight of the body, he gasped and took a few steps backward.

"You gonna be okay?" Starr said, and shared another look with Dr. Moore.

"Me? Yes, yes," Minkey stuttered. "Fine."

"Usually this takes longer," Dr. Moore said, "but I put a rush on it."

Starr nodded. She knew the medical examiner had done her a favor, and was grateful. By the time Dr. Moore's forensic photographer had reached the remote site earlier that day, Starr had marked all the potential evidence. She'd sent Chak to the main road to watch for the photographer's vehicle and signal where to turn. She had to admit, he'd been a trouper.

"I'll skim the things you already know. Female. Young, probably about twenty, maybe twenty-two. No evidence of sexual assault. No defensive wounds. No broken nails to indicate a fight. Nothing under the nails at all, really."

Even with the damage brought on by the young woman's recent death, Starr knew she had been pretty. Starr wondered about her, this woman on the table, and thought of the movie posters on Chenoa's bedroom wall, the life she must have outgrown. What had this woman desired that had died with her? And Quinn, what future had she dreamed of? What parts of her adolescence would she have left behind for adulthood? Her room, always such a mess. Emptying her closet onto the floor only to find an outfit she was never quite satisfied with. Or the endless stacks of cereal bowls on her bedside table, the Lucky Charms bloating and beginning to decay. Who would Quinn have become? A shot of pain, physical as anything Starr had ever felt, pulsed through her chest.

". . . and that's about it," Dr. Moore concluded.

Shit, thought Starr. *What did I miss? Fucking pay attention.*

"What else?" Starr said, rubbing her sternum. "Anything unusual?"

"That's just it," Dr. Moore said. "There's a lot we can't know after the fact, but the usual things we look for—they're not there. The interesting thing is the back of her head. Multiple skull fractures, but all along the back. Only on the back of her skull."

Starr looked at Dr. Moore—someone who seemed to have it all together—more blankly than she wanted to.

"So, when people are struck with a blunt object," Dr. Moore explained, "or when they have blunt force trauma—particularly to the skull—and the blow is from behind, most people, if they aren't knocked unconscious, will turn their head toward the attacker behind them. This means any subsequent blows, if there are any, will usually fall along the side of the head."

Starr was catching on.

"And these blows," said Starr, "were all in the same place?"

"Exactly. Multiple blows landing sequentially, same location."

"Then she must have been—"

"Unconscious. Maybe passed out, possibly deceased. We'll know more when I get the blood work back. Not sleeping. Even in a deep sleep, there would have been head movement after the first blow."

Minkey was nodding along but looking pointedly at a spot below an old round clock—Starr could hear it ticking like a metronome—and a row of framed credentials on the wall. Looking anywhere but at the body.

"The real problem, though, is that I don't have any other find-ings that are very helpful."

"I see," Starr said. "Tell me what your experience says about this body." She could feel the hope she'd had, of getting an easy lead, slide down toward her boots.

"When it comes to fibers, DNA or anything else that might give us some identification of who might be responsible"—Dr. Moore turned from the body and looked directly at Starr—"we don't have anything notable. Like I mentioned earlier, there is nothing under the nails, nothing around the nail beds. If there were foreign fibers or hairs, the elements she was exposed to may have eliminated them."

Starr looked at Minkey, who was taking short, shallow breaths and glancing alternately at the victim and at the wall.

"Time of death?"

"Based on rigidity and other factors, I would place it between midnight and six o'clock Thursday morning, but most likely sometime in the early-morning hours."

"Any luck with an ID?" Starr asked.

"Not yet. There is one thing, though."

Starr followed Dr. Moore to the end of the table where the girl's neck was propped on a U-shaped stand to keep her head positioned.

"The soil that had been placed in her mouth was probably put there after death. We'll take a closer look at it, but it doesn't seem consistent with the type of soil where she was found."

Stuffing a victim's mouth with soil revealed a lot about the crime. Intentionality, for one thing. Could even be a calling card left by a repeat offender. And the soil in the mouth and throat looked different from the soil where the body had been found, so where had it come from? Had the killer brought it with him or her? Taken the time to put it in a baggie and carry it in a pocket? Chosen this woman as a victim? Or had her murder been a crime of opportunity?

The bonfire, discarded beer cans, empty bottles and cigarette stubs were signs of a party. Chak had even confirmed that older kids partied at Turkey Creek. Had the killer been one of them? Waited until the party was breaking up and taken advantage of someone left there alone, vulnerable? Starr would have to wait for the blood tests, but wondered whether the victim had been incapacitated, passed out or drunk or drugged. What other clues or signs did her body hold?

Starr peered more closely, trying to make sense of the girl's blood-matted hair, which was still full of debris.

"What is this?" Starr asked. "Bark? Wood chips?" She thought of the logs, the firewood. The fire.

"It looks, to me at least, like these blows to the skull came from two different blunt objects. See here? There are two kinds of patterns. One is long and rather narrow, from a thin metal object, like a pipe or maybe a golf club. The other object was wide and left some debris behind. See how the splinters are embedded here?"

Dr. Moore pointed to the thick splinters that had pushed into the mass of bone, skin, flesh and hair. The campfire log Starr had collected from the scene. It was time to call in a favor—if she still could.

CHAPTER SIXTEEN

Hey, I got a weird one for you," Starr said into the landline at the marshal's office. It was late afternoon and she still felt like she was at the starting line of this investigation.

After she and Minkey left the morgue, they'd grabbed drive-through burgers, and then she'd sent him to canvass the rez. He probably wouldn't get anywhere, but she figured word had already started to spread about the death by the creek. No one had been reported missing, but that didn't mean the body didn't belong to someone who lived on the reservation. Starr was learning that, in many ways, the reservation operated like an extended family with young adults who weren't always tied to one home. She had picked up her phone and dialed a Chicago number by memory.

"Send over the file." The voice that answered at the other end of the line was brisk and cool.

"Earlie? It's me, Starr. Good to know you're still a phone call away."

"Girl, what you up to?" Earlie's tone changed immediately.

"Been a minute. Been a hot minute . . . been a lotta minutes . . . thought you might have disappeared on me."

Hearing Earlie—the name was short for Earlene—was both a balm and a sting to Starr. She felt a sudden longing for her old life, for her friend. It was painful, the way a once-broken bone aches before a storm.

"Yeah, I'm here," Starr said, "and you won't believe where."

After she'd filled Earlie in about escaping to the reservation, for reasons she planned never to divulge fully, Starr moved to the purpose for her call.

"Okay, here's the deal," Starr said, leaning back in the office chair at her desk and twisting her neck toward the door, even though she'd sent Winnie home an hour earlier. She wanted to keep this conversation private. "Remember that case you told me about last year, the one where they grabbed DNA from a board and it ended up being the reason they could charge the perp?"

"Oh yeah," Earlie said, slowly. Then she sped up as it came back to her. "Yes, yes. A forensic team presented that at that conference I went to in Detroit . . . two, maybe three years ago. Fascinating. So, what have you gotten yourself into?"

Starr could feel Earlie's mind working as she let the silence drag on a beat too long. She could picture Earlie in her lab coat and Doc Martens, safety glasses propped up in the mass of dark curls she wore cropped close to her head. Listening intently for whatever Starr had to say next.

"Well, here's the thing," Starr said. "I've got a body, and I've got a piece of campfire wood—a cut log, really—with what looks like some blood on one end. Maybe, if we're lucky, there are some fibers, maybe hair follicles that didn't belong to the vic. Victim was struck in the head with something, maybe this log we put in evidence, and I'd like to see what we can get off of it," Starr said, then added, "If you're up for it."

It was a favor, after all, one that she wasn't owed. Especially after leaving the detective ranks in Chicago under questionable circumstances. Not that many people knew the whole story.

"Shit, girl," Earlene said immediately. "Bag it and FedEx it. As long as you lock down the chain of custody, I have no problem seeing where it leads."

Starr laughed a little, despite herself. *Same ol' Earlie,* she thought, grateful for her friend. Maybe the only one she still had left after . . .

"I'll let you know what I find out, but I have to warn you: Don't get your hopes up. It's a long shot. I'll need to track down some specialized equipment, and then talk that department into lending it so we can give this a try. Like I'm saying, if this were a horse race, the odds aren't great."

"Hey, Earlie, thank you," said Starr, and she meant it. "Really. I know it might not go anywhere, but I think I may have someone going around bashing skulls. First a dog's, now a female vic's, pretty young."

"Yikes," said Earlie. "So, how are you, really? You know, after your daughter . . ."

Starr was quiet for so long, Earlie finally asked if they'd been disconnected.

"I'm doing okay. Getting by."

It wasn't the first lie she'd told since taking this job, but it was the first one she regretted. Earlie could probably handle the truth, but now didn't feel like the time to come clean. Something was shifting.

Lucy Cloud might explain it differently, but to Starr it felt like the old rush, the salve of an open investigation that brought relief by requiring laser focus. Work allowed her to set down everything else. Starr wanted to cling to the feeling as long as she could. It was the only reason she'd gotten out of bed that morning.

"Uh-huh," Earlie said, sounding doubtful. Starr could tell Earlie's bullshit meter was ranging into the red but she said nothing more, and Starr was grateful when the conversation moved on.

"It'll take a while," Earlie said.

For a second Starr thought Earlie was talking about her; then she realized she meant the forensic examination.

"It's our busy season," Earlie added before they hung up, "but I'll do my darndest to work it in."

Satisfied that if anything of value could be extracted it would be, Starr shuffled some of the mess of papers on her desk into stacks, and eyed Minkey as he came into the office.

"Anything?"

"Couldn't get anyone to come to the door," he said, "but I can go back out, keep trying."

Starr pulled from her desk drawer the evidence bag containing the firewood. When she'd gathered it from the scene by the creek in Crawl Canyon, she didn't know how—or if—it might factor into the investigation. Now she planned to overnight it to Earlie as soon as she got to town. When she looked up, Minkey was standing next to an old metal filing cabinet, trying to make sense of the coffee situation.

"Got too many pieces to be just one coffee machine," he said, holding up a mesh cylinder that looked to be part of a percolator from circa 1965.

Starr shrugged, dug the heels of her boots into the floor, and pushed. She grabbed the Bronco keys as her chair careened back from the desk.

Too bad, Starr thought. The hope that he'd be able to do some useful legwork for her was fading.

In the morning she would straighten out this officer-on-loan situation with the Dexter Springs mayor, find out just what the hell the mayor was thinking. But before that, as soon as the sun came up, she planned to do some fishing.

"Leave the coffee," she said. "Let's go see if we can get anyone to talk."

CHAPTER SEVENTEEN

The door swung open just as Starr made the third knock with the hard edge of a fist, and the flash of fur had her leg in its teeth before she understood what was happening. Her brain had just enough time to form the word *dog*, but already she'd been knocked from the porch stairs with her hands behind her, scrabbling away from the teeth that writhed over her boot and tore through her pant leg.

Starr was pushing her other boot into its furious mouth when a big man emerged and tried to wedge a broom handle between her and the dog. From a series of outdoor kennels behind the house that Starr couldn't see, a chorus of barks and howls sliced through the thin autumn air.

"Damn it," the man said. "Damn it all to hell. Chak, get the leash."

Starr, on her back, could see inside the trailer: a massive TV flickering light across the dim interior, the curtains closed. Under the snarling she heard the ticking of a *Wheel of Fortune* spin, then the sound of disappointment from the crowd, then stuttering applause. By the time she thought to reach for her sidearm, the dog was gone, yanked back by its collar. It wasn't the friendly dog that had ridden with Chak in her truck when they'd driven to the crime scene by the creek, but a different one, a missile shaped like a German shepherd with humorless eyes.

A hand reached down to pull her up, and she stood three feet from the dog, which was now wagging its tail, panting for approval from the mountain of a man. Adrenaline shook her legs.

"Sorry." It was Chak. He appeared between her and the Mountain, who must be his father, Chak looking as animated as she'd ever seen him, more so even than when he'd told her how he found the body.

"Come in, come on in," said the Mountain. "Let's get a good look at that leg."

Inside, Starr sank onto a kitchen chair, its vinyl cushion whooshing air, and surveyed her leg. The uniform pants were torn and there were teeth marks in the leather of her boot. She felt the wet heat of blood on her calf, but when she lifted the fabric there were only welts where the teeth had scraped.

"Lucky," said the Mountain, peering down at her leg. "Coulda been a lot worse." He ruffled the dog's ears. It sat beside him, satisfied, its eyes following Starr's movements. Then the Mountain took in her badge.

"I hear you already met my son, Chak. Now what do you want?"

What had she wanted? Some strange need, some winged thing? The sound of her pulse rushed in her ears. She wondered briefly where she was. What she was.

The dog watched her, curious.

Starr exhaled, put a hand inside her pocket and drew out her phone.

"You know this girl?"

A dead girl stared out from a grainy crime-scene picture. Starr observed the Mountain's eyes, his reaction, that split second of truth before the mask slid on.

"What are you asking me for? He's the one who found her."

"Asking everybody. When was the last time you saw her?"

"Don't even know her."

"You sure about that?"

Starr could feel Chak watching the Mountain, watching her.

"You're not gonna put this on me. Not on me, not on my boy. I said he could help you, could show you what he found, but that's as far as we go." He turned his back to her, opened an almond-colored refrigerator and stood in the rectangle of light that poured over the peeling linoleum floor. "In fact, what you're gonna do is get out of my house."

"Yeah," Starr said, pushing off the chair and standing to her full height. If he turned on her, she'd be ready. "Yeah, okay. How long have you lived here?"

"Sixteen years, thereabouts. Now get out."

The Mountain slowly pulled a Pepsi from the refrigerator and cracked it, but he didn't turn around. Instead, Chak rushed past Starr to the front door and opened it.

"Your dad's a real charmer," she said, looking back at the Mountain as she made her exit. "He have a name?"

"Denny. Uh, Dennis. Same last name as me. Spicer." Another dog ran from behind the trailer and nosed Chak, wagging its tail. It was the same liver-spotted hound she and Chak had taken to the creek so Chak could show her the body. "Hey, uh, sorry about my dad's dog. Princess is kind of scrappy when it comes to strangers."

"Anybody else live with you two?"

"Just us." Chak's dog saw a trio of deer move across the road and went still, its muzzle and one of its front paws extended like an arrow aimed at a target.

"Oh, hey, you see them deers, don't ya, boy?" He looked up at Starr. "You see them deers too? Don't let them spook ya like last time."

Starr waited until he was done laughing, until the deer moved off and the dog relaxed into a lean against Chak's leg. She pulled from her jacket a photo she'd found in Chenoa's room; it was of the girl and her van.

"Seen her around?"

"Nope." Chak shook his head.

"You see this van or hear anything, from anyone around here, you come talk to me," she said. "Come by the marshal's office. We can talk outside, or anywhere you want. The important thing is that you tell me."

"You're not gonna get me in trouble, right?" Chak glanced back at the trailer door.

"Absolutely not."

Starr left the porch and looked to make sure the curtains didn't part, then limped around the corner of the trailer to reinspect her leg.

Chak's dad was the only one who had answered when she'd knocked on the half dozen or so houses lining the road. She hoped Minkey was having better luck down the street.

She was surveying the surrounding houses and mapping out a plan when the sound of conversation caught her attention. Starr stepped back, pulling herself into the shadows at the end of the trailer, and watched as Minkey exited a brick house three doors down. A woman holding a child by the hand ducked under his arm, and Minkey reached back to retrieve a laundry basket that he then hefted to a clothesline strung between the house and a garden shed. While the child crouched to watch something intently in the grass, Minkey balanced the basket on a lawn chair and together he and the woman started to hang wet clothing on the line.

It was so surprisingly domestic, so companionable, that it sent an unmistakable ache through Starr. Where she'd been turned away, Minkey had gone easily.

And he too was a stranger. Or so she'd thought. Did he know this woman? She watched the ease of their interaction, Minkey stooping to tousle the child's hair as he walked away, and then turning to offer a wave.

Starr backed farther into the shadows and then retraced her steps through a side yard to the Bronco parked a road over. A noisy flock of Canada geese created a loose V overhead, the stragglers rushing to catch up as twilight set in. They were leaving. Like she should.

Later, after she and Minkey had both been at the marshal's office for an hour, Starr rubbed her leg, which still stung from the dog bite, and thought of Junior, his yellow dog and its strange death. And now the girl. Starr had already sorted through one box of cold cases, hoping to find a connection, anything, while Minkey hunched over a notepad, flipping through pages, at an otherwise empty desk. She walked over to him.

"Let's head out. Start again tomorrow morning. You make any progress?"

He shoved the notepad into a pocket, then tapped a pen on the desk and leaned back in his chair, trying for all the world to look casual.

"Nothing much. You know what it was like on that street we walked. Nobody wanted to talk. I did show the picture to one woman who recognized the vic but didn't know her name. Hadn't seen her in about a year. I didn't really get anywhere."

"Nobody you knew?"

Minkey's head snapped up in surprise. "Not a soul," he said carefully.

Ah, there's the lie. Minkey, she decided, would be one to watch—along with everyone else.

CHAPTER EIGHTEEN

✳

Junior stood on the bank of Turkey Creek in the dark, shining a flashlight beam onto yards of yellow tape crackling in the night wind. He'd hoped to pick up more empty bottles, this time without any onlookers like before. But this was new. This was bad.

He didn't remember leaving the creek last night, but he did recall setting out after he'd had the whiskey, and wishing for Yella dog to lick his hands, to run in the tall grass alongside him, to bark at things he couldn't see. Yella lived for the two-mile walk from the cabin to the creek bed, a cattywampus trek they'd taken so often that they'd nearly worn a trail.

Junior had heard the party before he saw it, and wasn't a bit surprised to see a bonfire and find a crowd full of faces he didn't recognize anymore. The party was why he went there, after all. It was a sure thing, discovering discarded cans and bottles at the creek. He must have collected them before he left, because just that morning he'd woken up on Odeina's couch with shoes full of sand and a sack stuffed with glass, the old woman watching him patiently from across the room.

"Grandmother."

"Another one" was all she would say. "Another one taken from the living."

Junior had spent most of the day's remaining light getting home by hitching a ride, then walking the rest of the way. He expected Yella to bark a greeting, then remembered the dog was dead; he trudged inside, made a bologna sandwich and set out once more for the creek.

Where he wanted to be now, where he felt alive, was in the wide open. Junior pulled a long stalk of feather grass as he walked and worked it with his teeth, the fluffy head bending in the wind to tickle his neck, his chin. His fear of the land becoming blighted with a mining camp was the only thing that could have brought him out of hiding, caused him to speak at tribal council, made him break his commitment to solitude.

He'd kept to himself for ten long years, making only occasional visits to the Trading Post, where he sometimes drank too much and let his fists make contact with skin, with blood, with bone. It was the pain he kept coming back to, pulling it around himself like a blanket and using it to ward away memories of those long-ago high school kids always hanging around.

He'd liked the company in those days. Liked the girls especially, with their dangerous looks, the way they paraded as women but were still tender flesh in their unlined beauty and the soft way they tried too hard to be ready for the world. In the night there was always some group outside his cabin, not at the creek like now, and they had swapped smokes and sips around a burn barrel. Or squeezed onto his broken couch, touching at the shoulders and thighs.

Those old days. He didn't think of them often, not anymore. Kept them partitioned in a part of himself that locked up things that hurt: losing Starr's father, a war, his loneliness, Loxie.

He'd withdrawn after Loxie disappeared. Disappeared in that bad way. Maybe it was not knowing what happened to her that caused him to be cautious. Or maybe it was the eye of suspicion cast over his life that made him want to hide away. And that was what he'd done with the cabin, made it a den he could hole up in like an animal. Like some foul yeasty thing hibernating until a thaw.

Where had his mind gone on those nights he couldn't remember? What about his hands, those strange creatures that had a mind of their own when he drank, making fists or love? What about the rest of him, the hidden parts that longed for contact, to be made real in what they pushed against?

Had Loxie been at the cabin when he lost himself? Yes. Of course she had. He remembered that clearly, the beginnings of those nights, those hazy next days. But had she been there *that* night? The last night she was seen? What was he capable of? But that was one question to which he knew the answer. War had tapped a part of him that had been resting in his DNA for generations; it had unleashed the spirit of ancestors who whispered that it was time to kill.

He'd found no evidence of having done an unspeakable thing, not to Loxie. Not to any of those girls, or the boys who tagged along with them, hopeful for their shot. No clothing left behind, no spatters of blood; and with relief, no body. And he would remember a body, wouldn't he? The only things left of those days, of Loxie, were the muddled memories he couldn't see his way through, and the fairy rings—those dried flowers she'd woven again and again into circles. Once, they'd been everywhere. He'd found them hanging on the arms of camp chairs, lying on tired transmissions, in the place where Yella slept. He was down to only one now, the others gone to the wind and rain and whatever other elements broke things down into their most basic parts, returned them to earth—to biome, to microbe, to resurrection in a future life, riding in the cell of a creature furred or fanged or feathered. He longed suddenly for that flower ring, to know her long brown fingers had plucked each stem, pulled it into a weave, fashioned it into something more.

Junior walked down the creek, skirting the caution tape and the spent firewood, hoping for an answer. He heard rustling in the bushes near the woods and flashed a beam of light at it, expecting a possum or maybe a skunk, but instead it was a woman, motioning for him to come near. He couldn't believe what he saw in the circle of light. Had she been at the party the night before? Did she need help? Was she looking for answers too?

She turned away from him.

"Wait," he croaked. "Wait. I need to . . . who are . . ."

He followed, his flashlight waving as he hurried, its beam catching a pair of antlers against bare branches.

His knees went out and he dropped the light, felt the gritty surface run under his skin as he buckled into the sand.

"What have I done?" Junior screamed into the pitch.

Here it was at last. What he'd always feared. Deer Woman had come for him.

CHAPTER NINETEEN

FRIDAY

Starr caught the scent of coffee beans from the sidewalk well before she reached the entrance to Dexter Springs' only downtown coffee shop. As she entered Rita's Roast, the jangle of sleigh bells hanging from the door didn't even get on her nerves. She was thinking about Chak's sketch and the half dozen or so black pickups she'd spotted that morning alone.

There was a Route 66 placard mounted prominently above a counter fronted by four empty stools that kept watch over several tables, most of them occupied at this time of day. The chatter of old men who had settled in for a morning of coffee refills, and of young mothers momentarily free of their school-age children, ceased at the sight of Starr's uniform, but she smiled and nodded as she made her way to the counter. It was time to cast a line.

Starr looked over a plastic-covered menu, then ordered a maple long john and a brewed coffee from a woman whose name tag said MAGGIE. Starr added a splash of cream when the coffee arrived, and casually clocked the room while stirring it to the color of mahogany. Her stomach growled, loudly enough that Maggie laughed good-naturedly as she handed her the bar-shaped doughnut.

Starr took a careful sip from the paper cup. It was coffee, all right, but not the best she'd ever had. She sat at a two-person table, with her back to the empty counter, and offered a friendly smile to anyone who made eye contact. *That should do it,* she thought, and settled in until it was time to set the hook.

The moms finished and went on their way, but they weren't the pond Starr was fishing in. It was the old men. Her first partner on the Chicago police force, long since retired, said the local co-op where farmers gathered was the place for gossip. Turned out he was right, and not just about the co-op. Eventually she discovered that his advice translated to all kinds of settings, even this one.

As Starr sipped her coffee, she knew she'd guessed right: The local men gathered here every morning, and hashed out news, rumors and more. And they were a curious lot, eager for fodder. It was only a matter of time.

She watched as a lanky fellow in worn blue jeans and dirty cowboy boots stood from where he'd been parked at a crowded table.

"Crazy Horse," he said, coming toward her, carrying his cup of coffee. "Or are you Sitting Bull?" Starr made a show of glancing confusedly behind her, then pointed to her chest and mouthed, *Me?*

"Horace-Wayne Holder." He stuck out a hand, level with the detail of his silver-plated belt buckle. "I'm just jokin' with ya—take it easy. You can call me Holder."

Starr gave his hand a hard shake, then leaned back in her chair to cross her right boot on her left knee. *Don't jerk the line yet,* she thought.

"So, you're the law in these here parts." He shook his head as if he couldn't believe it. "I mean, those reservation parts. Not *here* here." He looked at his posse, who were pretending not to watch. "You don't look Indian. Or maybe you do. Hard to tell anymore. Surprised you have time to relax, with that girl who's gone missing." He pointed to a grainy flyer. "Probably drugs. Lots of that out there. Big problem."

Starr peered at the flyer and Chenoa's eyes stared back at her, ink on paper. How had Chenoa dealt with this kind of racism? Starr knew Odeina had plastered flyers all around the Trading Post, where she worked, and it looked like she'd been here too. Were the flyers all over town?

"Ah, you know, getting the lay of the land. Gotta figure out what's what. Fuel up."

"Well, what I figure is with that new pipeline business going through there, all them Indians can afford to spend a little money on a policeman of their own, get their hands off our tax dollars."

Starr raised her eyebrows.

"Marshal," she said. "Bureau of Indian Affairs, more like it."

Holder pulled up a chair from the table behind him and sat backward in it, leaning his chin on the backrest, balancing a cup of coffee on his knee.

"Is that so? Hope you know what you got yourself into. It's rough out there, not like in town where we're all civilized and such."

"Oh, here we go," said a white-haired man at a nearby table, goading him on. "It's getting deep in here." He looked at Starr's feet. "Good thing you got boots on." The men at the table erupted in laughter.

Starr took an enormous bite of the long john, shards of maple icing falling to the plate. She smiled at him around the food as she chewed.

"See, to me it don't make no sense," Holder continued. "Why they ain't done it sooner. Found a way to make some money, stop scrimping through life. Damn near every other tribe around here has a casino at least. But what do I know? Maybe they just don't care how they live."

Starr shrugged and took another bite. Let him keep talking.

"This latest girl, she's what . . . the eighth, ninth girl that's run off from the reservation? Or gone missing. Whatever."

"You tell me," Starr said. "I'm new here."

"Well, don't you think you oughta know?" He looked her over. "Ain't that your business now?" He leaned back in the chair. "Way I see it, it ain't got nothing to do with us. Not with Dexter Springs, not with anyone who isn't on the rez."

The door to the coffee shop jingled and Holder turned his attention to the entrance, long enough for Starr to take the temperature of the room. Everyone had relaxed into their conversations again. Time to jerk the line, set the hook. "Why's that?"

"Meth, mostly. If they're not making it, they're taking it. Bad doin's out there, ain't no place for a nice girl."

Starr wondered whether he meant her—although she hadn't thought of herself as a *girl* in a long time—or the young women who were missing.

"Think about it. Why not girls from town? It's just the Indian ones go missing, because they're the ones either get messed up, mixed up or just plain run away."

"Refill?" She stuffed the last of the long john into her mouth, wiped her hands on her uniform pants, stood and picked up a carafe of drip coffee from the counter, then topped off both their cups.

"Yeah, like I was saying, seems like it's something real bad going on out there."

"You don't think they're getting picked up," Starr said, "maybe trying to hitchhike their way out?"

"Could be." He blew on his coffee, contemplating. "I still keep on the chatter. Got a CB and scanner in my truck. I think if there was someone picking up girls wanting a ride somewhere, somebody would have seen or heard something. If I were a bettin' man, I'd put money on a bad Indian going after his own."

"You're that sure." Starr considered this for a moment. "What about around here?"

"I don't know nothing about that. I'm just a simple man." He winked. "Run a few head of cattle, drive a route checking oil wells for one of them outfits out of Oklahoma City. It's not like we've got some crazy fool, somebody real bad, running around Dexter Springs. If we did, we'd all know about it by now."

Starr shifted. Word gets around in a small town. And Holder had a point about the rez. Two girls who were thought to be missing a year ago had turned up with a known dealer. Not everyone who was believed to be in danger ended up with their name in a BIA file, which made the number of cold cases Starr had in her office all the more astonishing. Come to think of it, Junior Echo's name had been in those files too. Petty stuff, warnings for public drunkenness or fighting. Maybe it was time to pay him another visit.

"Hey, you still with me, Crazy Horse?"

She laid a twenty on the counter. She had what she'd come for, an arrow of thought that would send her in a new direction.

"Yeah," Starr said. "See you around."

CHAPTER TWENTY

✳

A block west of the coffee shop, Starr noticed Minkey pacing on the sidewalk in front of city hall, where they'd agreed to meet. She looked at her watch. Nine a.m. He was punctual; she'd give him that.

Starr had planned to march into the mayor's office to ask why the hell she'd been gifted a deputy, but after talking to Holder she'd decided on a different approach. This wasn't Chicago. Starr shook her head at the thought of a loan like this happening in Chicago. No one she knew would willingly take a bite out of their own budget, so she'd decided to sniff around first and find out who she was dealing with. Especially now that the work was piling up, not to mention the boxes of cold-case files lining her office that she had yet to investigate.

The mayor's office was part of a new complex that housed Dexter Springs' fire and police departments as well as its city administration. *Fancy for a small town*, Starr thought as she followed Minkey inside.

The lobby was artificially cool, bright and quiet. A windowed dome overhead gave cathedral height to the open rotunda and flooded it with sun. As Starr's boots sounded across the tiles she thought of the PBS documentary she'd zoned out to last night. The Missouri State Capitol had a rotunda whose curved walls carried sound, enabling visitors to hear whispered exchanges—even from across the hundred-foot space. A whisper gallery. A lion's den.

A receptionist, who Starr later learned doubled as a payroll clerk, hit a buzzer and came around a counter to open a security door.

"I'll be back. You can wait here," Starr told Minkey. Although she'd planned to bring him along as evidence, she now thought better of it. He looked surprised but nodded agreeably.

The receptionist led her through an office-lined corridor where she caught glimpses of people peering at computer screens. Near the mayor's door, at the end of the hall, Starr could see an exit that must also serve as a private entrance.

"Marshal," said a friendly voice. Starr turned into a large office in time to see a woman rise from behind a flimsy-looking folding table.

"My desk," the woman said. "How do you like it?"

"I've seen worse."

"It's in next year's budget, I think—I hope—but I'm glad to make do. We've been busy, as you can see," she said, and raised both arms in a gracious sweep, indicating, Starr thought, the entire complex. "Please, sit down."

Starr sat on the edge of a folding chair. The room smelled of fresh paint and new carpet. There was an engraved nameplate on the makeshift desk: MAYOR HELEN TAYLOR.

"It will all be done in good time. This building—this entire complex, really—has been years in the making. Taking another year to outfit my office won't hurt."

None of this had been what Starr expected. The cavernous lobby, the layers of security, the poorhouse furniture amid grand, new construction, and least of all, the mayor. She was Quinn's size—no more than five feet four inches, with thick blond hair tied back in a simple ponytail. Starr had pictured an old white guy in a too-small suit coat, but this mayor looked like she might be leaving in a few minutes to coach a Little League soccer team or play a round of golf on her lunch hour. She wore jeans and a white T-shirt, her toned arms tan.

This, as much as anything, made Starr decide to dive right in.

"Look, this Minkey thing. I was surprised to find an officer on loan in the marshal's office. My office. It wasn't exactly welcome, and I'd planned to come here and"—she hesitated—"read you the riot act for interference, influence, you name it. . . ."

At the sound of a quick knock the mayor looked over Starr's shoulder.

"Oh, yes, Bernard," the mayor said brightly, "come in. I'd like you to meet Marshal Starr, from over at the reservation."

Starr gritted her teeth through a series of awkward niceties and avoided saying that she already knew who he was. She'd witnessed his nervous presentation at the tribal council meeting. She was eager to get to business and felt like pushing Bernard back out into the hallway and slamming the door shut.

"I'll be back later. Nothing urgent," he said.

Starr stood and closed the door behind him.

"Turns out I could use the help, temporarily. So thank you, but there is something else too. I'd like to keep this under wraps until we make more progress on this case. The body we found—" she began, but the mayor interrupted.

"Is it the missing girl?"

Well-informed, Starr thought, but the mayor had probably seen Chenoa's face on the flyers, like everybody else who went into Rita's Roast.

"Maybe," Starr said. "Could be." No sense in giving too much away, not until she knew who she was dealing with. The only thing she knew so far was that the homicide victim wasn't Chenoa, but she was keeping that to herself for now.

"She was found on tribal land? Was there foul play? Terrible shame. I can't imagine, as a mother, what her family must be going through. You'll let me know when you have her identified?"

"As a courtesy, sure," Starr said. "Now, about this loaned officer. You may not be aware, but my post as marshal is funded by the BIA, and as part of that job, I'm tasked with hiring a—"

"Couldn't agree more," said the mayor, waving off Starr's words. "Glad there's some attention being given to this . . . this epidemic of missing Indigenous women. And what happens to our neighbors on the reservation affects Dexter Springs too. It has taken me years to get the city to this point. But finally we have the right people in the right place at the right time to make some progress."

Starr pictured the dais in the city hall public meeting room, each chair filled by a consort to the mayor, their ruling queen.

"And now that we've gotten the community support to build this complex, the process by which we've been successful can function as a blueprint for future projects. Transparency builds trust, and trust is essential to making progress. But it takes so little for the public trust to waver."

Starr hadn't come for a civics lesson, but she was starting to understand why a town the size of Dexter Springs had a brand-new city hall. The wall behind the mayor's temporary desk was thick with plaques and award certificates.

"And one of those future projects is to attract a major employer to the area. We have a company on the line, an international energy company, and we're already mapping out infrastructure. But do you know what happens when there's trouble on the reservation?"

She paused, and Starr wondered briefly if it was a practiced affectation. She could envision the mayor making earnest and impassioned speeches to sway doubters toward her pet projects.

"Deals fall through; that's what. And we just can't have that, now, can we?"

Was it the ponytail that reminded her of Quinn? Starr tried to pull her thoughts back, hated the way she'd changed, the way she was only partially there at any given time. Now it was Quinn who filled her mind, face down on the bank of a dirty creek, her thick hair spread around her like a halo, like a crown, the blond turned the color of dried blood. *No.* Starr shook her head. *That wasn't Quinn. That was another girl, that other crime scene.* She'd come here to discuss the officer she'd left in the lobby.

The mayor reached behind another table, also temporary, and moved a bag of golf clubs out of the way to search through rolls of huge engineering prints.

"Those your clubs?" Starr thought of the dead girl, of blunt objects, of blows to a skull in the dark.

"Hmm?" Helen said absently as she unfurled a large map across the table. "Oh, those? Yes, I play a little. Love the putting green, especially now that my favorite driver seems to have walked off. Callaway too. That'll teach me to keep track." She studied the map for a moment, then shook her head, rolled it up and reached for another.

"Ah, that's the one," she said.

She spread the map and stopped the ends from curling by

placing a stapler on one side of the map and her cell phone on the other.

Starr watched as the mayor unrolled other maps, laying them out in order. The letters GCIS were printed along the bottom of each, along with the date on which the topographical survey occurred. There was one for each section of town, and if Starr could have oriented herself to the streets and buildings, she was sure she'd find the filling station turned café where she'd met Holder.

"Here are the initial proposed plans." The mayor ran one tan index finger along the printed ink.

Starr moved around to the mayor's side of the table. She smelled expensive. She was probably wearing Chanel No. 5, which always made Starr think of her mother.

"Here's the highway from Dexter Springs to the reservation," the mayor said.

"What's the yellow?"

"That highlighted route is something you should be familiar with," Helen said, turning her head to look at Starr. From this vantage point her eyes were gray, Starr decided. She could make out individual flecks of gold around the edges.

"Or you will be soon, I imagine. That's the proposed highway the city will be constructing. Are you familiar with the reservation's partnership with Blackstream Oil? This is Dexter Springs' contribution to the project, building this access road right to the edge of the drilling field, and, with Chief Byrd's permission, into the reservation."

Starr traced two yellow stripes running into the open territory of the reservation's wilderness area.

The pipeline, this road, the murdered girl and Chenoa, who might be missing. Were any of these things connected? She couldn't see how they all fit together, but she didn't believe in coincidences either. She'd long ago decided that if she heard hooves she was going to bet on a horse, not a zebra.

The most likely explanation was usually the truth, but she was beginning to think everything here would be far more complicated than she'd assumed.

Maybe that was why she followed through with her new plan and, before she left the mayor's office, agreed to keep Minkey on loan for a few weeks. Or maybe the fog of grief had turned her soft.

She spotted Minkey inside the lobby entrance and waved him out. As soon as they reached the sidewalk, her cell buzzed.

"Marshal Starr."

"Dr. Moore here. I have some preliminary results on the soil found in the victim's mouth. I knew it didn't look right for Oklahoma, but I wasn't sure where it originated. See, our dirt is usually reddish brown, sometimes quite red. Iron oxide gives Oklahoma soil its color. The iron oxide dates back to the Permian geological era, about three hundred million years ago, and leaches out of sandstone and shale. This red dirt has special significance for the Native people here. It's not only a representation of Indigenous blood spilled during their forced relocation, but also a reminder of their connection to the earth."

"Okay, but what we saw in the vic's mouth was white, not red," Starr said.

"Exactly. That's what I'm saying. This victim was found on the reservation, correct?"

"Yes, by a dry creek bed."

"What we found in her mouth is not our red soil at all, but kaolin. Pure kaolin."

"What is that, a new kind of drug or something?"

"No, not at all," said Dr. Moore. Starr could hear something behind her words, an upswell. "This white dirt is a type of clay, soft and chalky. I did a little research, and while there isn't a sizable deposit of kaolin in northeast Oklahoma, it's common in the southeastern United States. The thing is, kaolin is quite valuable. There's a huge demand for it, everything from cosmetics to pharmaceuticals."

Blinking in the bright midmorning sun, Starr paused on the sidewalk. Kaolin. This added a new layer to the investigation. Why had it been important to the killer to fill the victim's mouth with kaolin? And where had it come from? The soil could be crucial to the investigation. She would add it to Minkey's line of questioning when he went door to door on the rez. She hoped today's knock-and-talk would yield more information than the day before, at least for her. She'd received the same frosty welcome she had on Wednesday, when her official vehicle had been tagged with *colonizer*. Meanwhile, Minkey seemed to have a way with people. He was an outsider too, even more than she was. Yet she'd seen him get a woman not only to answer the door but to invite him in. What did Starr have to do so that someone, anyone, would open up to her? What was she missing that Minkey seemed to understand?

"Thanks, Doc," she said, and hung up. She turned to Minkey. "Interview everyone on the rez that you can. Get a bead on people. Flash the picture; find out what anyone knows about a young woman fitting our vic's description. There was a white chalklike particulate in her mouth that Dr. Moore says is kaolin. It's valuable, so someone could be keeping a small amount of it in a bowl, a bucket, a baggie, that sort of thing. Keep an eye out for it. Find out if anyone's heard of it. Oh, and ask about Chenoa, when they last saw her."

Starr shaded her eyes. A reflection was making her squint, and she tracked it across the street, where a window washer was soaping and scraping the glass on an old limestone building until it shone. The library.

It was time to find a better map.

CHAPTER TWENTY-ONE

✳

In the refuge of Dexter Springs Public Library's reference section, Bernard Gilfoil sat crisply in a hard-backed chair at a long table punctuated with dividers. He'd just left city hall, where he'd officially met the new marshal—though he'd already seen her at the tribal council meeting earlier that week. And, thanks to his long practice of eavesdropping, he'd learned that a body had been found.

He'd seen the grainy pictures of a missing rez woman on tacked-up flyers, same as everyone else in town. Now he was scanning the local newspaper.

"Bernie! B-Man!"

Bernard cringed at the sound of his high school nickname, something he'd left behind the day he graduated. That had been ten not-long-enough years ago, before a series of low-level city-government jobs stymied by a now-rotten economy had propelled him back to Dexter Springs with all the subtle force of gravitational pull. Six months ago he'd completed the final course for a master's degree in public administration, and six weeks ago he'd taken the first managerial job he'd been offered. His orbit around Dexter Springs felt inescapable.

Bernard didn't need to glance at his watch to know his morning break was nearly over. He was new to the city-manager role, but already he excelled at the work—the puzzle of bringing together funding sources and engineering plans, the specific skill of soothing a city council. He understood the rhythm of his day.

When he left Dexter Springs after high school, Bernard thought he'd never come back, and in the interim he'd worked hard to cultivate a different life for himself. In the decade he'd been gone, he had transformed from high school burnout to buttoned-up professional, even if it felt like a costume he stepped into every morning.

Still, history followed him.

History was, in fact, now tromping through an aisle between shelves, whispering his name more loudly than if she'd just spoken at a normal volume.

"Bernie!"

And there she was, rounding the corner, having entirely passed Biographies E–M on her left and the How To section on her right: Mitzie Gatz, who'd been the singular source of scandalous activity in his high school class.

"Oh, Bernie, I thought I saw you. Did you—"

He held up his hand like a stop sign. "I will not be in attendance."

"But you got my text?" Mitzie said. "I ran into your mother and she gave me your number. I thought, of course you'd like to see if any of the old crowd was still around. Paul and Stacy are gonna grab a pony keg and—"

She turned and crouched as a toddler tumbled from behind a shelf, dangling a book by one side of its cover.

"Dang it, Paisley girl," she said, and glanced around for the librarian. "Gimme that."

When she knelt with her back to him, Bernard could see right down the gap of her jeans. A crimson thong the shade of their high school mascot—the Fighting Cardinal—stretched across the horizon of her hips.

She stood and faced him, giving him a long, hard look.

"Well, I sure didn't think I'd find you here, in this dusty ol' place. Don't you know how to google?" she said.

But Bernard was too careful for that. Not that he was up to anything, really. He just liked to keep the different parts of his life in clean, separate compartments, everything in its own neat little box. He used his city computer for work-related tasks only. Everything he did on it was subject to public scrutiny, so he liked to play it safe. Sure, he had a personal laptop, but that he kept quarantined for his off-duty pursuits. Looking up hiking trails, mostly. The outdoors was a good antidote to life under fluorescent lighting. And he considered himself a bit of a naturalist, so he also used it to look up the interesting rock specimens he came across, which he had been assembling into a collection.

Since his return to Dexter Springs he'd taken to trails on the reservation. He enjoyed mapping the reserve in his mind as he walked, connecting it to what he had once known of the area. Although, he had to admit, a decade ago he'd been less interested in hiking and more dedicated to binge drinking.

And getting close to the rez girls. Like the beautiful woman he'd seen in the crowd gathered around the fighting men at the tribal council meeting. The man next to him said she could be Deer Woman. At first he'd thought it was a title awarded to a gorgeous rez girl, kind of like *Rodeo Queen* but for the Saliquaw Nation, but then he'd decided that probably wasn't right. She looked more like an influencer in that fine coat she'd worn. He couldn't get to the bottom of it on his own, so he'd come to the library to search Glenna's Indigenous lore collection. At least he'd have something to talk about if he had the pleasure of seeing the woman again.

"You sure look different," Mitzie said. "Clean-cut and all. Like a real city manager, I guess. Who would've thought?"

Bernard had developed a penchant for sand-colored slacks with sharp vertical creases and had tamed his fuzzy blond curls into a straight and severe style parted to the left. He wore a pair of glasses with thick black rims.

Bernard didn't like the way she studied him, so he concentrated on the veneer of a nearby card catalog.

The Dexter Springs Public Library card catalog contained alphabetically organized drawers full of ancient three-by-five index cards, and Bernard found them orderly and soothing. Often, as he thought about how to integrate all the parts of himself into one cohesive personlike assemblage, he ran his fingers across the handwritten titles and synopses that were the divination of that first librarian.

Bernard could picture her, following the rules of proper conduct in a time when men wore hats and women carried clasp-top purses.

He eyed Mitzie's crop top and said, "The city's launching its first major infrastructure project in fifteen years, and I've been brought in to manage it. We're constructing a new highway that will run from here through the west end of the reservation." He hesitated, then added, hopefully, "It's the kind of project that makes a city manager's career."

Mitzie, who'd lifted the child to her hip, slowly shook her head.

"Bernie, you're just the man for the job," she said. "Sounds like it, anyway."

He agreed. With any luck, this road project would propel Dexter Springs into the future. It would put a win on his résumé, so he could get hired in a larger city. Larger, and far away from here.

"Earth to Bernie," Mitzie said, waving a hand in front of his face. "B-Man, you're an odd duck. C'mon. Just come out for a few minutes. See the gang. We could use a—"

"It's Bernard now," he said. "Bernard. Not Bernie, not B-Man. Bernard."

She ignored him, reaching into the pocket of her jeans for a stick of gum.

"Did you hear another girl might have gone missing from the rez?" she said, her face turning serious.

She popped the gum into her mouth and rolled the wrapper between her thumb and forefinger, then furrowed her brow at a smear of marker on her forearm. She put the balled-up wrapper in her pocket and licked her thumb to rub the smudge off.

"Shoot, forgot about my spray tan," she said, more to herself than to Bernard. "So scary. I just can't believe another girl has gone missing."

Mitzie held up one finger to pause the conversation and set the toddler back down.

"Anyway," she resumed, "these missing girls. It's terrifying, right? What is that, seven in the last decade? Actually, I think it's up to nine since we graduated. Remember Loxie, from high school? It's like when she disappeared it kicked off some kind of curse. This is terrible to say, but"—she leaned in close; Bernard could smell the mint of her gum—"I'm glad it's not happening in town. I mean, all these missing girls have been from the rez, but still . . . I don't go anywhere at night without someone with me, especially when I have this little one."

She turned to smile at the toddler, who was lying on her belly halfway under the table, gnawing on a book she'd pulled from a shelf.

Bernard looked blankly back at Mitzie, his face a disinterested mask. Of course he remembered Loxie. Of course he'd heard about the missing girls. He wasn't stupid.

"Can't be too careful," he said, finally.

Bernard eyed the library's entrance, thinking of escape. He noticed the marshal entering, tall enough that she nearly had to duck the doorframe. He watched as she removed her cap and bent the bill like he'd seen farmers do when they were breaking in free hats from seed dealers.

Mitzie followed his gaze.

"Oh, her? Yeah, that's the—Oh, Pais, get out of there. I mean it!—that's the new marshal from the rez."

Bernard watched as the marshal looked around to get her bearings. He imagined the impression the library made. The ornate ceiling, the marble floors, the shelves filled with volumes of material no one needed anymore: dictionaries, reference manuals, three different sets of encyclopedias. Beside them, more shelves, with dog-eared paperbacks that, judging by their covers, contained stories of windswept lovers—some on land, some at sea, others inexplicably on mountaintops. He knew that from her vantage point she couldn't see the children's section but could hear it: the little chirps and staccato outbursts of toddlers that echoed off the limestone walls.

As announced by the date carved above its door, the stone building that housed the library had been erected on the corner of Main and Birch in 1888. It had served as the Dexter Springs Bank for half a century before sitting empty so long that a colony of bats took up residence in the attic. Briefly, it was used by the dwindling number of members who belonged to the local Masonic lodge, who did nothing about the bats. Then, at the behest of concerned citizens who, in 1968, raised money through bake sales, car washes and a father-daughter dance at the Methodist church, it was turned into a library.

There had been only two librarians. Mrs. Crabtree, a former substitute teacher with a reputation for sending kindergartners to the principal's office, had lasted longer as a librarian than anyone had expected. She considered it a lifetime position, like being appointed to the Supreme Court, and approached it with all the seriousness of an undertaker. For the first two decades of the library's existence there were strictly enforced late fees and a code of conduct for all who entered.

Glenna Mossman had been a welcome change when she became the next librarian, in the late 1980s. She had white hair and was of indeterminate age—she could be fifty or seventy-five—and she was not only the librarian but the town's unofficial historian and an avid genealogist. Most days, she wore blue jeans, sneakers that still looked new and a shirt with *Genealogy: organizing the dead and confusing the living* emblazoned on its front. She seemed never to tire of the joke.

Bernard watched as the marshal's gaze settled on the circulation desk and on Glenna, who was inspecting due dates stamped on the forward interiors of returned books and sorting them into categories so volunteers could shelve them for future readers.

He strained to hear the marshal's conversation with Glenna over Mitzie's continued chatter.

"We were all surprised when we heard you came back," Mitzie

said. "It was a real shame the way you just dropped off the earth. . . ."

Bernard was focused on the marshal, on Glenna. What could they be talking about?

"Bernie?"

Mitzie brought him back to her.

"What? Oh," he said. "Yeah, a shame."

Glenna walked briskly toward Bernard and Mitzie, the marshal following, taking in the library—not like a tourist but like someone used to looking at a crime scene and committing it to memory.

Bernard could see the patch on the front of her uniform. Starr looked him in the eye and gave him a nod as she passed. A shiver crawled over him. He thought of ride-alongs in official police vehicles, of watching her work a case. It awoke within him that early fascination with law enforcement. The methodic learning and filing of details would have suited him.

"And here you'll find what you're looking for," Glenna said, walking the marshal to a carousel of weathered hardbound books. "This one will give you a bit of the history of the Saliquaw Nation, although as you can imagine, it also has plenty of omissions, considering that there are few written records directly from the nation's members. Here you'll see a few of the Indigenous maps in our collection. Go back far enough and you'll see the size of the reservation after their forced relocation to Oklahoma on the Trail of Tears, and over there is an official compilation of the area's family histories—mostly white, since that was obviously more important to the city's founding fathers."

Starr nodded stiffly and shifted from one foot to the other.

"Relax," Glenna said, looking at her. "Local humor. Unfortunate, to be sure, but pretty accurate. You'll have to forgive me.

With the genealogy I do, including my own, I've come to realize that anyone part Native like me has half her family's history written down by white folks and the other half lost to the wind. Unless an elder remembers it, but there aren't many left now. I've been working for years on the library's collection of Native authors and I've recorded some of the oral stories of the reservation. Real doozies. Magic, really.

"Anyway, here's what you need, and if you can't find it here, or if you can't find the maps you need, then check the vault," she said. "Welcome to Dexter. Let me know if I can help you find anything else."

The vault was where the library kept its archives and its most delicate historical documents, but copies of them were alive in Glenna's head. The vault also doubled as a storm shelter, where patrons and townsfolk sought refuge from tornadoes—like the most recent one, which had skirted most of Dexter Springs but touched down briefly in a pasture, picking up one of the Nixons' Jersey milk cows and depositing her relatively unscathed in front of Lynwood Drug.

Bernard watched Starr log the details of the small collection. When she got within a foot of him, her gaze stopped roaming and locked on his. He smiled nervously.

"Really, Bernie, you wouldn't believe our last class reunion," Mitzie continued. "Hardly anybody showed up. I was one of the officers when we were seniors. Maybe you don't remember, but officers have to plan the reunions, so if you don't want that job, steer clear of getting elected, I tell the kids. Well, not my Paisley girl—she's too young to understand all that. But I do tell the ones I run into, like her babysitter, or the carryouts at the grocery. . . ."

Her voice droned on as Bernard's fountain pen, a turned-wood masterpiece and the most expensive thing he owned, weighed heavily in his shirt pocket and put pressure on his heart. He could feel it thump, thump, thumping, heating up. Blistering the pen, the ink, his skin.

The marshal looked through historical Indian Territory maps from the library's archival collection, then turned her attention to a current topographical map of the region. Was the marshal's research related to the missing girl? Or maybe she was an outdoors enthusiast, like him. Bernard scanned the marshal's firm backside.

They could go for a hike together, he told himself.

The fire that had sparked the rabbit thump of his heart had spread to his hands. He swiped his sweaty palms across his khaki pants, where they left dark, wet blotches. He smelled smoke, but how could that be? Maybe it was coming from inside; he was combusting.

A bead of sweat broke loose from Bernard's hairline and traveled across the terrain of his morning shave, taking a final dive off the cleft of his chin. He looked around the library and his vision became brighter, his eyes clearer from the anxious liquid of his tear glands.

Bernard made himself stare down at the newspaper in front of him. *Keep it together, man. Keep it together.* It was a plea, not a command.

He stood, folded the newspaper and placed it back on the library table.

"Yes, well, I've got to head back," Bernard said. "It was, uh, nice to see you."

Bernard started moving toward the exit, Mitzie's voice still ringing in his ears. He felt like he'd forgotten how to walk.

"Um, okay, bye," Mitzie said, and shook her head. She glanced at the marshal and smiled, then retrieved Paisley and went to the circulation desk.

"You seeing this?" Mitzie said to Glenna.

Through the library's picture windows overlooking Main Street they watched Bernard run across the street without looking, a horn sounding as he raced in front of a car and toward city hall.

"He was always a smart one," Mitzie said, "but a little weird. I think he might have a crush on the new marshal."

"He did get a little worked up," Glenna said, "but he's always wound too tight, if you ask me."

"He is kinda cute, though," said Mitzie.

"Interesting guy, from what I understand. Keeps the city's projects organized, or at least that's what they tell me. Comes here about every day on his morning break. I keep a list of questions patrons ask about the city and he answers—explains, more like it—and I pass it on."

"Yeah? I think all these projects have folks curious. We're finally getting some things done around here, progress people can count on."

"Me, I only count by generations," Glenna said, then shrugged. "Takes all kinds."

Mitzie nodded and perched the child atop an old wooden cabinet. The library now had a digital circulation system to track due dates, but Glenna had retained the depository with its many drawers full of checkout cards for their history: signatures penned over decades—impermanent promises to return.

CHAPTER TWENTY-TWO

✳

After the library, Starr spent Friday afternoon at her desk in the marshal's office going through file after file from the BIA, discovering one missing girl after another—probably a decade's worth—until her head swam with bodies found and not.

Winnie was gone for the afternoon, home with one of her grandchildren, who was sick with a stomach virus. Minkey had called to report that his door-to-door questioning on the rez had led to nothing, so she'd sent him to the station in Dexter Springs to search police reports for any crimes linked to the rez, but he hadn't found anything. He'd been away only a couple of hours when she heard the door to the marshal's office open.

"Hey, boss," Minkey said. "This yours?" He held up a leather pouch secured with string.

"Nope."

"Found it hanging from the door handle."

"You look inside?"

Minkey shook his head and walked to her desk, where he gingerly set the object down and stepped away.

"Well, let's hope somebody's not sending us anthrax," Starr said, trying to make a joke. Minkey blanched. She pulled on a pair of latex gloves, supplies she'd taken from the morgue the previous day, and loosened the string on the pouch so she could spill the contents onto the desktop.

"Huh," she said. It didn't look like much of anything. A handful of sand along with a rusted bottle cap. Some flowers with small white petals and yellow centers, dried and starting to crumble. A feather in variegated shades of blue.

"That's a tail feather," said Minkey, "from a blue jay. Did you know the pigment in that feather is actually brown, but it looks blue to us because of the way it reflects light?"

"You're a regular Audubon field guide."

Minkey's face reddened. "What do you think this is? Some Indian thing?"

"Indigenous," Starr said.

The office phone trilled.

"Marshal," said Starr, then cradled the landline's old receiver between her ear and shoulder as she listened. "How long? Where exactly? Okay, we'll be right there."

She hung up, grabbed the Bronco keys and motioned Minkey to the door.

"Trading Post," she said. "Drunk and disorderly."

In the Bronco, Minkey clicked on the passenger seat belt as Starr threw the vehicle into reverse.

"Minkey," she said, shifting into drive, "how long have you lived here?"

"Here?" He looked out the window, across the open land slipping away to the west. "Oh, you mean Dexter Springs? Well"—he scratched his chin—"I moved here after I graduated from the police academy. For the job, you know. That's been about two years."

"I'm sorry," Starr said. "That's too bad."

"Oh, it's been okay. I mean, I like it here."

"Give it time."

"No, I really do. I know I'm still considered new, but I'm trying to work my way in."

"Working in how?"

"Community-policing stuff. You know, volunteering when I'm off shift, joining the Lions Club, that kind of thing."

"Why? Don't you have better things to do on your own time? Like get rowdy, get around?"

Minkey laughed. "Not saying I don't kick up a little, but I try to keep my head on straight. Don't want to screw up my career."

"In Dexter? You want to make detective?"

"Yeah, something like that."

They drove on in silence, Starr considering her next question.

"My granddad, see, he was a Ranger," Minkey said.

"Like a Texas Ranger?"

"Yeah, exactly. And he kinda raised me, well, not raised exactly, but had a big influence on me, the kind of man I wanted to be."

"So why not become a Ranger?"

"Thought about it, but the police academy was more in my reach. I was figuring out how to pay for it, sending out a few applications for rookie-officer openings, and then I heard from Dexter Springs. It was the one municipality that offered to pay for my training at the police academy, so I took them up on it. I just can't quit or take another job for three years, or I'll have to pay the city back. Got about a year to go."

Starr thought about the domestic scene she'd seen play out with Minkey and the woman on the rez. While Starr had been met with resistance at every turn, Minkey had settled into easy conversation. It was possible he was personable, even likable, but it was too coincidental, the way he showed up the day the body was found.

"Did you know the deceased?" She watched him closely, noticed how his hands moved.

"No, ma'am. But that doesn't mean much. I don't really know anyone from the rez."

"Then why the hell did the mayor volunteer you for this?"

He shrugged. "Maybe I volunteered myself."

Starr pressed the brake, parking outside the Trading Post's front doors, and faced him.

"What?" he said. "I had my reasons."

"You gonna tell me what they are?"

"I don't see what that has to do with my ability to—"

Starr scoffed, then realized he was serious.

"I thought I could make a difference," Minkey continued, "out here. More than writing citations for driving too fast down a city street. People on the rez could use someone on their side, someone who cares about the law. Who cares about them."

"Well, you dumb bastard," she said. This was some howdy doody shit if she'd ever heard it. "We'll see how far that gets you. Nobody takes a job here unless they're one of three things: desperate, delusional or both."

Minkey turned a shade of red that matched the University of Oklahoma crimson she'd seen on stadium pennants, T-shirts, hats and license plates, and now a lawn flag hanging in the window of the Trading Post. Starr could see Junior inside, gesturing wildly at a cashier.

"Come on," she said. "We got a live one."

CHAPTER TWENTY-THREE

✳

A thin layer of sand crunched under the soles of Starr's boots. Outside the Trading Post, two boys on bicycles circled the Bronco, gold chains swinging from their necks as they angled over the handlebars to gain speed. The glass door of the Trading Post, spotted with stickers, flyers and handprints, set off a metallic ding when Starr walked through it, Minkey following.

Junior was agitated. That much was clear.

Starr asked the man behind the counter if he'd been the one to call, and he answered by uncrossing his arms and sweeping both hands in Junior's direction.

"What is it today, Junior?" Starr said.

Junior's lips curled into a snarl, and Starr stepped away from the glass behind her. One look at Junior, with his shoulders hunched forward like a defensive lineman's, and she decided she wasn't going to be tackled through a window. Not today.

"You feeling all right, Junior? Tell me what's going on."

The man behind the counter opened his mouth to speak, but Starr held up a hand to silence him.

Junior's chest heaved, but he said nothing. On the counter, and overflowing onto the floor where he stood, were supplies: a sleeping bag, a fishing net, several lures and a roll of filament, cans of Van Camp's pork and beans, a can opener and an empty canteen.

"You going somewhere? Looks like you might be thinking about going out of town. Not what you want to be doing right now. Trust me on this."

Junior looked past Starr, locking on Minkey.

"This is Officer Minkey—er, Minkle—so take it easy, Junior. He's from Dexter Springs, lending a hand so we can cover more ground on the cases we're working. You step outside with him, and he'll listen to whatever you have to say. I'll be right out."

Minkey moved to the door and held it open, which sent out another metallic ding from behind the register.

"Junior, is it?" Minkey said. "Let's talk out here."

"Go on," Starr said, eyeing Junior and stepping aside. "You don't need this kind of trouble. Just head out and cool off."

Starr waited until Minkey and Junior were standing outside, the boys on bicycles leaning into the wind as they curved closer and closer to the men, before she turned her attention to the man behind the counter. He'd taken a seat in a kitchen chair stationed where he could watch the gas pumps. The register area was a mess: crooked stacks of single-leaf papers and copies of the *Sentinel-Times* newspaper out of Dexter Springs, along with a block of wood with a single nail, bloated with impaled receipts.

"You gotta do something about him," said the man. "He's come in here more in the last twenty-four hours than I've seen in years, and he's worse than ever. Talking crazy, scaring off my customers."

Starr looked around at the empty store. There were shelves stretching out along one side of the Trading Post, and refrigerator cases along the back. She could hear the whir of an ICEE machine. Separated from the convenience shop by a half-wall of warped paneling were a dozen hard-surfaced orange booths, the tabletops scattered with crumbs and condiments. Beyond the booths was a narrow pass-through window that looked into an empty kitchen.

"You always this busy?"

He scoffed.

"Look, I do all right. Got this place I run during the day, until I switch out with my night manager. Then I head to my place over on Route 66. Imagine you've heard of the Red Garter. But now I got this guy hanging around, talking to every woman who tries to get gas, telling them stuff that doesn't make sense, showing them something in his pocket."

"Like what?"

"Hell if I know." He leaned closer, and Starr could see the shine of his pink scalp through a thin layer of combed-over hair. "I got this one lady, runs the diner side of things, and I been trying to be delicate about this because of her. Junior's a relation to her, and I can respect that. Family's gotta stick together. But this, this is too much. He's been in here or out in the parking lot for hours, and I can't have him harassing people. Bad for business."

"You got a name?" Starr asked, taking her notepad from her uniform.

"JJ," he said. "Jake Johnson."

The boys who'd been wheeling their bikes came in, preening and casting their eyes. They split off, one going down an aisle, examining bags of chips, the other spinning a display of sunglasses. JJ called after them.

"Boys, I know you're trying to take something. I told you not to come in here unless you have some money to spend."

"Nice of you," Starr said.

"I'm positively a ray of sunshine," he said flatly.

Starr took in his beaded belt, his bolo tie, his Western shirt with mother-of-pearl snaps straining at his paunchy belly. Behind him, the restaurant's menu, a white board with black letters slotted into linear grooves, hung over the pass-through window. Even from where she stood, she could see a layer of grease that clung like film to the menu board, building up dust. On the bottom it read: POP DR PEPPER SHASTA COKE SPRITE REFILLS EXTRA.

Starr noticed movement in the kitchen. It was Odeina, carrying a pan of silverware.

"Hang tight," Starr said, and walked toward the kitchen, her leg still aching from the dog bite the day before.

Starr rang the bell on the window counter and Odeina's voice came out of the kitchen: "Be with you in a minute."

When Odeina appeared through the saloon doors beside the window, her hand was reaching into an apron pocket for a pen. When she saw Starr, she came to a halt.

"You got—" Odeina swallowed hard. "Do you have news for me?"

"No. No, nothing like that. Still investigating."

Odeina slammed her pen and order pad onto the counter. "Oh, so you're finally looking into it? Exactly what are you doing here, then?"

"I have a couple of questions for you. We received a complaint about Junior, and he seems pretty spun up. How long has he been here today, and what is he up to?"

Odeina looked over Starr's shoulder, scanning for Junior. Starr pointed outside, where Minkey and Junior were talking, and noticed that JJ had repositioned himself in his chair by the window to watch them.

"He's doing what he can. Trying to get people's attention, urge them to stick together, be safe. It's a hell of a lot more than you're doing."

"So he's talking to people. That's it?"

"Women, mostly. He's trying to give them protection."

"Protection?"

"Look, you wouldn't understand, but he took it hard when you found that young woman by the creek. I mean, we know it's not Chenoa, and I'll be forever grateful for that, but this is someone's daughter. Do you understand me? I care about that. And so does Junior. He's really been through it, his own losses you would know nothing about."

"So, this protection he's offering is . . ."

"It's a medicine bundle, wards off harm." She pulled out of her pocket a leather bag, same as the one Minkey had found hanging from the door handle at the marshal's office. "But don't you forget who you're supposed to be looking for. Nothing can help that girl by the creek now. You should be out there looking for my daughter, not wasting your time up here about Junior."

"Those supplies he's buying. That doesn't look good. Maybe he's running. Maybe it has something to do with that girl's death."

"Doubt it."

"What about Chenoa? Were they close? Has he been acting strangely since you last saw her?"

"What is it about you that makes you so incompetent? I'm trying to keep my head above water, working doubles, and when I'm not doing that I'm looking after Grandmother or putting up flyers or driving around to ask if anyone has seen my daughter. But you know who they haven't seen? You. What good are you if you aren't even looking?"

Starr clocked Minkey and Junior in the parking lot, something serious in the way they were talking, Junior leaning toward Minkey, then surprise on Minkey's face. And something else. Fear?

Starr retraced her steps to the front door, motioning JJ to stay where he was. The moment the door opened, Minkey straightened.

"So, no cable, then?" Minkey said.

"Just rabbit ears. Keep it on for the noise. Gets quiet out here, so at night I'll try to pick up a show," Junior said. He nodded to Starr, then looked directly at Minkey. "Truth is, maybe that TV is watching me more than I'm watching it."

The boys on their bikes were gone and there weren't any cars at the gas pumps. A purple-black bird hopped toward Starr, cocking its head to catch the gleam of late-afternoon sun, its feathers a mass of unruly angles, looking as scrappy and damaged as everything else.

"Junior," she said, "let's see what you've been up to. Empty your pockets."

CHAPTER TWENTY-FOUR

Finally, at a quarter to seven—after Starr had released Minkey from duty, settled Junior and taken him home—she lugged a file box to the old Bronco and drove to the rental house in Dexter Springs, where she pulled a card table from the garage and set it up in the empty living room. She laid out the maps she'd borrowed from the library or spirited from Odeina, and used empty Jameson bottles to pin down the corners.

One of the maps showed looped trails in reds and blues, with icons by a few isolated trailheads; the other showed the reservation's varied geography. Different than she'd thought. She had imagined that the area was a wide, flat plain with more cowboys than careers, but Oklahoma was full of surprises. She thought of Junior trailing women who entered the Trading Post, offering them protection bundles from his pockets, desperate gifts he believed could change their fates.

Starr had known there was a problem with missing Indigenous women. This was why she'd been hired to take the marshal position. Qualified, even.

But now. There were so many. Gone.

They could be here, she thought, and used a finger to trace across the acres plotted on the paper maps. *Or somewhere far from here,* and she thought of interstate highways. The women could have been picked up by a driver catching I-44 to Oklahoma City and beyond.

Any one of these girls could still be alive.

The itch was starting; Starr could feel it under her skin. It would grow and grow until there was nothing to do but think about the cases. Go over every detail again and again.

She didn't understand her own process, even after all these years. Most people thought the work went in a straight line. A murder. An investigation. Clues. An arrest.

Starr knew better. Sure, in hindsight a completed investigation made sense. She'd distilled her own actions into reports enough times to know what to leave out and what to put in. But she also knew there was a wasteland between starting and closing an investigation, and that sometimes you wandered in it, lost.

It was too late for the girl at the morgue. No matter how fast Starr moved forward with an investigation, she could never bring her back.

She stared at the file box she'd brought from the rez. Most of the girls in the files it contained had disappeared under largely unknown circumstances, but there had been a few clues. Three of the girls had been seen walking along the road that leaves the reserve, which wasn't unusual. Nor was it out of the ordinary to hitch a ride. Four more seemed to vanish into the night. Another had been spotted six months after she was last seen but had never turned up again. And now there was the victim by Turkey Creek. Starr was looking for patterns in chaos and coming up empty;

sorting through details that could ultimately fit together, or mean nothing at all.

Starr took a file at random from the middle of the stack and sank into the camp chair she had stationed by the card table. She opened the file and slid the slick photographs around like a child shuffling playing cards. She needed new eyes, but the Jameson was starting to take hold. She'd been measured in her drinking that evening, allowing one shot, and then another one, only after she had thought about certain things.

The first file yielded no answers; nor did the second, third or fourth.

But here, in her hands now, was something different. Starr looked at the date on the file she held. This case was at least a decade old: A young Indigenous woman had been discovered buried and badly decomposed near a remote trail, too far gone to offer much information. Images of her body, pale and still, swam up at Starr. She skimmed the autopsy report. Posthumous skull fracture. And something else that sent Starr's heart racing. The victim's mouth had been filled with soil. But not just any soil. It was a white particulate—like what filled the mouth of the body she'd studied under the brush near a bend in Turkey Creek, with the vultures biding their time on the changing currents over Crawl Canyon.

Were there more victims who had been discovered with a similar calling card?

Starr flipped through file after file. *Missing. Missing. Still missing.*

Her uniform buzzed. Starr leapt from the chair and pulled her cell phone from a pants pocket. She checked the caller ID. Eight-four-seven area code. Earlene.

"Been hell trying to get hold of you."

Starr smiled. "Earlie, I knew I could count on you. Tell me something good."

"Aw, girl, I got nothing to say. Not what you want, anyway."

"Nothing?"

"Look, I went over that wood up, down and sideways. With a fine-tooth comb. If it was there, I would have gotten it."

Starr's gut wrenched. Not the news she wanted. More loose ends in a case that seemed to be made of them. She looked at her watch. Friday, nearly nine p.m. Time was moving too fast.

"Talk to me," Earlie said. "What else you got? You said it was a blunt object, so sure, it could be this wood here, but did the medical examiner find wood fibers?"

"Yep," Starr said. "All around the wound. Split the skin and frac-tured the skull, and internal damage too. Lacerations on the brain."

"Something solid. That's for sure," Earlie said.

The line was quiet, both women absorbed in their own thoughts. Starr's mind moved through the scene: the blows, the death—probably slow—and afterward, the burns. She knew that collecting DNA from the log had been a long shot, and even with-out the outcome she needed, she was grateful to be able to count on someone from her old life.

"I don't know what else to tell you," Earlie said. "What's going on out there, anyway?"

"Caught a case, that's all," Starr said.

"Just one?"

"For now."

When the call ended, Starr thought again of the striking sim-ilarity between the two cases, old and new: the white soil at the centers of both deaths. If there was a serial killer in the area, there were bound to be more victims.

She didn't want to go this route, thinking a serial killer was to blame, but she knew the statistics from the cases she'd worked in Chicago: At any given time, there were twenty-five to fifty-five serial killers operating in the US, and they often made use of the interstate highway system to move around.

She stared at the maps until the lines blurred.

There were so many cases, and none of them seemed to fit the two she'd flagged. So many files on murdered Indigenous women who were victims of domestic disputes, bad drugs, gun violence. And from the rez, even with its relatively small population, more than half a dozen women were currently missing. There could be so many reasons why. A driver with bad intentions offers a ride. A runaway runs into trouble. A trafficker is masked as a boyfriend.

Why was she always leaning into long odds? She had one old file with an MO that matched that of the murder by the creek, and even that link was tenuous. She had to keep an open mind, steer clear of tunnel vision.

From the start, this newest victim's death wasn't like any other case she'd worked. She was spinning in the wind, with no cooperating agencies to call to her aid in setting up a perimeter, interviewing all who came and went from the reservation. . . . And there wasn't a damn thing she could do about it.

Worse, she knew the BIA didn't have a comprehensive national database to track missing Indigenous women, even though Indigenous women were seven times more likely to be murdered than white women. The ratio of Indigenous women who were missing was even higher.

Starr reached into her shirt pocket, pulled out a joint bent and worn from the day. She opened a new bottle of Jameson and flicked fire from her silver lighter, wondering whether she cared about breaking the no-smoking rule that would forfeit her deposit.

What did the BIA think she was really going to accomplish out here? It was like they tried to make it easy for the bad guys. *Tried.* It was entirely possible for a killer to make a go of it on the rez virtually undetected.

But that didn't mean Chenoa was gone. Hell, maybe Chenoa was still out in some part of the reservation's wasteland, right under Starr's nose. She could still find Chenoa, even though she had not found Quinn in time . . . but that thread unspooled into dangerous territory, didn't it?

Starr took a long drag and held it like she was underwater.

CHAPTER TWENTY-FIVE

✴

S tarr had a name.

She'd been out cold in her camp chair, dreaming of paper trails and deer and missing women, when the cell phone on the card table buzzed her back into existence. In her confusion, Starr looked to the window for sunlight, but saw instead the pitch of night. Half past ten. It was Dr. Moore calling, the medical examiner, who'd run the victim's fingerprints through the state database and gotten a hit.

Sherry Ann Awiakta.

The woman's parents had not reported her missing; now Starr had to find them so she could tell them their daughter was dead. It took her several minutes to reach Winnie, who shouted into the phone over the noise of her grandchildren.

"*Aye!* Don't touch that! Too hot! Hello? Oh, Marshal, what do you need?"

When Starr said the girl's name, she heard Winnie's sharp intake of breath.

"No." She drew out the sound like the echo of ancestors. The receiver rustled. "Hush, you two! Go play. Leave me be."

A few minutes later, the image of a hand-drawn map pinged on Starr's cell phone. The Awiakta family lived on the reservation. Even though Winnie had repeated directions to their home, twice, Starr hadn't been able to understand. Winnie spoke in landmarks, and Starr needed specific instructions.

She squinted at Winnie's crooked pen strokes—a creek here, an abandoned house there, a lone oak where Starr needed to turn left. The route took her into a remote part of the rez, where unmaintained roads became impassable when it rained. She'd have to take the last stretch by foot. She'd have to say the words she'd once been felled by. Tell them their daughter was dead.

Starr didn't close her eyes again as she sat in the chair. And she didn't lie down on the bare mattress in the bedroom. Instead, she went to the garage, propped open the man door and stood among the boxes she doubted she'd ever unpack. The neighbor's Australian shepherd yapped on the other side of a short yard behind her house.

The weak glow of a security light gave her an unrelenting view of the sagging wooden deck on which the dog was penned. The sliding glass door that led to the deck was covered with tacked-up blankets and a Confederate flag. Whenever she was at her duplex, day or night, the dog barked, a monotonous note boring into her brain.

When she noticed the air rifle leaning against cardboard, she picked it up, pumped it a few times, sighted above the dog's head and fired into the night. It was a decent shot at sixty yards, the pellet pinging the siding of her neighbor's house and momentarily shocking the dog into silence.

Starr ran her hand over the gun's scarred wooden stock, her last name carved into it. She'd been so proud of the gift—the only one she could remember receiving from her father, even though they'd lived most of her childhood, just the two of them, in a four-story Chicago walk-up apartment building.

She set it aside and rifled through a welcome basket from the Dexter Springs Chamber of Commerce: a tattered library book that had been taken out of circulation, a coupon for the hardware store, an Avon business card stapled to a lipstick sample. She hadn't expected much from this little town, except that it be within the thirty-minute response area the rez required, but this was disappointing. Why not throw in a few spirits, like those little airplane-sized bottles, or maybe a fifth of whiskey? Now, that would have been welcoming.

A dog-eared brochure, fallen to the bottom of the basket, summarized the origins of Dexter Springs: *An Indian campsite next to iron-fortified natural springs that became a major battle scene in the Civil War.* No mention of the displacement of the Indigenous people who'd lived here first, or their massive land loss, or the forced relocation of other Indigenous families to this region. No cheery paragraphs about starvation or the pre–Civil War massacre in which two thousand people were killed at the hands of the US government. Hell, she *was* the US government, wasn't she?

Lucy Cloud's words rang through her mind: When Indigenous women disappeared, they disappeared twice. Once in life and once in the news. Where was the news coverage of Sherry Ann Awiakta? She was as invisible as all the others had been.

Starr let out a long breath, opened the lid of an old metal coffee container to retrieve a new joint and felt in the pocket of her stained bathrobe for a lighter. The evening was cold enough for a coat, but she'd gotten used to wearing the bathrobe for warmth and to ward off the smell of weed. A wool beanie kept the smoke from her hair, overdue for a cut and still black like her father's.

She needed to notify the Awiaktas, but she settled into a sagging lawn chair in front of a platform made of unpacked boxes. A persistent Kansas wind rattled the half-closed garage door, so she tuned the dial on her old radio to a jazz station out of Miami, Oklahoma. It began a run of songs, and she drew in long drags until each note was an isolated sound that unwound her coiled mind. She dropped her head between her elbows. *Fuck.* She didn't know whether to cry or laugh.

How did she wind up in a place that held the history of her father? She'd had no other choice. The job was all she had.

Starr used her boot to push at a dead and dried-out June bug, a summer leftover still on the garage's concrete floor. Thriving in heat, drawn by light, June bugs stuck awkwardly to screen doors and clothing and tangled in long hair. She'd once known a little girl who screamed every time one of these bugs got near her. Starr wondered if Quinn would still be scared of them today.

If... There was so much *if* that Starr could feel herself drowning in it.

Starr studied the June bug between drags and blew smoke out of the side of her mouth in slow, measured seconds. She had once lived a different life. Drank a beer or two, but only when watching the Bulls take the court. Felt disgust at a perp with a syringe or a bag of blow, or even a couple of pre-rolls. Shook down her daughter's room if there was a whiff of weed.

Then Quinn was gone, and the pain came on so strong that it moved through every cell, made her retch into wastebaskets, filled her with madness. And there would be no cure. Not for her. She knew then that if she didn't find some way to numb even a small part of the searing grief, she wouldn't live long enough to find Quinn's killer.

Starr knew who she was now, what she was capable of, what she required to see it through. She'd finish this joint and then start again on the whiskey. Get so fucked-up that her brain would turn off, so blasted that she'd fall asleep before her body even knew what was happening. And right before she lost herself there might even be a few moments when everything felt right again— or at least felt unavoidable in a way that released her from duty as she slipped into the long, aching night.

Or she could do what she'd been hired to do. What her sworn duty was. She could tell them. She left the garage and shed the bathrobe in the house, then added her cell phone to the backpack where she stored her scant necessities. Her Glock, now holstered on her service belt, offered a weighty comfort.

Starr stashed a bottle of whiskey under the driver's seat and turned the Bronco's ignition, bracing for the news she'd have to deliver and the terrain she'd have to cover in the process. The dark spaces of whatever was out there. Caves. Old mines. Her own mind.

She pulled on her seat belt and inched the Bronco onto the deserted roadway. Any heat that had been trapped inside the cab left through the open windows as she drove a route that crossed Dexter Springs from north to south, through an area where tour- ist guides still retold the story of Bonnie and Clyde robbing— twice in one week—Eden's Grocery Store. Now Dexter Springs had a closed-down Walmart, a losing high school football team and 7,343 people probably wondering why they hadn't taken off a long time ago.

Starr caught the fishy scent of the river that ran from Dexter Springs to the reservation. She wondered what it would be like to sink into the cool, rushing current until her lungs screamed for air and then pulled the water in.

I have got to get it together, she thought. *Focus on the road.*

She trained her eyes on the asphalt illuminated by waxy headlights, the pitch so faded that the white lines no longer showed. The glow of the city dimmed in the rearview mirror and no other vehicles were in sight, so she relaxed her grip on the steering wheel and concentrated on keeping between the ditches. She lit another joint and stowed the lighter, blowing smoke out of the open window. When she passed the signs announcing her departure from Kansas and arrival in Oklahoma, Starr honked the horn for good measure.

Side roads clicked by, there and then gone in the dark. Without the benefit of street signs, it was difficult to know when to turn onto any of the dirt roads that intersected the highway. Starr slowed when she saw a sign, impossible to read because of damage from shotgun pellets, that marked the reservation turnoff. She was close to the remote west end of the reservation, so she steered the Bronco onto the dusty shoulder and then veered left onto the next dirt road.

The transition was so severe that it jolted the lighter out of her shirt pocket. Starr kept one hand on the wheel and felt with her other along the coarse twill of the torn bench seat for the lighter, then took a right at the next corner. Even in her muddled state, she knew this road was worse than the last one, if it was maintained at all.

Starr glanced at the road in front of her to make sure it was clear. "You little fucker," she said, stretching across the seat and wrapping the fingers of her right hand around the lighter. She sat up behind the wheel, happy to have won a battle for once.

She squinted through the windshield, unsure where she was. A road? Lake Michigan? A dream?

Suddenly, in what had been the space of headlights tearing weakly into an abyss, two eyes shined yellow. *Driving!* She put both hands on the wheel. She was driving. The pulse of her heart drummed in her neck as the road rose into the distance as if it went only up and up and up, into space. Starr's mind began to register that the yellow eyes belonged to an animal, but her hands were already moving, cranking the wheel to the right. *This monster's too big for a direct hit.* The thought came to her from a distance.

Starr punched the brake with both feet as the Bronco careened into a steep ditch carved out by a road grader under a thick hedge of trees. The right front wheel came to a hard stop on the far bank and Starr felt a sickening lift into air. Then gravity whipped her back to earth.

Starr sat shocked, her mind playing catch-up. She reached a hand up to rub the side of her head where it had smacked against the doorframe. Her head felt loose on her neck, unstable.

Through the open window she could see in the peripheral glow of the headlights that the yellow eyes belonged to a deer, the antlered creature still on the road. It stared at her, frozen in place.

Son of a bitch, she thought. *Fucking son of a bitch.*

Fury rose, and ached for the satisfaction she hadn't given it since Chicago. The familiar rage flushed through her, lighting neurons with flash fires that sent her body into action.

Starr pulled the Glock from her side and aimed it at the deer, her finger on the trigger. She sighted, but the deer had come to its senses and was already in motion. Down the barrel of her gun,

Starr watched the deer turn its slender neck to the future and bound into the darkness. The only target left for her to see was the upright flag of its white tail swishing back and forth as it faded into the distance.

Starr put the gun in her lap, thumped her forehead against the steering wheel until she felt the pain cut through. She felt for the ignition and turned the key. There was a reassuring noise . . . and then silence. She tried again. The engine didn't catch.

She turned the key once more, knowing she risked running the battery down. Nothing.

Around her, the noises of night insects whirred. Starr reached to the floorboard and pulled her backpack to the seat, then unzipped it and searched her phone for the sketch from Winnie. How far was she from the end of the road? Maybe she was already there? If she could find the right access point, she could go ahead on foot. But nothing on the map made sense. She reached under the seat to open the whiskey bottle.

A rangy, hardscrabble bug lured by heat and light climbed the backpack next to her. Starr reached for her flashlight to kill it, then looked at it closely. No red patches. Nothing endangered about this one. She swept the beetle into her hand and dropped it out the window. For a long time she stared out the windshield and into the branches of the hedgerow that scraped the hood of the Bronco in the November wind. She leaned her head out the open window. She'd forgotten the night sky could look like this, with stars so close she could graze them with her fingertips. More stars than she had ever seen. She tried to find constellations. She pointed at the Big Dipper, or maybe it was the Little Dipper. Everything was a mystery.

She was so far from home. And so far from telling Sherry Ann's family the truth.

CHAPTER TWENTY-SIX

SATURDAY

Holder swallowed the dregs of lukewarm coffee in the cup he'd carried out from Rita's Roast, and stepped out of his truck. He'd meant to glass some deer as the sun rose, but he'd spent too long at his usual table, trying to learn what the regulars knew about the new marshal.

Sure, he'd also been worried that crazy Odeina Cloud might show up with more missing person flyers, still searching for her daughter, who, just a few days ago, had been alive and walking along the ridge. At least he'd had the sense to ask Cloud a few questions, all caring-like, and find out that her daughter was looking for some kind of nocturnal insect on the rez. Had anyone in Dexter Springs seen her? *Sorry, darlin',* he'd said.

Then he'd given the mayor a heads-up, just like he'd promised, trying to minimize the potential fallout of what the supposedly missing girl might find, insect-wise. If the future drilling site or the area designated for access roads or—God forbid—any of his adjacent land was home to an endangered species, he was screwed.

If that rez girl discovered an endangered species, the land would be tagged as a critical habitat under the Endangered Species Act, and in a flash it would come under government control. Even the rez land, which was held in trust by the Bureau of Indian Affairs. And especially his land, which the federal government could easily seize for preservation—and he'd pay the expense. It was a scenario that had already played out in neighboring states.

Just this year, the federal government had surveyed a Texas rancher's land as part of a proposed highway expansion and found eyeless spiders the size of dimes living in cave fissures. If the rancher wanted to use the land where the spiders lived—his own land—he had to apply for federal permits that cost hundreds of thousands of dollars. And if he didn't? The fines would start to pile up: at least fifty thousand dollars for each time he disturbed the species.

Hell, he had more on the line than the mayor ever would. The land he'd borrowed against would become essentially useless if the Blackstream Oil deal fell through. He'd end up holding the bag.

Holder tossed his paper coffee cup onto the ground and reached for his binoculars. The sun had been up for a few hours, making it too late in the day to catch deer on their early-morning routes, but they weren't the signs of life he was searching for.

He hadn't been able to spot the rez girl for the last couple of days. He was worried that she'd moved on or hunkered down and he wouldn't know where to find her or be able to learn what she'd found, so he'd changed locations. This morning he'd come in on a back road—if you could call it that—and bumped over it as far as it would take him. He couldn't see much from where he was, just a bend in Turkey Creek, where it washed through Crawl Canyon, and he wished, once again, that he'd brought an ATV in the back of the truck so he could cover more ground, but he couldn't risk the attention the noise might attract, even out here in the boonies. Hell, even a trail horse, if he had one of those, would be better than his truck. What did these folks have against roads, anyway?

Holder zipped his coat against the wind, then steadied the binoculars and dialed them in until he could see clearly to the far bank of the creek and to the grassy rise above it. He scanned the line where land met silver sky, but he detected no movement. Finding this girl was like looking for a needle in a thousand haystacks.

He wanted—no, he needed—to know whether the rez girl had found any endangered bugs and then, if she had, stop her from telling anyone. His future depended on it. He was so close. Months ago he'd sold the mayor on his plan to frack the rez land for oil and let her take the credit. Now she was days away from winning the next election, and he was watching his future come together in just the way he wanted, for the first time in his life.

The mayor had agreed to his plan because he'd sold her the only benefits she cared about; she didn't know it yet, but she was playing only a bit part in Holder's drama.

Holder settled his Stetson and raised the binoculars to take one last look before heading out, and this time the view was different. He spotted a hunting dog tracking along the banks of the creek, then followed the rise behind it until he saw a figure coming after it. His heart thumped at the thought of seeing the girl . . . but it wasn't her. He could tell, even at that distance, that it wasn't her, and when he focused he realized it was only a boy. Holder set the binoculars back in the truck and watched the boy and the dog work their way along the creek until they were out of sight.

Even though he was, technically, trespassing on rez land, maybe he should have talked to the kid. Asked him if he'd seen the girl.

But this wasn't the time to call attention to himself or his movements on the rez. If this girl was right, it was just a matter of time before the Bureau of Indian Affairs sent a government official. His gut churned behind his belt buckle. He'd met the new marshal. The threat was already here.

CHAPTER TWENTY-SEVEN

I t was the birds that woke her, but when Starr reached for a pillow to muffle the sound all she felt was the torn bench seat of
the Bronco.

"What the . . ." she mumbled, and shot upright, sending a bottle of whiskey onto the floorboards and her head into a tailspin.
"Ooh. Fuck."

Her neck was stiff; her bladder ached; her teeth felt furry. And
as Starr pried open the passenger door to climb out, she realized
she was in the same ditch as the night before. *The incident with the
deer.* After the wreck she'd tried to call for a tow, but the cell reception was so poor that she'd finally given up and decided to
walk the dirt roads back to the highway. Then she'd opened the
bottle.

Starr held up her phone, checking service, and then tried the
marshal's office. It was early for Winnie to be there, but maybe . . .

"Good morn . . . Marshal's . . . How can . . . serve you?"

Starr caught the gist, though the line cut out.

"Minkey. Listen. It's Marshal Starr. Get the map to the Awiak-tas' from Winnie and drive the route. You'll find the Bronco. Tow it. I'm walking in to do the notification, and I'll call for a ride when I'm back out by the road."

"What? You're walking to the Bronco?"

Starr held the phone to her chest for a moment. She was going to murder this idiot sooner or later.

"Follow the map. From Winnie. I'm walking to the Awiaktas'."

"Oh, Winnie. I'll get a map from her. Got it. But, Marshal—"

The call dropped, so Starr stowed the cell phone in her back-pack and rummaged for a bottle of water and something to settle her stomach. What had she put in here the night before?

The main track leading to the Awiaktas' was impassable by car for weeks after every big rain because the reservation didn't have the funding or heavy equipment to make repairs to the sections that washed out. The unmaintained road had become so chroni-cally problematic that the Awiaktas had figured out an alternate path, which backtracked over prairie land, but that route was too complicated for Starr to follow, Winnie warned. "Easier if you walk."

The morning was cool and bright, the air crisp, as Starr pulled a bottle of water and a bag of Cheetos from the backpack, glad she'd thought to bring supplies. Then she settled the backpack's straps over her shoulders and set out to find the Awiaktas.

Starr knew from Winnie that a home in this remote area wouldn't have a telephone line, and she'd learned for herself that cell reception wasn't reliable. Her head ached for relief as she walked, stepping over the puddles of a nearly dry creek and tak-ing in the pleasant, earthy scent that hung above them. She never broke the surface of the water, not if she could help it. It was a habit that had started in childhood, when her father told her about the Little People, elflike creatures who pulled disobedient children underwater. Starr now knew they were made-up bullshit. But women disappearing on the reservation? *Too fucking real,* she thought.

Starr knew the staggering national statistics that turned murdered Indigenous women into numbers, categorized by the types of violence they'd endured, illustrated only a fraction of the truth. Most reported cases involved women who did not live on reservations, which meant the crimes had been recorded by local or state officials and added to the Department of Justice's limited data. Crimes against women who lived on the rez weren't usually reported, and if they were, many potential investigations were quickly eclipsed by jurisdictional finger-pointing.

Starr had been sent to the Saliquaw Nation to make a difference, but she wasn't sure she could. Here, no one asked questions about Quinn or avoided Starr's eyes or offered glum smiles—because they didn't know. Starr's grief took on a vaporous quality that left her unmoored in this new place.

Sometimes, when she was exceptionally high, Starr had a queer feeling that Quinn had never existed. More often, Starr could feel how all seventeen years of her daughter's weight had pressed against her own body in that last moment when she'd held her; how her daughter's frame had slumped against her, the unnatural loll of her beautiful head.

It was a feeling Starr had worn like skin, until she'd crawled right out of it and landed with her gun trained on a fleeing man. She'd given him a Chicago six, emptying a half dozen bullets into his back.

The investigation into her actions had ended a job she was relieved to lose. The Indigenous blood she'd gotten from her father had given her an edge with the BIA, but not a future. There wasn't room for possibility on the land of his people. Not the kind of possibility she needed. She needed to figure out where she would go next.

Ahead, caves and hollers had been carved out long ago, and within that vast space of the rez was the family of a murder victim. And maybe—just maybe—there was, as Odeina insisted, a missing girl recording the lives of coal-and-crimson beetles.

Starr still figured Odeina was wrong. Her daughter was probably a runner. Maybe it was a good thing, Chenoa leaving the rez for another life.

The rez spanned nearly fifty-eight thousand acres. Starr didn't feel particularly hopeful about scouring the area even if she narrowed her search to the Manitou caves, the location Chenoa had noted.

Starr knew little about the terrain other than what a map could show her, but she knew that, as in many sovereign tribal nations, some of the land had been stripped and mined in the previous century, then returned to the tribe after the EPA shut down mining operations because of groundwater contamination. Now it was fallow, a wilderness crisscrossed with hundreds of game trails, home to predator and prey.

An hour after she'd started walking, Starr had finished the Cheetos and half the water. If she didn't spot the Awiakta family home soon, she was going to lie down in the grass, with her backpack as a pillow, and rest. Maybe take a little hair of the dog, start on the whiskey again. Then, at the top of a distant rise bordered by prairie grass as high as her thighs, she noticed the dull shine of a single-wide trailer with a faded blue stripe running its length. When she closed in, Starr could make out other details: a maroon two-door Buick LeSabre with the hood missing; a half dozen riding lawn mowers that looked like they were used for parts; and a couple of dogs soaking up the morning sun. She hoped they were friendly.

They weren't.

As Starr approached, the dogs—a gray and white husky and a smaller chihuahua mix—ran at her and barked furiously. She was enormously relieved to see they were chained, but then realized they stood between her and the front door. She skirted the dogs to go behind the trailer, and saw a man running an arc welder that spit sparks into the air around him. He jumped when he spotted her, then slowly flipped up his welding visor.

"Marshal Carrie Starr," she offered, holding out a hand.

"What do you want?"

"Are you the father of Sherry Ann Awiakta?"

He nodded. She could tell by the way his shoulders stiffened that he knew it was bad. She waded in. There was nowhere to go but through—through the shock and fury and pain—and then she'd ask the questions.

By the time she'd clawed her way back, feeling as if she'd nearly drowned, Starr didn't know more than when she started. There weren't answers here. Yes, Sherry Ann had lived there— until she took off last year. No, he didn't know where she'd been, or who she'd been with. Could Starr leave now? Yes, she knew the way.

The last of the morning faded as Starr set out, intent to trace her steps back to the Bronco, but somewhere in those first miles after the Awiaktas' trailer she took a wrong turn.

She emerged from a thicket to find a blocky shape she could have sworn hadn't been on the horizon when she'd hiked her way in. An abandoned house. The kind that lingers on the landscape, windows broken out, wildlife wandering in. She pulled off her backpack and walked closer, glass shards reflecting constellations around her feet.

Starr wondered why a family had left the house behind and how long it would stand before animals and earth broke it down into useful pieces. *Dust to dust* reverberated in Starr's mind, and she thought about Quinn's perfect body, formed inside her own. She had watched what was left of her daughter disappear under six feet of dark soil.

Starr circled the house. The metal roof was the best preserved part of this square structure that was hunkered at the top of a hill. It had probably never had electricity, she figured, being so remote.

She spied a well at the base of a windmill that no longer turned, and behind the house at a respectable distance, an outhouse. She stood for a long time staring at the door. It was partially open, and she wondered what she would find inside. Probably stuffed full of raccoons, she thought, and almost laughed at the idea. Raccoons playing poker. Rabbits tending bar. Deer . . . *Better not to think about deer,* she decided.

She was . . . not lost. She wouldn't admit that. But she was off course. Maybe she could shelter inside the house, get out of the sun, get her bearings, get sober before starting off again.

Starr set one foot gingerly on the sill of the open door—the porch steps had given way long ago—and pulled herself up. She searched the front room, dim even in the daylight, with the beam of her flashlight before stepping all the way in. It was a simple foursquare, its rooms divided around a plus sign at its center, and there was nothing but what she expected: graffiti on the walls, a couple of busted chairs, empty beer bottles, an improvised pipe made from a Coke can, left-behind trash. She could smell urine and the musty stench of mildew. The house had the obvious look of a party hangout, but nothing seemed recent.

Starr was making one last sweep when her foot caught an edge and she went down hard on her hands and knees. At this new vantage point she was inches from a dark smear on the wall above a baseboard. Red, like blood. Like the mess that had been made of Sherry Ann's scalp. Like the spotted beetles Chenoa sought. Like the color of murdered women. She took a pocket-knife from her backpack and scraped a few flakes into an evidence tube. *Probably nothing.*

The ceilings, low and marred with water stains, were making her feel claustrophobic. She didn't want to run into any meth heads who might pick today to start using the house again, or worse, wild animals that might see her as competition, so she stowed the tube in her backpack and hurried out the front door. She'd rather face whatever was waiting for her outside.

Starr drew a deep breath of fresh air, then withdrew a bottle from her front coat pocket. The familiar Jameson warmed her chest while she considered what to do next.

She consulted the cheap compass sewn onto a strap of her backpack. She had to be near the swell of granite she'd traced on the map. Generally, she knew she should be moving east.

Even with the sun at its zenith, there was a circle of moon in the sky as Starr walked across a great plain and opened another bag of Cheetos. She wiped orange dust off her fingers and onto her pants. Starr wondered if an uprise to the north was Manitou caves. If Chenoa was out there, did she really expect to find her? Would it be a recovery or a rescue?

She was always looking for a body; she wasn't always sure whose.

CHAPTER TWENTY-EIGHT

Bernard left ajar the door to his office in city hall. Closing it would be . . . what? Suspicious? Yes, better to leave it open. Besides, it was Saturday morning, and if any other employees happened to walk by, he would see them from his desk chair.

From the start of this new job, just six weeks ago, Bernard had arranged his desk so that he faced the door. He had never liked surprises. But just yesterday the reservation's new marshal had been an unexpected visitor in the mayor's office. And, less than an hour later, there she was again: interrupting his morning break at the library.

Although Bernard had agreed, as part of his job, to handle the logistics of the city's partnership with the reservation and Blackstream Oil, it would be better for him—infinitely better—if the deal fell through. The catch? He couldn't be the one to scuttle it.

Bernard took a deep breath, settled his glasses on the bridge of his nose, rolled his neck to release as much tension as he could and began to study the budget files for every department of the city.

Bernard was good with numbers. Numbers always made

sense. He never had to wonder what they were thinking. Not usually, anyway. He always looked forward to losing himself in their certainty.

The next few hours that passed were an extension of the last few weeks that he'd spent poring over the budget. A bit obsessively, even he had to admit.

It wasn't until he'd worked through lunch and the numbers on his computer screen had begun to blur that Bernard stopped to remove his glasses and rub his eyes. It was there, and he'd finally found it, elegantly hidden and nefariously off-kilter. Numbers never lied, and now he knew what they had been trying to tell him. The mayor—definitely the mayor—had been skimming thousands upon thousands of dollars, and also, somehow, covering it up. The answer had eluded him for weeks, but he had it now. Clear as day.

Bernard congratulated himself as he took an external hard drive the size of his palm from his pocket and transferred the city's budget files onto it.

He thought of Mitzie. About his awkward exchange with her in the library yesterday, his morning respite ruined by the appearance of Marshal Starr. How nervous they both made him.

He'd invested a lot of time in presenting just the right information to put the partnership between the rez, the city and Blackstream Oil in a good light, not that Mayor Taylor had noticed. She was always watching him, which put him on edge. And when he felt on edge, he liked to be prepared for anything.

It wasn't that Bernard liked secrets. It was that he found them necessary. He tried locking them away in tight compartments so that he could go on with his life, but he had discovered, during those years of college and then grad school, that keeping a secret was terribly stressful.

He came back to Dexter Springs because of the job, Bernard

told himself. And that was partly true. He had come back because of the job and because the economy was bad and because he had to take what he could get.

But there was something else that was true too. The reservation had pulled him back. It was like a missing tooth, and he couldn't stop touching his tongue to its absence, to the sweet pain of it. He couldn't stop.

He.

Couldn't.

Stop.

Bernard watched the computer screen as the file transfer finished; then he removed the drive and palmed it into his pocket. He looked at his watch: one fifty-five p.m. He had five minutes to make it across the street to the library, where Saturday afternoon's story time was ending.

As Bernard left city hall through its rear exit, the cool air of an autumn afternoon rushed around him, soothing the heat that had worked its way up his neck, mounted his cheeks and beaded perspiration on his forehead.

He exhaled and used one hand to straighten the collar of his shirt, anxious to put things in motion. He set a course to the library's street-level double doors, and once inside, he traversed the stone floor to the main collection. Soon he was weaving his way between shelves to the children's section, where a half dozen toddlers had just been released like doves at a wedding, scattering down the aisles carrying books or toys.

"Oh my gosh, Paisley. Come back here. Yes, girl, and give me that book. Sorry, Glenna." Bernard could hear Mitzie's voice. "At least she'll be a reader someday."

And with that Mitzie burst around the corner, trailing a wobbly toddler.

"Well, Bernie! I didn't expect to see you again so soon. How are you?" She took him in, the sharply creased slacks, the tucked-in shirt. "Still no Google, huh?"

Bernard shrugged off the joke and, looking around, said, "Have a minute? Wondering if we could talk." Then he quickly leaned in and added, "Quietly."

This was a risk and he knew it. Maybe trusting Mitzie was too large a risk, but when he recalled the years that she'd spent patiently explaining calculus to him in high school, he had acquiesced. What choice did he have?

Numbers were a language he had learned to adore, and Mitzie was even more fluent than he was. Also, he'd never known her to keep a secret.

It's what he was counting on.

"Sure thing, B-man," she said. "Let's do this. Here, Paisley. Come to Mama."

She slung the child across one hip and followed Bernard to a study room at the back of the library, away from the rest of the patrons, who were paying no attention at all.

They entered the small room and Bernard shut the door, Mitzie setting Paisley on the floor with a hardcover of *The Pictorial Guide to Tarot Wisdom*, yet another book the toddler must have pulled from a shelf as she passed by. The little girl, her soft curls falling into her eyes, gurgled and pointed at the brightly colored cover.

"Whatcha got?" Mitzie said.

"Um, okay, here's the thing." He had practiced this, but now the words he had intended to say didn't come to him. "You're really good with numbers." He stumbled. "I mean, really good."

Mitzie crossed her arms over her chest and smiled, snapping her gum and waiting. She was the town's unofficial tax accountant and ran an office out of her home, with small-business owners dropping off fat envelopes stuffed with disorganized receipts, hoping she would save them.

Bernard pulled the external hard drive from his pocket, his palm clammy.

"I'm wondering if you could take a look at this, but keep it between us. Really, Mitzie, *only* between us. If what I think is happening is happening, this is bad. Very bad."

Mitzie's eyes grew wide as she used a thumb and finger to pluck the device from his open hand.

"What is this?"

"The entirety of our city budget for the last three years. Every file. From every department. And something's off. I can't point to it, but it's there, and if anyone can find it, you can."

Mitzie laughed. Paisley dropped her book to the floor.

"Bern," she said, "you're not going to believe this." She shook her head. "I'm one step ahead of you. I just made copies of this year's published budget and had intended to go over it line by line, but this? This is so much better."

They smiled at each other then, and a secret happiness welled inside Bernard. They were two conspirators on the right side of everything: honor, the law, their town. And, with any luck, they had the power to right this wrongdoing.

Bernard had his own reasons, and he hoped that Mitzie, who was making a life in Dexter Springs, would be a dog with a bone. Everything around the mayor turned to gold while the edges of town, including real estate and people, fell into decline, and soon Mitzie would know why. Bernard was filled with something he could think of only as joy.

Meanwhile, he knew he had an image to uphold.

Bernard was steady, reliable, composed, diligent. All the things that made him a good city manager made him good at other things too. He shook the thought out of his head.

"So you'll take a look? Thing is, if you find something amiss, you can't use these files to prove it. You'll have to find the problem, if there is one, and somehow correlate it with the published budget. I can't be involved. This could go to the highest level."

He didn't say things like *fraud* or *embezzlement*, but the words hung in the air.

"Ooh, I'm a forensic accountant now, B-man." Then she saw his worried expression and leaned in close, whispering, "It's okay. I'm on the case. Meet me back here next week. After story time."

She slipped the external hard drive into her bag, scooped up Paisley and opened the door. Bernard watched her hips swing toward the circulation desk and then the exit. With any luck, he'd just transferred the heat to Mitzie, which would keep him where he needed to be: far, far from suspicion.

He looked out the library's windows to city hall across the street, the parking lot a ghost town. The rest of the day stretched with possibility, and he had plenty of time for a hike.

CHAPTER TWENTY-NINE

✳

After walking in what she believed to be generally the right direction, Starr again crossed the creek bed with the puddles she'd avoided. She'd managed to escape the Little People. And there'd been no signs of Deer Woman, if any of that had been real.

She could see how growing up on the rez messed with people. It was isolated. Beautiful. Deadly. She'd done her terrible duty and notified Sherry Ann's father of his daughter's death. Now she couldn't stop thinking about who was to blame, nor could she get Chenoa out of her mind. Chenoa, chasing forgotten beetles through the night; Chenoa who, like Sherry Ann, was young enough to have been her daughter.

When Starr reached the road where she'd left the Bronco, she could see that Minkey had been there. Inside the cab she found a note explaining that he'd pulled the Bronco from the ditch, then given it a jump start, and that he was running a basketball practice for the boys he coached but he'd come back if she needed anything. She was relieved when the Bronco roared to life. She'd done enough hiking for one day.

Twenty minutes later, when Starr pulled the old Bronco up to Chief Elmore Byrd's house in the heart of the reservation, she could see the lawn was verdant despite the onset of autumn. There was a garden hose set out to water it, a sprinkler flipping lazily. A small herd of children waited, giggling and holding hands, then all at once plunged together through the cold spray. They shivered on the other side, their clothes dripping.

One of the children waved shyly, but the rest paid Starr no mind as she got out of the Bronco, settled the keys in the front pocket of her uniform pants and walked from the side of the dirt road to the cinder-block house. Its rectangular footprint wasn't unlike that of the community center, but there were decorative plants holding on to life on either side of the front door, and there was a wreath dotted with tiny turkeys and tied with a faded orange ribbon. The children's laughter as they ran through the sprinkler on the lawn, the Thanksgiving decoration on the door: It felt like too much joy all at once. *The world's gone mad,* she thought.

"*Ha-we,*" Byrd said when he opened the front door. Starr knew it to be the nation's word for *hello,* and returned the greeting.

Byrd looked past Starr at the children and smiled. "They'll feel the cold one day," he said. "Not today, but one day."

He motioned for Starr to come inside and take a seat at a table stationed in the combined kitchen and dining room. He reached for a coffeepot on the counter and raised his eyebrows at her. Starr nodded, and soon they were drinking a strong black brew with generous amounts of heavy cream that would remain in her memory for the rest of her days. It was unexpectedly perfect. The peace she felt sitting at Byrd's table was nothing like the feeling of being in Odeina's scarred trailer with the old woman cackling warnings at her.

She still felt like an interloper. Not only because she was BIA sent, a reminder of the tribe's contentious and traumatic dealings with the federal government, but because her father's culture— his family—was so unfamiliar to her.

"You've come about our young women," Byrd said finally, after they'd both sipped their coffee in comfortable silence. "And I want more than anything to help."

This openness was rare on the rez. If she was going to get anywhere, she needed more people like Byrd. She needed history, anything that could help her learn what wasn't in those files, both the old ones she'd pored over and the new ones she would have to make.

"But what I think," he said with a sigh, "is that you are too little an effort, too late, and that, like everyone else, you are not enough."

It was a punch in the gut, but it was at least familiar territory. She knew how fast people could go from the respite of welcome to straight-out rancor. Most of the people she'd met on the rez had skipped the welcome part.

"Look, I can imagine how you must be feeling," she said, "but I can—"

He held up a hand and waved it, cutting her off.

"These missing girls," he started to say, then corrected himself. "I call them girls, but really they are women. They slip through the cracks. All these law enforcement agencies—city, county, state, federal like you—spend days arguing over what to do and who should do it. Whose responsibility is it? Meanwhile, weeks, months, years pass without someone conducting even the most basic investigation."

Starr opened her mouth in defense, but she knew he was right. Why should she try to say anything different? She knew, from the half-hearted research she'd done before the interview that led to this job, that on the 326 reservations in the United States, the disappearances of women were more frequent, less visible in the media and, ultimately, more difficult to solve than in other populations.

Territorial disputes between law enforcement agencies were largely to blame, with few tribes able to afford their own police forces. And because most reservations were in remote locations, neighboring law enforcement agencies were usually county sheriff offices, which did not have jurisdiction on the reservations. The pattern followed with municipalities, which was why a few days ago Starr had been stunned to see a Dexter Springs officer on temporary loan in her office.

Those weren't the only issues, though. Alcohol, drugs, domestic violence, all the usual suspects that went hand in hand with violence against women, were in full force on the rez, so law enforcement dismissed concerned mothers and aunties. There was the standard *Runaways come back.* Or the classic *Over eighteen? Yeah, they can be gone as long as they want to be.* Starr had said it herself. To Odeina, just this week.

"We need something to keep our young people here, to keep them engaged," Byrd said, and Starr realized she hadn't been listening. "That's why Blackstream Oil is so important to us." He stood and walked to the kitchen window, setting his coffee cup in the sink. "Yes, yes, oil. Fracking. Everyone hates it."

It was as if he was talking to himself now.

"But," he said, returning to meet her gaze, "with this new deal with Blackstream Oil we can begin to heal. We'll have money for school supplies and equipment, funding for a medical clinic—

maybe even a permanent doctor—and we'll be able to provide help for families who cannot find hope anywhere else. And"—he looked now at a wall of pictures behind her—"we can call home the spirits of our missing young people, their souls that are wandering and lost."

Fuck, if he starts making antlers out of his hands and telling me about killer deer . . . Starr longed to light the tip of a big, fat joint. It was Saturday, after all. She thought of the bottle in her backpack, the inch that was left of its contents. It would bridge the gap in a pinch. All the new hope was dissipating.

In Byrd's eagerness to partner with Blackstream Oil, a new danger was being introduced. Starr wondered whether he knowingly overlooked it.

Bringing transient workers to a remote setting, where they would likely live in temporary housing units called "man camps" on tribal land, would cause a new slate of problems. Their crimes, when they happened, would fall between jurisdictional cracks. They'd need more than just one BIA marshal on the rez when that happened. There would be more victims and more families without recourse.

Byrd began pacing from one end of the kitchen to the other. What had she wanted to ask him? Everything felt far away. It felt wrong now to be at his table, drinking his coffee, when she couldn't focus on what he was saying. She wasn't high. Not drunk. It was as if Deer Woman was in her head.

"Even in normal times, convincing people to come together, to share a ceremony for healing, is more challenging than it used to be," Byrd said, walking to a framed picture and pulling it from the wall.

He handed it to Starr, who stared at the face in the frozen image. Dark eyes, dark hair. A face rounder than Chenoa's, but like Chenoa's just the same.

"That was our Loxie," Byrd said. "She went missing ten years and two months ago."

Starr rifled through her memory. Had she seen this face in an old case file she'd pulled from one of the BIA boxes in the marshal's office? She couldn't trust her mind right now, not when it was crowded by a beautiful woman with antlers. The vision smiled at her. *Can deer smile?* She was losing her mind. The room around her shimmered, charged with electricity.

"She walked out this front door one day and vanished right into thin air," he said. "She was only seventeen."

Quinn, Starr thought, and shook her head. She took a deep breath to ward off the panic building in her chest, the feeling of suffocation at her own helplessness.

"We were closer then, all of us, more of a community," Byrd continued. "There were search parties. Relatives went out on horseback or took ATVs on all the roads leading into or out of the reservation. We set up a tip line. One caller said she saw Loxie get into a blue pickup but wasn't sure when. It might have been the week before she went missing."

He sighed.

"We searched. But look around us. There is so much ground to cover. How would we look over every hill, under each tree? You can't imagine the futility."

Starr nodded. She could imagine, actually.

"My cousin spotted a pink sweater in the ditch near the highway as he was driving into Dexter Springs. I thought it looked like something of Loxie's. We asked—begged—for an investigation, but Dexter Springs said they didn't have the capacity. Two years after Loxie's disappearance, there was a vote to disband our tribal police force because we couldn't fund it any longer. But I," Byrd said, "never stopped looking."

Starr swirled the dregs of coffee in her cup.

"My wife, though," Byrd said, "she wasted away after Loxie disappeared, stopped taking care of herself. Refused her diabetes medications. Everyone became a suspect to us. Do you know how it is to think your friends, your family, your neighbors, even strangers you see in a store or on the street, may know something about your daughter's disappearance?"

Oh, she knew all right.

"Anyone in particular?" Starr said.

"You were at the tribal council meeting," he said. "The oil deal? And afterward, the fight? I warned you about Junior. After Loxie . . ." He took a deep breath, blew it out slowly. "After she was gone I learned that Junior bought beer and who knows what else for high school kids, just so they'd spend time with him. And Loxie was one of those kids."

Byrd gripped the counter.

"I went after him," he said. "I mean, I really did. I dogged him at every turn, sure he had answers."

"And?"

"And I wanted to kill him with my bare hands, because he wouldn't say a word. He holed up in his cabin, stopped coming around. Hell, first time I heard him speak in years was at the tribal council meeting. I couldn't believe it had drawn him out."

Byrd pulled out a chair at the dining table and sank into it.

"I was so angry. I knew after a while that I had to do something with that anger," he said, "so I campaigned for tribal chief. Anything to escape that pain, right? I knew I had to stay busy, and I knew there had to be a way to get the resources we needed. I learned how to find government grants, how to apply for them, spent hours putting them together."

"Grants," Starr said. "Grants like the BIA offers? That's how . . ."

"Yes." Byrd nodded. "I'm the reason your job exists."

Starr blinked. This was news. She'd always assumed Chief Byrd was opposed to a BIA presence on the rez, to outside interference. He'd kept her at arm's length, separate from everyone, from everything.

She felt the room spin.

"But it's only a Band-Aid, having a marshal on-site who can conduct an investigation. What we really need is to address what lies underneath. The poverty, the crime. Our unemployment rate is three times the state average. What do you think young people do if they have no hope?"

Starr knew. So did Byrd.

"Even if one of our young people finds work, guess what. The average annual income on the rez is less than seventeen thousand dollars. It's the continued oppression of our people. Do I need to tell you the stories of our ancestors? The genocide? The residential government schools?"

Numbers danced in front of Starr's eyes, somehow real in the dim interior light.

"I am going to pull this reservation into the future with oil money. I'm not selling mineral rights. Hope, Marshal Starr. I am selling hope."

A child's burst of laughter caught on the wind and pushed inside the house, through the cinder blocks and mortar, the insulation and drywall, the paint and pictures on the wall.

CHAPTER THIRTY

Junior was sitting on the top step of the rickety wooden stairs leading up to his front door Saturday afternoon when Starr cut the engine and left the old Bronco cooling.

Telling Sherry Ann Awiakta's father about her death had been hell that morning, and the miles she'd walked were still with her. She could feel the ache of them in her shoulders, where the backpack straps had dug in, and there was something else now too. Learning about Byrd's missing daughter and his suspicions about Junior made things notch into place. He was related to Chenoa, so he obviously knew her. And where had he been when Sherry Ann was murdered?

"See you got your door patched."

Junior glanced at the thin slab of plywood covering the space where a door had been.

"No thanks to you."

They were both quiet for a while, Starr watching the knife in his hands work the end of a stick.

It seemed like forever since she'd taken him home, found the dead dog and watched him bury it, but only three days had spanned the interim. Starr was still shaken by what she'd seen in his cabin, but even a haunt like that seemed harmless in the clear, bright afternoon sun. She was relieved that Deer Woman, if that's what she had really seen at Junior's that night, was an omen that fled in the light of day.

"You want something?"

"You know Odeina is worried about Chenoa. And yesterday at the Trading Post, you obviously knew about the Awiakta homicide, saying that's why you were handing out those protection things you made. I also have it on good authority that another missing girl used to spend a lot of time out here, about ten years ago." Better that she came in soft. "So, now I've told you what I know at this point, and you know this is an ongoing investigation, right? You've got a pretty good perspective on these girls from the rez. And I'd obviously like to hear it."

"I don't know shit about nothing."

"You hang out with a younger crowd a lot?"

"Used to. I was younger too, then."

"Maybe you buy beer for some high school kids once in a while. Happens all the time. Young girls not too shy to ask for a favor, and the next thing you know, they're staying over, running around your house like they don't care who's wondering where they are. Maybe they get older. Maybe you still keep tabs on them, or maybe they don't want to hang out with you anymore and that makes you mad. So, who comes out here now?"

"Nobody. Keep to myself." He set down the knife and the wood. "You don't know how it is here. My side of things. I was there for those kids, mostly rez kids. Watched out for them."

"How?"

"Look, this was a long time ago, but sure, we partied. Safer here than anywhere else."

"Safer? It wasn't safe for those girls. Maybe you liked them; maybe it went wrong. I know you get upset."

"Trouble happens when I get out. People getting in the way of my fist, that sort of thing. So now I keep to myself. Don't want trouble. Don't want it coming around either." He stared pointedly at Starr. "I've been in a lot of bad situations. I regret that. But now you're suddenly the 'law'? I guess pinning this on me would be a pretty big get for you, huh? Way to prove yourself?"

"Yeah, I'm not worried about that. I'm worried about what happened to Sherry Ann. You walk down to the creek after you buried the dog Wednesday night, Junior? You know where Chenoa might be right now? What about Loxie? What can you tell me about her?"

Junior couldn't hide his surprise quickly enough when she said Loxie's name. Starr saw it flash across his face.

"When I left you here Wednesday night, what did you do? I need to know your whereabouts from the moment you walked back into your cabin until—let's just say—Thursday noon."

Junior's body tensed, his hands flexing while he eyed the ground. Beside him, the knife caught the light. Starr took a step back, unclipped her service weapon.

"If you move on me," she said, "I will draw. If you come at me, rest assured, I will put you down."

Junior didn't respond.

"You need to talk to me, Junior, because I promise you that if I leave here without the information I need, I will pick apart your life. You want me to do that?"

"Odeina."

"What about Odeina?"

"I was on her couch until Thursday morning, and then I made my way back home." He didn't tell Starr about the creek, the way he'd woken up with sand in his shoes, on his clothes.

"You better be sure about that, because I'm going to check. And you'd better know where you were when Loxie disappeared. And, Junior?" Starr said, walking backward to the Bronco. "If you know anything about Chenoa that you're keeping from me, I will come for you." She patted her Glock. "Like you said, I'm the law. Anything can happen on the rez."

CHAPTER THIRTY-ONE

✳

When Starr pulled up to the Trading Post she could see Odeina inside, running an order to the only occupied table. The sight of food made her stomach growl and she realized the only things she'd eaten that day were Cheetos. It was nearly ten p.m., and even though the restaurant was open an hour later on Saturday nights, it would still be closing in a few minutes. Same as on Wednesday, when Starr had left Junior's after watching him bury the dog, after hearing the sound of a distant party at the creek and before Chak had discovered Sherry Ann's body less than eight hours later. If Junior was telling the truth about being with Odeina, that would steer the investigation in an entirely different direction.

Odeina looked up when the door chime sounded. She grimaced at the sight of Starr, and then walked toward her with an order pad.

"What can I get you? Or have you actually been doing your job and have something new to say?"

"Need to ask you a few questions about Junior. Won't take long."

"Junior? He hasn't been here all day." She looked back at the lone customer, who was biting into a cheeseburger. "What do you want with Junior?"

"Last Wednesday, were you working here?"

"Wednesday . . ." She looked to the ceiling, remembering. "I was. Worked a split shift, so I closed."

"And what did you do, where did you go, after you left here?"

"Well, that would have been our meat loaf special, so I boxed a meal for Grandmother, and then I closed up at about eleven thirty and . . . Wait. I did see Junior when I was driving home. He'd been out picking up bottles."

"Okay, good. And what happened after you saw him?"

"Well, I stopped to see if he needed a ride and then took him to my place. He slept on the couch until I dropped him at his cabin the next morning."

"How was he? What was his, you know, state of mind?"

Odeina looked down at the order pad she was holding.

"Junior has a good heart. He's rough, sure, but people don't know him. If they would just give him a chance . . ."

"Did anything seem unusual about him at the time? Did he seem off?"

"I don't think he even remembers getting in my car, to tell you the truth. He was in a bad way, and I could tell he'd been drinking. He was crying, saying something about Yella and I don't know what all. I figured he could sleep it off and at least I'd know where he was, that he was warm. Left sand all over my car."

"Sand? From where, did he say?"

"No, but it looked like he'd been down at the creek. He goes down there to get cans, bottles, recycling stuff. Kids are always trashing it."

"But he was with you, the entire time, from eleven thirty Wednesday night until when the next morning?"

"Would have been about ten thirty the next morning, since I came here after that for the lunch shift." She glared at Starr. "Don't believe me? Ask Verlyn there." She pointed to the customer dogging the burger.

"I can hear you," he said, and gave Starr a thumbs-up. "I hitched a ride with her that night, helped her get Junior in the car and practically carried him to her couch. And that wasn't easy, I tell you. I walked home from there. I guarantee you that after Junior's head hit the pillow he wasn't going anywhere."

"Thanks," Starr said, and turned toward the exit. "Be in touch." The medical examiner put the time of death after midnight. If it wasn't Junior, then who was it?

"Chenoa," Odeina called after her. Louder: "Chenoa. Find her!"

Later, when Starr reached Dexter Springs and settled herself in the garage, wearing her bathrobe over her uniform, she lit a joint and thought about the party at the creek, about everyone who might have been there, about Junior tucked safely away at Odeina's as Sherry Ann's life had slipped away. Sherry Ann, who'd been days from her twentieth birthday.

Quinn would never reach that age.

Chenoa had, but only to have her future become a question. She was twenty-two, old enough to go where she liked for as long as she wanted, but practically still a child.

Starr stopped herself. *Don't go there.* She could feel the tendrils of loss and shame tightening their grip.

She grabbed an old desk lamp protruding from a cardboard box, plugged it in and switched it on. She opened the three-ring binder she'd taken from Chenoa's room and flipped through its contents. Pictures of beetles with red patches on their wing covers, a few with markings that verged into an OU crimson. Starr peered at a diagram that pointed out a protective plate between the beetle's head and wings; the plate was covered with a Rorschach-looking patch of red.

She didn't usually mind bugs, but these things were huge. Unsettling. In the binder she found a snapshot that had a ruler next to a beetle for scale. Two inches. A carrion beetle the length of her thumb, it buried itself in soil during the day and fed on small dead animals at night.

Starr flipped a few more pages, then stopped. She read part of a report, which Chenoa had gleaned from the Oklahoma Department of Wildlife Conservation's website:

> American burying beetles are nocturnal. To prepare for reproduction, male and female pairs seek out a carcass under the cover of darkness, and then defend it against other burying beetles and competing scavengers. They bury the carcass in the soil, removing all fur or feathers from the body, and the female lays twelve to eighteen eggs near the carcass. When the eggs hatch, larvae feed on the carcass until they pupate and emerge as adults, approximately eight weeks later. American burying beetles are unique among insects in that they exhibit a large amount of parental care for their offspring.

Parental care. Starr recalled the silences her father would sink into, forcing her to spend hours alone. She'd wished for her mother then, even though her mother was long gone from depression or cancer or whatever ate her up when Starr was too young to understand and her father too drunk to tell the truth.

Starr closed her eyes and sounds turned to color. Something was clicking into place, but what? She was only halfway through the joint, but she unscrewed the cap on a bottle of Jameson and took a swallow. She knew that soon her shoulders would release the tension they'd stored all day. Another drag. A few more. A drink. She turned off the lamp and sat in the darkness. A thready thought made her chase its tail: night.

At night. The beetles are active at night. Odeina said Chenoa searched for them at night.

If there was a chance of finding her, it would require a plan that was the opposite of a search that needed daylight to succeed. Yes, that was it. She needed to find the girl at night. Quinn. *No, not Quinn,* Starr thought. *Chenoa.* She repeated the name in her head. *Chenoa. Chenoa.*

Starr flipped on the overhead light and stumbled around the garage, peering into boxes. Starr had seen an old trail on one of Chenoa's maps, one that would veer into the reservation's most remote areas and lead her to the Manitou caves. She remembered Odeina's angry, condescending rant the day she'd showed Starr the map. She thought of the graffiti on her service vehicle. She would never feel like she belonged on the rez. There was a big difference between having enough heritage to get a rez job and being part of the community.

She imagined how quickly word would spread across the rez after she'd found the girl, saved her, how everything would be different then. She'd find Qui— She shook the cobwebs from her head. Who was she looking for? *Chenoa.* Chenoa, *right.*

Maybe she could win one. She'd find Chenoa, who, like the beetles, was out in the dark. Maybe she'd twisted her ankle or had some other small thing happen and she needed to be rescued. *That would turn 'em around,* Starr thought. Everyone on the rez would practically volunteer to scrub the spray paint off the MAR-SHAL decal on her service vehicle. There would be a celebration, and she'd walk down the potluck line filling a plate so high it would need sideboards to contain it all: fry bread like Winnie described, venison stew like the recipe that scented Odeina's kitchen, buttery new potatoes that tasted faintly of the soil they were grown in. All the food her dad had ever made. What would it feel like to be home?

CHAPTER THIRTY-TWO

SUNDAY

By seven o'clock Sunday morning, Starr was parked outside her office, watching pink fingers of light stretch across the sky. She'd stayed in the garage the night before, poring over Chenoa's maps, studying her research, the newspaper articles she'd clipped. Starr had slept three hours, maybe four.

She felt for the joint in her pocket, swigged a series of long draws from the whiskey she kept stowed under the seat and rested her forehead on the steering wheel.

With any luck the building would be empty, at least for a while. She needed time to think, time to go through more files. She already knew Winnie would be in Dexter Springs most of the day, taking her grandchildren to their Biddy basketball games. Minkey was busy that morning too, but she'd asked him to come in to work for the afternoon.

For the time being, though, Starr was glad to be alone. She didn't think she could stand being on the rez one more second, not any part of it. This job had brought the worst kind of trouble. Missing women. Murdered women. Memories of her own daughter.

She got out of the truck, slammed the door and walked around the back of the building. A pair of plastic lawn chairs were upended near the rear entrance to her office, the door rusted shut. She righted one of the chairs, brushed off a spider and settled in. The other chair, she pulled directly in front of her knees and then propped her legs on it. The wind picked up and rattled the brittle grass that had grown over the summer. She faced the wide expanse behind the building, her eyes drifting over russet and gold waves of long prairie grasses that undulated with the rise and fall of wind and earth. Beyond the grasses were ravines, their edges thick with trees and carpets of fallen leaves, the hollows dank and cold where the sun didn't linger; instead, it passed over as quickly as a life. As quickly as her daughter's life. Blink and it's gone.

The old pain was there, swallowing her whole, and Starr wondered why she was still alive. She knew what had fueled her in those first days and weeks after Quinn's death, but she'd killed that problem and left him as a warning in a South Side alley. She'd never been charged with the crime, which meant there were still people in Internal Affairs who knew Chicago was better with one less bad guy. The fact that their ruling came on the heels of Quinn's funeral had been a small mercy.

Starr brought the joint out from her pocket and fired it, listening to the chatter of dark little birds that flocked from branch to grass and back again. She had no idea what type of birds they were, but the crest of a red cardinal was unmistakable when it alighted in a tangle of hedge trees to her left. Osage orange, Minkey called them, hardwood trees that dropped knobby green fruit the size of softballs. He seemed to know every living thing here.

For Starr, coming to the rez had been as much about losing herself as about finding someone, anyone. Chenoa. Maybe it was hubris, thinking she could walk out there and be the hero of someone else's story. Why stand against the world and delay the death you crave when there's no way to set anything right?

Her cell phone buzzed, cutting her thoughts.

"Starr." She answered on the fourth ring, not even checking the caller ID.

"Please hold for Director Randall."

Starr immediately straightened in her chair, then stood. Steve Randall was director of the Southern Plains regional office of the BIA, stationed out of Anadarko, Oklahoma. Her reporting agency.

After a few moments of silence and a couple of clicks that made her sure the call had dropped, Randall came on the line. Starr knew reception behind the building was spotty, but if she moved to a better location she'd risk losing the call altogether. She decided not to take her chances, so she stood still and erect, her attention focused.

"Director Randall here. Marshal Starr? Good." He didn't wait for her response. "Listen, how's it going down there?"

"Good, sir, very good. Not fully equipped when I arrived, but that's been handled and I—" she lied.

He cut her off.

"Here's the deal. I recognize it's highly unusual to ring you on a Sunday, it being the Lord's day, but it's come back to us that you've got a homicide down there. A vic from the rez and found on the rez?"

"Yes, and—"

"Okay, good intel, then. Haven't seen a report yet, so that better be on my desk by noon tomorrow. Listen, I've got a committee meeting on the horizon with some higher-ups and I'm going to need you to get a handle on this. Not looking good for what we're trying to do here, which is the right thing, of course, sending aid where aid is needed. But how well that aid works falls on you. It's why we hired you, you know, with this being part of your"—he hesitated—"heritage and all."

"Right," said Starr, hoping she sounded convincing. She couldn't tell him she'd been shut out of inner circles, turned away from doors on which she'd knocked, that the official BIA vehicle was vandalized during her first week on the job. Or that she had no idea who had killed the girl whose body had been discovered by the creek bed.

"I'm actually working that case right now, making progress. Good progress," she added, hoping it didn't sound like an afterthought.

She pictured the dead girl's mouth, filled with white, chalky substrate. There was Chenoa, of course, who was probably missing. There were other young women, gone for years—and in the mouth of one victim, the same white substance found in Sherry Ann Awiakta's throat. One more invisible girl whose family would never be the same.

"Better be progress," said Director Randall, "because you've got one week to make this case, or we'll have to go in a different direction. It's not something I'd anticipated, necessarily, but there it is."

"Different direction?" she said numbly.

"Yeah, hope you haven't unpacked."

Then he was gone. Whether the call dropped or he ended it didn't matter.

Starr slumped back into the lawn chair. This job was her last resort. Her. Last. Resort. What was she going to do now? Where would she go from here? She couldn't go back to Chicago and she didn't have the money to set up anywhere else. Even if she did, detective work was all she knew.

Starr stayed in the lawn chair for an hour, then spent three more scanning the BIA cold cases still left in her office; she was searching for any kind of clue that could lead her to Sherry Ann's killer. When it was nearly noon, she left for the Trading Post, where she grabbed a cellophane-wrapped turkey sandwich. No sign of Odeina.

She decided to head to Junior's shack. So far he'd been the most talkative of everyone she'd questioned, even when she was threatening to take him in. Maybe he would tell her more about Chenoa. What she liked. Her secret hopes. Her plans. Maybe understanding Chenoa could lead her to something—anything—that would advance her search for Sherry Ann's killer. Maybe it was a waste of time to think about Sherry Ann when Chenoa might be out there, alive.

Tracking information on the rez felt like wandering into a maze of funhouse mirrors. She'd learned that she couldn't get anywhere by barraging anyone with questions. Every time she asked direct questions, their faces would turn to stone, the light in their eyes retreating in some way, and they would say nothing. Nothing of value.

Starr washed down the sandwich with three gulps of whiskey as she drove; then she rolled the window of the Bronco down to feel the brace of cool air. A local radio announcer rattled off the forecast: unseasonably warm today, with a cold front moving in; by Monday evening much of the region would see its first ice and snow, with heavier amounts along a line running parallel to Route 66. Starr wondered whether the cold snap would be anything to rival the lake-effect wind and snow that rolled off Lake Michigan into Chicago. She doubted it.

Director Randall had given her a week. Sherry Ann's trail had already gone cold. And he had no idea that she had a more pressing problem. Chenoa. Maybe—just maybe—she could save at least one lost girl.

CHAPTER THIRTY-THREE

✳

As Junior's shack came into view, Starr saw him on the front steps again. It was like he'd stayed where she'd left him the day before, mad as hell and swearing he had an alibi. Now he scowled when he saw her drive in.

"Alibi checks out," Starr said as she left the Bronco. "Talked to Odeina."

She approached him slowly and pointed to a camp chair that leaned against the cabin. When he nodded, she shook dried leaves off its nylon seat, set it up and tested her weight until she was confident it would hold.

"You ever see any deposits of white dirt around here? Has a really fine, chalklike texture? It's called kaolin, I believe."

Then she waited.

If Starr hoped to make some headway, ask questions about Chenoa or find out who else he might have seen at the creek the night before Sherry Ann's body was found, she needed a different approach. Nothing too direct, not yet. The turkey sandwich roiled in her belly and she adjusted the belt on her uniform. What she wouldn't give to have eaten a Portillo's Chicago dog instead.

Junior was silent for a long time, his eyes narrowing as he considered the question.

"Don't think so."

Another dead end.

Jays flitted in and out of the tires in Junior's yard, the birds' loud calls competing with the chatter of at least a dozen finches. The wind picked up and Starr pulled her jacket up against her chin.

"Sometimes you don't really know a place until you leave it," she said.

Junior nodded.

"I was gone for a while myself," Junior said finally. "Started building this place about fifteen years ago." She studied his bare forearms, tracking the tattoos. Prison, probably. Military, maybe. She'd pulled his record, but there was a lot about Junior she didn't know.

"I know it don't look like much." He tilted his head toward the cabin behind him. In the daylight, Starr could see that it listed to the west like a cargo ship with an uneven load. "It ain't much, to put it plainly. I built it from scrap, leftover construction materials, things thrown away."

Starr looked around the yard. Among the towers of bald tires were other things: wood pallets, piles of scrap metal, a fifty-gallon drum overflowing with crushed aluminum cans, wilting cardboard boxes full of rusty nails, a mountain of discarded green and amber bottles with faded labels. It looked like chaos, like a scene from one of those hoarding shows Quinn sometimes watched on repeat. Yet it wasn't. Not exactly.

Now that Starr studied it in the daylight, there might be an order to it. She could feel him watching her, still wary.

"Did you collect all this?" she said. "To recycle?"

"C'mon."

Junior pushed off the porch steps and walked toward a shed beyond the mess. It stood under a natural awning of bare tree branches, its wood so weathered that it blended in with the landscape.

"I have something to show you," Junior called back to her.

Starr followed him along a path that wound through the yard, thinking of the questions she had, wondering how she'd convince him to elaborate on life here, to explain every dead end, each closed door; all the while, she was questioning whether she could trust him. His criminal offenses were minor, but she'd known plenty of men who tipped further and further until there was no coming back.

"I was a lot younger then, a decade at least," he said as she caught up with him. "When those kids were coming around."

"I get it."

"No," Junior said. "You don't." He stopped and turned to face her. "Those kids I used to know, they've moved on. Because of me. Because I gave them a place to be when their mama or their daddy took off or got too drunk or there wasn't any food at home. You think I haven't already been through this? The suspicion? I was here when Loxie disappeared. Not you. Not your dad. Me. It changed me. Don't nobody come around here no more. Not this girl that got killed at the creek, not anyone."

Junior stalked to the shed and pulled back its sliding door, but Starr motioned for him to go first.

"Ooh," she whispered, her eyes traveling upward. "Oh."

She'd expected the building to be as cluttered as his house. But this . . . There were no words.

The rustic walls of the shed gave way to a ceiling that served as a window to the gnarled branches and blue sky above. The window was made entirely of emerald and amber bottles. Starr thought of the piles of recycling materials outside. Here, they'd been cut and pieced together, transformed into a kaleidoscope. Light filtered through the glass, dappling their faces and the floor on which they stood.

This was stunning. A cathedral. A shrine. Starr felt the kind of wonderment that arrives, unbidden, the first time a truly magnificent sight is beheld. Like witnessing the power of Niagara Falls, or feeling a newborn warm and slippery on her chest with eyes that held the ages.

Art is only a poor imitation of nature, no matter how skilled its creator, but this was the most breathtaking thing she'd ever seen. Quinn, with her sketchbooks and art pencils, would have loved it.

"Y-you—" she stammered. "You made this?"

That's when she knew. This . . . what could she call it? This architectural sculpture. It was the heart of the man. Junior had invited her in. There was nothing that would still be hidden to her in his closed-up spaces.

Starr looked up through the ceiling, watched the light change colors as the trees shifted in the wind, feeling for a moment the pure kind of joy she had been sure would elude her the rest of her life.

She was on the land of her father's people. An outsider. For the first time, she could admit there might be another reason she was here: to discover where she belonged in this great web of people, to understand how their collective history materialized in her life in ways she'd never been able to connect. A part of her that wanted to belong.

"Whoa," said a voice from the doorway. Starr and Junior both flinched, and were surprised to see Minkey standing there, looking skyward. "Looks like a lot of work. Can't believe you can do that. You use, what, old bottles that you melt down? I saw this *How It's Made* episode—you ever watch that show?—where it showed how beer bottles are made, filled and packaged. Man, I love that show. Answers all these questions you don't even know you have, like how the filling is put inside Twinkies."

Starr glanced at her watch. It was later than she'd thought. Well past the time she'd told Minkey she'd return to the office. She'd left him a note saying where she was, and didn't realize he'd know how to find Junior's place. She decided to use him as the distraction he was.

"Yeah, uh, no," said Junior. "Don't get that programming out here."

"Junior, mind if I look around a bit?" Starr said. "I'd like to get the lay of the land around here. See what's what."

Junior shrugged. She left the workshop, Minkey bumping into a stack of bottles, then looking at her while Junior was distracted by the fallen glass. Starr rolled her hand for Minkey to keep the conversation going.

"I am so sorry," Minkey said, turning to Junior and chattering on for Starr's benefit. "I got tied up thinking about that show. Let's just go back to how you make this stuff."

Starr walked behind the shed, surveying Junior's junkyard, feeling like she'd come to her senses. Junior might have an alibi for Sherry Ann, but she still had questions about Chenoa. Maybe there was evidence that Chenoa had been here, voluntarily or otherwise. Maybe she'd just left, or maybe she was here now.

Inside the workshop, the conversation shifted.

"The other day at the Trading Post," Junior said, "sure thought you looked familiar."

"I get that a lot. Got one of those faces, I guess."

Junior stepped toward Minkey, so close he could smell the man's breath, minty and warm.

"I'm gonna ask you this real quiet. You ever go down to the creek?" He registered the shock on Minkey's face. "I seen you there that night. Getting that fire going, weren't you? Bet the marshal doesn't know you were getting cozy with Sherry Ann. I'll bet she'd be real interested to find out. Somebody like me might be tempted to tell her the truth."

Minkey stayed rooted in shock as Junior stepped back and took a long, deep breath. Junior knew this was all wrong, in that bad way, speaking of the dead in this sacred place where he tried to release whatever was trapped inside him, his own quickening that he hoped would birth a new life. But now Deer Woman was coming for him.

At least he wasn't responsible for Sherry Ann. At least the innocence he'd projected had turned out to be real. Junior thought of Byrd, Loxie's father, and how he would have hated her being at Junior's place back then, like all parents hated the secret lives teenagers hid. She'd been the seed that germinated who he was to become. Her hands making, ever making: weaving flower crowns, bracelets, necklaces that hung to her waist. His desire for her had been so free of artifice, so pure, that she caused creation to bubble up from inside him. It was as if some greater instruction had been downloaded directly into his body and he'd fought against it. The drinking had caused him to miss so much time then, to do things for which he couldn't account. What happened during those long blackout hours? Did he become a monster?

CHAPTER THIRTY-FOUR

Eating out of my hand," Mayor Helen Taylor said into her cell phone as she smiled and waved at passersby from the plush interior of her Lincoln. It was Sunday afternoon and she'd just finished a meet and greet at the Dexter Springs senior center.

"You know what they say about successful politicians. The first thing you have to do is win. If you don't win, you can't do any good."

"I'll win, Wink," she said. With the completed city hall construction project she'd caught the attention of Wink Parkman, a gas and oil lobbyist, who had driven her interest in bringing fracking to the reservation. "And once we break ground on the oil project, I'm bulletproof."

She stared out the driver's window at a series of campaign signs with her face on them. Two days until the election. Work on the access roads to the reservation would start the following week; then the oil workers would set up camp on the rez and, with her plan moving past the point of no return, she'd start planning her bid for a senate seat. Halfway through her next term as mayor, she'd be able to blow this burg.

"People are watching, Helen. You have my support, and now the people with the means to build your political future are talking about how far you'll go."

She smiled. Everything was going to plan. Of course, Holder thought it had been his idea when he'd arrived in her office bursting with a scheme to get rich. His "discovery," as he called it, of tapping into a little-known reservoir beneath reservation land had already been floated to her by Parkman, along with an offer to connect her to a network of backers who could craft a political career that would go higher than she'd ever imagined. All she had to do was work with Blackstream Oil—specifically, their man on the ground, Antell—and ensure Chief Byrd's cooperation. She was using Holder to smooth out any bumps along the way. And she had Minkey in place to report on the reservation's new marshal.

"But there's concern," Parkman said, "that maybe you won't be able to keep things handled. That it's got too many moving parts. That maybe you're not capable of it."

"Is that some kind of threat?"

"It's a warning. You think you're my only source of information?" Parkman laughed, his voice velvet smooth. "I wouldn't be good at what I do if I didn't have eyes and ears everywhere. We need you to be our local leader who supports the oil project. Don't get me wrong, Helen: You've done a fine job of that. I even agreed when you wanted to bring that rancher on board. But my opinion has, shall we say, shifted. I have it on good authority that Holder is a loose cannon. And what I do not want is the involvement of someone who cannot act predictably in my—our—best interests."

Holder. How could Wink know about Holder's increasingly erratic behavior? She'd done her best to keep that from him.

"We're going to need you to be very careful, Helen. You can't afford to have anything backfire over the next forty-eight hours. Or down the line. If you need my assistance in cutting him loose, say the word."

"I'll handle this my way."

"Understood. But risking this election, risking this project, would jeopardize your path to the senate. Our backers could get cold feet, and it would be wrong to risk it all when you could do a lot of good for a lot more people. When we could all do more together."

"It's all going to plan; don't you worry about that. I built city hall, didn't I? Added a modern public safety facility to it, right? Something that no one else had been able to do for twenty years, Wink. Frankly, no one could have accomplished this but me."

"Helen, how do I put this . . . ? Since our first conversation, all those months ago, I've believed you deserve our support and that you could get the backing for a senate seat. Or go higher. Maybe all the way."

"I'm doing it," she said. "I don't understand why you think I'm not."

"Don't let a smell become attached to your campaign."

"What? Now you're not making sense. From the start I've been your political ally. It's who I am."

"Who you are, Mayor Helen Taylor, will depend on what happens on Election Day."

When she heard the click Helen slammed the phone against the dash, then tossed it onto the passenger seat and revved the engine. She took a deep breath, gave a friendly wave to a dog walker who had stopped to stare, and willed herself to stay calm.

In two days, the election would be over. Her city council already was lined up just the way she wanted it. The road construction and the oil project were nearly in motion. Now all she had to do was make sure Holder played his part.

Helen took a deep breath, summoned all the tranquility she could muster and eased the Lincoln onto Main Street to make her way to the linear park. At least she could get some exercise while on her way to see that infuriating man.

Helen's routine of running at the park had become just one more activity in the tapestry of normalcy she'd woven. It was perfectly fine for her to be at the park. That was what her husband thought. And, technically, she *was* getting those miles in.

But the weather was shifting. She could feel it in her bones.

Helen parked, cut the engine, slid the phone into her jacket pocket and set out on her run. She let her mind wander. Holder might be nearly a foot taller than her, but if she could get her hands around his neck . . . It was a fantasy she'd had more often as the city and tribal councils had worked through lease details, and as she'd become a buffer between them and Antell at Blackstream Oil.

She took the path to the wooden-slat bridge, water running silently below as she mulled over her strategy. First things first. Parkman didn't know as much as he thought he did. She'd been able to negotiate a sizable kickback from Antell, an off-the-books bonus no one knew about—not even Holder—which would allow her to pay back what she'd taken from city coffers. It was the only solution. Without Antell's payout, her budding political career would be all but over; it wasn't exactly easy to win an election from a jail cell. But she had only a small window in which to pay the money back before someone looked closely enough to uncover the fake vendors and falsified expenses. While Bernard seemed harmless, there was something about him—his watchful eyes, maybe—that made her wonder whether she'd read him right during the hiring process. He'd seemed quiet, docile, desperate for a job: all the qualities she liked to exploit in her employees.

Holder. He was a different story.

Her feet sounded across the wooden planks, a comfort she'd come to appreciate on her way to the secret meetings with Holder. He'd made sure his land was the best option for the site of the city road project to access reservation acreage into which Blackstream would inject high-pressure salt solutions to crack underground rock formations and retrieve previously unreachable oil, maybe even natural gas. Holder's land value would increase astronomically; he would be rich beyond measure. In return, he identified and removed obstacles.

And there was Chief Byrd, so intent on offering his people a better future that he didn't notice her machinations. Or he turned a blind eye. No one wanted to know how the sausage was made.

Helen's pocket buzzed. She pulled her phone free and clocked the number: Byrd's.

She didn't answer. He would have to wait.

Holder was just over the bridge, the smoke from a cigarette pluming above his head as he waited by a barbed wire fence. Holder was a wild card, but she'd make sure he worked to her benefit. Because of him, she knew that a rez girl was researching bugs, that if she found an endangered species it would doom the oil deal. Doom Helen's future.

Holder crushed the cigarette under the toe of a boot as she ran toward him.

"You do know," she said, waving off the smoke, "that a murdered girl on the rez is already strike two. And if anyone gets even a whiff of some rez girl locating a bug that could bring in the EPA or the FBI or whatever protects bugs, that will be strike three. Blackstream Oil will run in the other direction. And take all their money with them."

"Whoa, whoa, whoa," Holder said, stepping back and raising his palms. "Easy there, Lady Mayor. Comin' in hot. I told you I'm a problem-solver."

Helen sighed. Holder had proved useful by gleaning information from the town's rumormongers and keeping her privy to anything that might impact the oil deal. Somehow Holder had been even better at exporting information off the rez than Minkey, even though Minkey was a part of the murder investigation.

"What's the update on the rez girl and those . . . whatever bugs?" she said.

"Burying beetles. She's still looking for them, but she won't be for long. I scared the hell outta her. I been watching where she's searchin' and . . ."

Holder ran through his activity of the past few days. He'd searched the reservation's wilderness area until he spotted the girl hiking a ridge. Later, when he figured out where she was camping in her van, he'd gone after her on foot. The rest had been so easy. First he'd dropped the cell phone she'd left in the van into a cup of water. No working phone, no way to call for help even if she could have picked up a signal. Better still, no one could track her location.

After he rifled through her belongings, Holder sat in the driver's seat of the van, staring out the windshield. It came to him in a flash. He disengaged the parking brake, hopped out and gave the van a shove. It rolled, picking up speed until it tipped into a slough a hundred yards away, the driver's side listing into earth. It was a message she wouldn't be able to ignore.

"What's new with the murder investigation?" Helen said. She reminded herself to call Minkey into her office to quiz him in the morning.

"Don't know why they can't keep them rez girls supervised." Holder pulled a pack of Marlboro Reds from his jacket and tapped one into his hand. "Nothing to report. Investigation's going nowhere, is what I heard."

"A death on the rez means questions. Questions aren't something I'm too fond of. Antell doesn't like having a federal marshal on-site. I know that much."

"I'm keeping an eye out. Most action I've seen so far is that marshal drinking coffee at Rita's Roast. She's trying to close the barn door after the horses are out." Holder turned away from the wind to light his cigarette. "Speaking of the coffee shop, I'm doing my best to make sure you get the votes you need."

Helen crossed her arms and frowned up at Holder.

"Why would anyone vote against me?" Ungrateful plebeians. Because of her there would be dozens of oil workers with money to burn, which would boost the local economy; those dollars would transform into new businesses and new homes.

"I'm just saying, you better win that election. I don't wanna have my ass handed to me by Blackstream Oil when Antell wants to know how this will work with someone else as mayor."

"Go calm Antell down. Feed him your usual line of bullshit. And put out that cigarette. Who even smokes anymore? Gross."

"Wow, talking dirty now. I like it." Holder snuffed the Marlboro and snapped the butt over the fence line. "So, if a murdered rez girl was strike two and a rare bug was strike three, what was strike one?"

"You."

CHAPTER THIRTY-FIVE

✳

While Minkey was keeping Junior busy in the workshop, Starr checked for signs of Chenoa along the tree line and peered through the windows of the cabin. *Nothing.* When she heard Minkey's truck take off down the two-track she walked back to Junior's workshop.

Inside, she found him absently spinning a pottery wheel with one hand.

"Where's he going?"

"Don't know," said Junior.

Maybe there's something in the water, thought Starr. Minkey was as unpredictable as the rest.

The sun was about to set on Junior and his junkyard. Starr corrected herself. *Art.* She leaned against a workbench and watched light play across the glass-bottle ceiling as Junior left the pottery wheel and began sorting wine bottles.

The art Junior created was extraordinary. As good as, even better than, anything she'd seen in an art gallery. Not that she haunted that type of fine establishment, but art had been an interest of Quinn's. *If it's important to you, it's important to me,* she'd always said to her daughter, and that had fueled all kinds of new things.

Quinn had convinced her to take a kayak onto Lake Michigan and to volunteer to rehabilitate day-old kittens with on-the-hour feedings. Starr had been tired all the time, but those years had gone so fast. She would do anything to have them back now. A familiar ache welled behind her eyes and she shut them hard against it.

"You don't remember anything about this place?" Junior said. "About the rez? From when you were little?"

"Yeah, not a thing. I didn't even know my father had ever left me here until this week. Guess I was too young."

"My mom, who lives with Odeina now, that's who kept you. Her and me. We traded off for maybe six months. Then, one day, he just showed up, your dad. Took you back to Chicago and we didn't hear another thing, except finally that he'd"—Junior hesitated—"died."

"Why did he leave?" Starr said. *No, that wasn't the right question.* She knew he'd enlisted in the army, been stationed in a war zone, then settled with her mother in the city. And that her mother didn't like it when he talked about his family. "Why didn't he ever come back?"

Starr thought about how different her life would have been if she had grown up here. Would she have fallen in love? Survived her teenage years? Would she have had Quinn, had other children? Been better off knowing her family? Even with her blood claim, the rez wasn't open to her. Maybe there was nothing left to give. If Indigenous people were going to preserve their cultures, to some degree that would require separation from the rest of the world. And that included her, didn't it?

"Who can say?" Junior fell silent. The wind picked up. It pushed against a south wall of the workshop, coming in through the cracks and tracing her face like fingers. "Why did you come back?"

"I need to know who I am." It was her first honest response, probably in years.

"And who are you, Carrie Starr?" Junior stopped his work. His dark eyes looked into hers. They were so much like her father's.

She broke his gaze. Who was she, indeed? She was broken. Incredibly broken. But still here. Still standing. Still pulling herself up through the abyss that enveloped her daily. She'd been eaten from the inside like her mother. Stunned by booze like her father. But still she stood. On this land. With her own two feet, which were not lost to diabetes or any of the other ailments that plagued her people. She was alive. Mercifully, painfully alive. But she was surrounded by secrets. If she could find the monster responsible for Sherry Ann's death . . . if she could find Chenoa . . . any of the missing girls at the center of those secrets, she could set them free. Maybe liberate herself too.

Junior turned toward her, outstretching his arms and putting a hand on each of her shoulders. For a moment she saw her father, with his easy laugh and wicked sense of humor, with his love for her and with his ability to hitch a ride on life's ever-changing current.

"You," Junior said, his voice filling the beautiful space he'd created out of discarded things. "You belong here too. We are all your family."

Starr wept, her tears making tiny stains the old wood of the floor would absorb and keep, like a mother saving a lock of her child's hair.

"There's something else too," he added as her crying waned.

"Your father . . . we were like brothers. Once. A long, long time ago." He scuffed the floor with his boot. "It was a different time then. When he didn't come back . . . I didn't even know about you until he dropped you off that day. So tiny. Whatever he hated about himself, he loved you. And I always hoped that he kept a place for me too. In here." Junior tapped his chest, then turned away and looked through the stained glass, the light stippling his face.

"He had to leave. Part of me understood that, of course I did. Your mother hated it here. Loved him, but there was nothing she liked or respected or wanted from his life or the rez. And by the time she was gone, it was too late for him. Too much life had passed by, and he had cut his ties with us. At least, he must have believed so."

An hour later Starr and Junior had left his workshop to sit in front of the shack he called home. The light was fading, the junk piles casting strange shadows. Junior was an artist. She still couldn't wrap her mind around it.

There was something nagging at her too, something about Odeina or about the beetles. Plus, she couldn't shake the feeling that Chenoa didn't fit with the other missing girls, who seemed to have gotten involved with bad crowds or bad drugs or maybe bad men who then became worse. She felt the old detectives' curse at work, the curse of a solution going unnoticed right under one's nose. It had probably been there all along. If only she could make sense of it.

"You ever seen a beetle like this?" Starr scrolled through her phone, finding a clear image of a two-inch beetle marked with OU red.

Junior set down the beer he was drinking and studied the picture for a long time.

"Nah, I don't think so," he said, "but that white dirt you asked me about? I kept thinking about it and realized I'd seen that before. Pretty sure, anyway. There's a whole deposit of it a few miles out from here." He motioned vaguely behind them, to the wilderness area. "Might be the same, might not, but that's what I seen."

"You think you could show me the place if I had a map?"

Was the kaolin a dead end? Starr wondered whether it had any cultural significance, but little information about the rez existed in any kind of formal way. No books, no internet articles, no documentaries chronicling its history. The Saliquaw Nation wasn't studied by anthropologists and it didn't have the draw of Oklahoma's 300-thousand-member Cherokee Nation. The only way she was going to learn the Saliquaw Nation's history was to ask the people who belonged to it.

"I go through that area, where the white dirt is, when I'm hunting," he said. "I've always been a hunter."

Starr felt the weight of the BIA's cold-case files at her office, at her home. She tapped her foot against the porch step it was propped on, then forced herself to stop. *Patience.* Everything on the rez unfolded at its own pace. Relevant information wrapped in unrelated stories.

"One thing most people don't know, especially if they don't dress their own game," said Junior, "is that each body holds a history, and with enough practice, a person can learn to read it. Maybe not entirely. It's not a thing to be fully known, but it is a story of a life—at least as much as we can understand of it. Shoot a duck, any kind of game bird, and butcher it. The second part of its stomach, called the gizzard, will tell you a story. Cut the gizzard open and you'll find not only half-digested seeds, but the small rocks that help pulverize the food. From the seeds you know what the bird has been eating, sure, but from the rocks you know where it has been eating. They are a map that marks its route." He looked at her, the corners of his mouth in a wry downturn. "Things you can't know from a package of meat at the grocery store."

"Right," she said, "but what's a duck got to do with—"

"That's what I'm getting to. There is always more information than you think there is. At least, when you realize the things that can be understood."

Starr shook her head. Although she'd been pleasantly surprised by Junior's art studio, she was frustrated, and she was eager to learn something—anything—that could lead to answers. Across the open land, the wind shifted and chilled, a sign of the winter storm the radio had predicted.

"The council meetings? They're like the meat you buy at the grocery store," Junior said. "Packaged, efficient, a good presentation, but not the whole story. Not the whole story at all."

Starr pictured the meeting at the community center. Chief Byrd with the gavel. The nervous-looking guy from Dexter Springs. What was his name? Bernard, that was it. And the tall, concise Norwegian named Antell who presented details on the contract between the reservation, the city and the oil company.

Seemed straightforward enough. People for it, people against it, the lure of fortune winning out in the end. Was there something more?

"Maybe I should talk to Chief Byrd," she said, solely to watch Junior's reaction. "Maybe Antell."

Junior stared at an ant crawling over the top of his left boot.

"Went hunting once, came across a guy named Holder. Owned some land bordering the reservation," Junior said. *"Pshht."* It was a derisive sound that started in the back of his throat and escaped through his nose.

"Holder," Starr repeated. "You mean Horace-Wayne Holder?"

"That's the one. Well, I was tracking a deer I'd hit with an arrow, and the blood trail ended at an old barbed wire fence, with his land on the other side of that fence and the tree row. I doubled back, got the old pickup to start—which it don't like to do when it's cold—and drove to his ranch house. He's nice enough, but I'm not the kind of fellow who traipses across land uninvited, so I figured I'd ask permission. He volunteered to help me, and we tried to pick up the trail until it got dark. Figured by then the deer had hunkered down somewhere. A shame too, because I knew by the time I found the deer—if I could find it—in the morning, the coyotes would already have had their fill. We parted ways, and I said I'd start early the next day."

Junior looked into the distance.

"So, I walked over to his house the next morning, just as the sun was coming over the hill, and I saw him. He was out in his shed, bay doors open, and I thought, *Great, he's ready to go.* Then I saw what he was doing. He had that doe trussed and half-skinned, hanging there. I could see the steam coming off her body. She was that fresh. He must have gone back without me and found her, and now she was bound for his freezer. Wasn't right. Still ain't right. I'd never trust a man who did something like that, no matter how good he seemed."

Later, and for a long time, Starr would think of that moment; think of it a thousand times over, turn it in her mind until its edges were worn smooth like a river rock. It lived in her consciousness with Junior and the deer, with Chief Byrd and Blackstream Oil, with Chenoa and white chalk, with Holder and the burying beetles making houses out of the dead.

CHAPTER THIRTY-SIX

✦

The sun was setting when Starr arrived at Odeina's trailer and knocked on the screen door. It bounced against its tracks, making a hollow metallic sound.

Starr disliked Odeina, which she knew was neither professional nor fair. Maybe she even hated her. But she understood her. Understood the fear and grief and burgeoning anger, all rolled into one big blunt that had to be smoked, even if you weren't into that sort of thing. Even if you were already so high you were sick with the spinning.

Nothing. Starr looked around from her perch on the top step in front of the trailer and quelled the urge to kick in the door. She needed a slug of whiskey, something to calm the rage that was starting to build. So much could have been different if her father had returned to the home of his people. She would have lived a different life, maybe even one in which she felt like she belonged to something larger than herself. It was an alternate history in which Quinn might still be alive.

Starr kicked at the door with the toe of her boot, then creaked

233

the screen open and peered through the door's tiny window. The living room TV threw color and light against the interior and was loud enough to block the sound of her knock. Slowly, Starr turned the knob and walked in. "Knock, knock," she announced. "Hello?"

She felt the soles of her boots land on the linoleum. The kitchen was as she remembered it. Clean. Worn. She searched for Odeina but found the old woman instead, settled in her usual place, a living room chair, under a mound of blankets.

"This was my dream," said Lucy Cloud.

"Odeina here? I was supposed to meet her." Starr had promised Odeina that if she stopped ringing her cell phone at two-hour intervals she would come to the trailer to talk. The last thing Starr needed right now was this old woman leveling fairy tales at her like a threat.

"My dream was that you were lost. But you were not alone. It was not a god with you, not as you think of a god," the old woman continued, as if Starr had not spoken at all. "She is a spirit. . . ."

Starr squeezed her eyes shut. She wanted to throw a kitchen chair through the window. She looked around to see who the woman was talking to. It was like stepping into the middle of a conversation.

"But Deer Woman is not one of the Little People," said the old woman, looking straight ahead at the masks on the opposite wall. "Little People are spirits that can be helpful or devious. They can move from one form to another. Like fairies they are, or maybe like your leprechauns."

This Starr understood, having read to Quinn every book she could find about fairies, which Quinn loved. And, having grown up in Chicago, land of the Saint Paddy's Day celebration, where even the river turned green, Starr knew leprechauns.

"Deer Woman too appears as she chooses. Half woman, half deer. A deer completely. A woman with hooves for feet. She stands at the boundary between worlds and is often a welcome visitor. But not always. Here—sit." Her crooked fingers came out from under the blankets and she pointed from Starr to the couch opposite her chair.

Starr obliged, sitting uncomfortably under the masks. She strained her neck to keep an eye on them.

"Like all of our people who have known pain, Deer Woman has a dark side. She has a thirst for vengeance. Do you know how she came to be?"

Starr shook her head, rubbing her hand across the back of her neck. This was exhausting. She didn't have time for the ramblings of this old woman right now. She'd done everything right, played by the rules, played her part, given her heart. Now her daughter was gone and she was here, among a people she would never understand. More young women were dying, going missing, and she felt powerless to save them.

What fresh hell was the Saliquaw Nation? Being here was like waking up from a twenty-year coma and realizing the world has changed, has gone on without you. And here she was. She'd toed the line to keep bad juju or karma or whatever at bay so that it wouldn't be visited on her daughter, her one good thing. For this reason, she'd taken every shift, worked every beat assignment, then every case that involved tailing a detective as a rookie; then she took on her own homicides, with the dedication of someone who knew the dead and wanted to hang the living. Dealt with the families of victims, too much even. Made a promise once; learned not to do it again, but still did in her head and in her heart, even if she never said it out loud.

She knew that somewhere deep down she'd already promised

she would find Chenoa. Give the family some closure, even though she had started to understand that closure might never come.

And she was hungry. Always hungry. The buzzing began at the back of her head while the old woman watched her expectantly. Maybe angry women were actually just hungry. *Fucking hungry.* Tired of counting and keeping track and doing it right and smiling when in the end it didn't matter anyway. We washed our faces and put on lipstick and wore uncomfortable shoes and didn't eat dessert and we fucking smiled and smiled and smiled until our interior spaces became molten.

Starr stood from where she'd been perched on the couch. Was Lucy Cloud speaking? Starr couldn't hear anything over the buzz in her ears, the way the floor swam under her boots. Maybe her problem was hunger. All the calculations to make sure she didn't take too much from this life, not more than she was owed, and now she was hollowed out and ravenous.

She turned to face the masks. Which one would she wear to become something else? What kept her in line other than the bounds of her own mind? What were expectations but a prison? The carved mouth of the deer mask turned higher at the corners. Starr was hungry now and she was going to take and take and take until she was satiated, her face pushed so far into her offender's flesh that the blood ran from her nose and chin, pushed so far that even her forehead was red.

The old woman began to cackle from her chair.

What if we took an eye for an eye? thought Starr. Would women still be raped, beaten, abused, taken, killed, hurt? What if women blew that shit up, stopped waiting for cops or detectives like her, who failed anyway?

Most people didn't realize that police, that detectives especially, were useful only after the fact. After the fight, the assault, the murder. After a million little deaths. They came later, always behind the eight ball. Always trying to undo a knot that had already been pulled tight. She was only a part of the cleanup crew. No matter how many killers were caught and, if their victims' families were lucky, sentenced, it was too few. Far too late. Her daughter was already dead. She felt the rage coming on like a sickness. *Fuck those motherfuckers.* A voice swirled in her head. *Fuck. Those. Motherfuckers.*

"You feel her," said the old woman. She lifted her arms, her fingers holding up tufts of hair.

Starr had forgotten Lucy was there. That she was still in Odeina's trailer. That she was the marshal in this godforsaken place. She was tired of keeping up appearances. Starr let her mask slip, and then reached for the one on the wall, the one always watching her, the one shifting and changing and bleeding.

"Deer Woman," said Lucy Cloud.

Both women looked at the mask Starr held in her hands.

"Once, long before my time in this body, there was a woman who was savagely raped and left for dead in the woods. The spirits sent a fawn to lie beside her so she would not die alone. She folded what was left of her battered body around the fawn, the way a mother curls around her baby, a comfort to them both. That might have been where it ended, with yet another woman's anonymous death."

The old woman gazed into the distance, into some other world.

"But the spirits knew what the woman did not, that with her death, her attackers would go unpunished. Her cries for justice became a transformation; the spirits granted the deepest wish of her angry heart. She was reborn. Time and again. She would appear in human form at powwows, at ceremonies, after too many passes of the bottle around fires that created the only light in the woods. She lured away men who were unaware of her true nature. They noticed only later, in that moment when death comes, that she had not feet but hooves; saw her details only when she trampled them to death. Do you know how long it takes to trample someone to death? To kick a man's belly and chest and skull until he lies twitching in the dirt and leaves? Long enough for him to realize he is going to die. Long enough."

Starr listened. Maybe for the first time, she listened to the old woman like she wasn't crazy. Shouldn't the young learn from the old? Wasn't her duty to respect her elders? And what had this woman seen? Her own hurts and transgressions, her own many deaths.

"See, they came for me too. I was young and nimble. When the truck stopped, and the men called to me, I ran. Across the open spaces, and then into the brush, fast as my legs could carry me. Still, they caught me. When they were done I understood what it was to be hunted, and I saw Deer Woman for myself. Her eyes were alive with a woman's sharp intelligence. There were antlers growing out of her hair. She had hooves."

Starr was fully present now, fully aware and fully listening. Could she grow hooves where her feet were, burst antlers out of her unlikely head, put her strong hands around a soft neck and crush until death met between their locked eyes?

"Deer Woman lives on. She continues to punish those who prey on innocence."

Starr nodded; the floor became firm again.

"You know it's true," the old woman continued. "You've seen her, haven't you? And you know where she is."

At this, the buzzing in Starr's head went still. The old woman was right—she had seen Deer Woman in the yolky light of Junior's window that first night—but she was also wrong. Starr had no idea where Deer Woman could be.

"Lead them to dance with her, Carrie Starr. They don't know that she can be banished through tobacco and chant, or that the only way to save themselves is to see her hooves before she has them alone. They don't know enough to be afraid. Deer Woman is in you—all that anger funneled through the ages."

"Okay, enough, enough," Starr said. A feeling ran, alive, just under her skin. The old woman folded her arms back under the blankets. The clock in the trailer's living room struck six and the old woman's neck twisted so her ear could catch the sound of chimes.

"Ah, it's only an old story," said Lucy Cloud, shaking her head as if she could see something far above the wall of masks.

Starr felt like she'd been at sea, her legs unsteady as she went from carpet to linoleum and opened the door to leave.

"If you want to find a girl," the old woman called, "you should follow a man."

CHAPTER THIRTY-SEVEN

MONDAY

The old woman's words were still on Starr's mind as she pulled up to the marshal's office the next morning. She extinguished what was left of a blunt before putting it in her shirt pocket, then spritzed a bottle of Febreze over her head, letting the droplets rain down in a fine mist. She'd taken the long way to the community building, smoking and watching the sky turn a turbid gray as she drove.

Follow a man, Lucy Cloud had said. The problem was knowing which one. Byrd carried enough anger about his daughter to be a danger, but that wrath was aimed at the reservation's stagnation—and at Junior. Starr had already cleared Junior. And she believed Junior's story about the deer, how Holder had stolen the kill. Holder had rubbed her wrong the first time she'd seen him, what with all his mansplaining and the meanness in his eyes. She pulled the whiskey from under the seat and took a slug—an antidote to the hours she'd stayed awake searching BIA case files; fortification for the long day ahead.

Starr left the Bronco and the weatherman's near hysterics about the early arrival of the first winter storm. When she entered the community building the cold followed her inside, sticking to her clothes, her hair, her exposed skin. Her boots tapped a familiar rhythm across the concrete floor to the marshal's office, where the door was ajar. She didn't expect Winnie this early. Then she noticed the smell. Beneath the musty odor of commodity boxes and BIA files, she caught the scent of cologne.

Starr swung the door open and Minkey stood from where he'd been crouching over a stack of files.

"Minkey," she said, her heart racing. "What are you doing here already?"

"Marshal, I was, uh, hoping that . . . well, what I mean is, I'd like to—" Minkey stammered. "I wanted the chance to talk to you this morning, you know, in private."

"Go for it," Starr said, settling the Bronco's keys in a desk drawer. "Got a lot to do today, so get cracking. Maybe start with why the hell you took off from Junior's yesterday."

"Yeah, that's what I want to talk about. That and . . ." He handed Starr a slip of paper with a woman's name and phone number on it. "You'll probably want to verify what I'm about to tell you. You can call this woman, Megan Begay. She lives here, on the reservation, and I coach her oldest son. See, he's on my basketball team, but it's just the mom and him and his little brother, and he's been getting into some trouble. She wanted me to look for him that night."

"What night? Look for him where?"

"The mom was worried about what he might be getting into.

He'd been hanging out with some older guys from Dexter Springs, coming in late, lying. When he wasn't home before dark that night, she was worried he'd ended up at the creek, maybe at a party out there. She asked me to see if he was there."

"Minkey," Starr said slowly. A shiver worked its way up the back of her neck. "What night were you at the creek?"

"Wednesday."

Sherry Ann had been found the next morning, just hours after her death. Minkey had been at Turkey Creek too, and now he stood between Starr and the door, an escape. She shifted, putting a hand to the weapon on her belt.

"You got something to tell me?"

"That's what I'm doing." Minkey backed away, palms up. A supplicant. "Why I'm here. To tell you. I went down to the creek, like I'm saying, and I looked around for the kid."

"Take it easy, Minkey." She pulled the Glock. "Just stay right there."

"The boy. He wasn't there. At the creek. But before I took off, I talked to this girl sitting by the fire. Never asked her name. It was only for a minute. Look, I didn't know who she was until—"

"The Awiakta girl."

"Yes, Sherry Ann. I didn't say anything the next day, at the autopsy, because," he said, "to be honest, I was trying not to get sick. I had no idea I knew the victim in the case you were working, or that anything had happened to her after I left the creek—not until later. It was a shock when I put it together, when I learned who she was, and that I'd met her in the hours before she died. Believe me—I wanted to tell you, but I knew how it looked. Suspicious."

"I need you to kneel now, Minkey. Get to your knees."

"I swear she was fine when I left. Said she was going to watch the fire for a while and then go home."

"Now, Minkey. Drop."

"Hey, you don't need to do this. I swear, you don't. Call this number too," he said, lowering himself to the floor while holding out another slip of paper. "Ask for Opal. She's the secretary over at the United Methodist, and she'll tell you, by eleven o'clock that night I was at the church."

"You have the right to remain—"

"It was a lock-in, a youth group lock-in! I'm one of the group leaders. I was inside the church all night, and I wasn't alone for more than a minute for twelve hours. You said it yourself, that Dr. Moore believed Sherry Ann was killed well after midnight."

"So why come to me now and confess, when you could have told me all along? When it would have been a hell of a lot more useful for you to—oh, I don't know—maybe give me a list of the people you saw at the party? Fuck." Starr holstered the Glock and glared at him. "Get the fuck up, Minkey."

"There's one more thing . . . about Junior. He was at the party. I didn't see him myself, but he must have seen me. The other day, at the Trading Post, he said some odd things while you were inside, talking to witnesses, and I didn't think too much about it. But yesterday, at his place, he threatened to tell you. Are you, uh, still looking at him for this?"

"Damn it, Minkey. You know that you've jeopardized this entire investigation. And that's the best-case scenario."

Starr paced to her desk. She had thought something was off about Minkey. Suspected it from the first time she saw him.

"I know it," he said, lowering his head. "I thought I could help, maybe make up for being in the wrong place at the wrong time, so I went back to her house when we canvassed the rez."

"Her who?" Starr said.

"Megan Begay, like I was saying. I mean, I saw a bunch of faces at the creek but not anyone I knew, so I went back to ask her who was in the usual crowd down there."

The woman with the little boy. Minkey hanging laundry on the line with her. That painfully domestic scene.

"And what did you find out?"

"Nothing. She didn't know. Like I told you, she said she'd seen Sherry Ann about a year ago but didn't know who she was, didn't even know her name. I wondered if there were any older cases that might shed light on this one. I wanted to find who did this so it wouldn't matter where I'd been, where I'd happened to be, that night."

"So that's why you were digging through my files when I came in this morning?"

"Yeah," he said, "it was. But I realized that it would follow me. Even if I got past this case, what about the next? The one after that? If it ever came out that I'd been dishonest about my where-abouts, every case I touched would come into question. Every single one."

Starr nodded. He wasn't wrong. She thought of the night in Chicago, the way she'd turned her career into a tightrope she walked every day.

"I wanted to look in the files, to see if there was any evidence that might link me to Sherry Ann. I mean, there shouldn't be," Minkey said. "And I guess I also need to resign."

"Since I never hired you in the first place, how about you run back to Mayor Taylor and tell her how well this went, how you're a real asset to the force? How I didn't need you here in the first place."

Starr looked at the BIA boxes filled with the names of missing women, murdered women, lost girls. Little paper coffins all their own.

CHAPTER THIRTY-EIGHT

✴

Starr spent the rest of the morning at the creek with Minkey, where she made him walk through his actions and conversations during the night he'd met Sherry Ann. Then she sent Minkey on his way and returned to the marshal's office, where she could hear Winnie laughing before she even entered the room.

"Must be some story," Starr said. Byrd was standing by the filing cabinets with Winnie, who was in stitches.

"Hoping I'd find you here," Byrd said as the phone rang and Winnie moved to take the call. "Can we talk?"

Starr shrugged a shoulder and motioned to the chair by her desk.

"Maybe take a walk outside? I could use a little exercise." He patted his protruding belly.

Starr held up five fingers to show Winnie how long she expected to be gone, and with that she and Byrd exited the building, leaving Winnie's raised brows behind.

Once outside, Byrd turned not toward the main road, but to circle behind the building. For a moment Starr thought they might make use of the two ragtag lawn chairs near the unusable back door.

Instead, Byrd kept walking, making his way through the tall grass that led north toward the trees, toward the ravines and the caves that cut a line through the miles upon miles of wilderness area that belonged to the reservation. Starr saw now how beautiful it was, a tonal palette of bronze and gold with the deep ocher of autumn mixed in, and how it seemed to stretch on forever.

"The other day," Byrd started slowly, so softly that she almost didn't hear him at first, "I may have come on a little strong." He made a noise meant to be a laugh, but it caught in his throat and he waved the sound away with his hand. He walked to her left, which she preferred, because she kept her service weapon on her right. He located a formerly invisible path that took them, step by step, away from the cinder-block building.

Starr glanced at the sky. It looked as though it might rain at any moment. A band of warmer air was trapped low among the clouds, keeping the moisture in limbo.

"Heard a winter storm warning on the radio this morning," Byrd said. "Freezing rain, windchill. We may get some snow, earlier than usual." He shook his head. "Climate's gone crazy."

They walked in silence a few minutes, Starr thinking of the old woman and watching for deer.

When Byrd stopped and turned around, the little rez town lay before them, her office at the outskirts as if it could keep the rest of the world at bay. She stayed silent, even longer than she had when interviewing suspects in Chicago. Silence. That's what kept people talking, not filling space with noise.

"We used to organize search parties," he said finally. "All volunteer, with people from our community, from Dexter Springs, anyone who would help. But you see what we're up against." He waved his arms at the expanse of land and pointed with his chin toward the main highway, which a few people from the rez still relied on to hitchhike to Dexter Springs. "I know what Odeina has been telling you, that we aren't willing to look. It's just that . . ." He trailed off.

Harmless, is he? Starr considered him on the sly. *Would he be able to grab someone?* Someone smaller, definitely. He probably didn't have much stamina, though. He would need a strategy to keep someone under control. And he would know about control. Most people in positions of power, no matter how little power, knew how to conceal or promote agendas of their own. But that day, at his house . . . It had been so . . . weird. She'd had that same strange and swirling feeling that overtook her at Odeina's when the old woman started telling her stories.

"Between you and me, I figure maybe it's just Odeina that Chenoa is avoiding. Odeina has her problems. I mean, we all do, but . . ."

Something in the way he said this set off Starr's radar.

"Ten years, and my daughter has never been found." He looked at his watch as if it were a calendar, but the time was on his tongue. "I've been waiting for her, waiting for answers ever since. I'm angry that she slipped through the cracks. She was gone, and there was so much change. It was a mess when the tribal police disbanded. There were jurisdictional issues with other agencies. Eventually the BIA sent someone to investigate, but they left without a word. Never heard another thing about her case."

Byrd pointed to the right and Starr saw that under the skeletal branches of a lone tree lay a large stone fronted with the worn colors of fake flower petals. Tears welled in Byrd's eyes, clung to his lashes before splashing down his cheeks.

"We made her this memorial on the first anniversary of her disappearance," he said, sweeping the back of a hand across his eyes. "We had to do something for . . . for closure. Now all this"—he cleared his throat—"life has passed by. I still come to talk to her here."

Starr saw a faded photograph encased in a plastic sheath, tied with string to a nearby branch. She thought of all the files still in boxes in her office. Of the handful of missing person files in her Dexter Springs duplex. Of the smiling school pictures on missing person flyers. Of autopsy photos.

"What I'm trying to say . . . what I'm not doing a very good job of telling you . . ." He swiped at his nose, which had begun to run. "There were years after Loxie went missing when we could not afford any type of law enforcement on the reservation. We weren't—we aren't—a wealthy nation. She was not the first to go missing, but she was young, healthy, good in school. Had even transferred to Dexter Springs to finish out high school. She wanted to go to college and was hoping for a scholarship."

"What do you think happened?"

"At first, it all seemed so normal. No, not normal. It was better than that. She was thriving, making new friends, relishing her studies. Then, one day, she went to a football game at the high school. . . ."

Starr nodded. She'd driven past the stadium on her way out of Dexter Springs every day, an aging gray monolith. She'd seen it light the sky on Friday night.

"She didn't come home. She—" He broke down then, sobbing into his hands, his belly shaking. "She never came home."

"Is there a file, any information?"

"Might be," he said. "I tried like hell to get copies of the investigation Dexter Springs started, but in the end they said it wasn't their jurisdiction, so they turned it over to the feds. Far as I know, the BIA didn't find any trace of her."

"Nothing?"

Byrd shook his head.

"A few years ago I started to meet with the mayor over in Dexter Springs. She was an outsider, seemed receptive to my ideas. I thought maybe we could work together, our two communities, prevent this from happening again."

"But you couldn't, could you?"

His shoulders sagged. "That wasn't the problem. We worked together just fine, as long as it involved the one thing Mayor Taylor really seemed to care about, which happened to be the same thing I finally realized was going to turn the tide for our people."

"Oh yeah? What was that?"

"Money. Fund a police force for our nation, or a marshal service"—he gestured toward her badge, which shined darkly under the dampening sky—"and properly equip our schools with teachers who are paid a living wage, with new books and enough chairs for the students. Right now, they carry their chairs from class to class because we don't have enough for all the rooms. There are so many things that will be made better with that oil money."

"So that's where you planned to get the funding, from Blackstream Oil?"

"Not at first. For a long time I didn't know how I would bring more money to our nation, but I knew there had to be a way— had to be." His voice grew more emphatic. "Then, one day, the mayor called me and I learned that it had been under our feet all along."

"The oil."

"Yes. Like everyone else, I thought the oil fields were tapped out around here. I didn't think there was any oil that hadn't already been drilled, but I learned that with fracking it was now possible to pull oil from places that had been unreachable before. Think of it: all that wealth trapped for millions and millions of years. And here we are, about to get rich from it."

"What does this have to do with—"

"The missing women? It's the other side of the coin, you see. It's holding on to the ones who are here. With education. Health care. Recreation. Full pantries and freezers. It's time to look after the living."

Starr left Byrd standing at Loxie's makeshift memorial; she wanted to chase a long shot. Inside her office, she sorted boxes, checking the dates marked on them, until she found what she was looking for: a water-damaged set of case files at least a decade old. She pulled a series of folders out and laid them on her desk.

Byrd said the BIA had briefly been on the rez after his daughter disappeared. *What if . . . ?* Starr shuffled through the stack as she stood, looking for any victim labeled a Jane Doe. She heard Winnie answer the phone as it rang.

"Marshal," said Winnie, covering the receiver with her hand. When Starr didn't answer, she said it again, in a stage whisper. "Marshal!"

"What?" Starr didn't look up. There were three bodies, three separate files, three possibilities—all from the time Byrd's daughter was last seen. The first two weren't a match. One victim was too old to be Byrd's daughter. The other hadn't even originated in Oklahoma but hours away, in Wichita, Kansas. Starr opened the third file.

"You have a call. From a director . . ." Winnie looked down at her own writing. "From a Director Randall. About a report he hasn't received yet?"

"I'm not here."

"But, Marshal, he can *hear* you."

Starr slumped into her desk chair, stunned by what she saw. The thought that had tickled the back of her brain at the sight of Byrd holding Loxie's picture had led her here, to this folder. Days ago she'd seen autopsy photos of a young female victim who, like the Awiakta girl, had a mouthful of white soil. But here, buried in paperwork, was the result of that BIA investigation on the rez that Byrd had mentioned. The victim had been unknown to Starr. Until now.

How difficult was it to complete an investigation, make proper notifications, pay a little fucking respect? The BIA had let all these files—*this* particular file—languish in some storage locker until she'd been hired on the rez. Now she had proof that Loxie's body had been found, that her remains were interred as evidence all those years ago.

Starr shoved the files into a desk drawer and headed for the door. Air slipped from the room, making it impossible to catch her breath.

"Marshal? What do I tell him?"

Starr slammed the door. Outside, she paced near the parked Bronco, stopping every few steps to brace her hands on her knees. She had to think about what to do next. How was she going to tell Byrd that his daughter wasn't missing? She'd already been dead for ten years—and found.

"Hungry?"

Starr leapt upright, reaching for her service weapon. It was Chak. He held a lifeless mallard by the neck, and waved it as his liver-spotted dog jumped at Starr's waist.

"Ducks spook you too?" he said, laughing. "Ah, don't worry. He can't hurt you. He's nothin' but good eatin' now."

"Don't you ever go to school? Truancy is against the law, you know, and I'm . . ." She tapped the badge on her uniform.

"Oh, hey, that van you were looking for the other day? When you talked to my dad? I seen it."

Starr reached into the Bronco for the photo of Chenoa standing next to a VW van. "This van?"

"Yeah, that's the one. Saw it out there." He pointed to the western edge of the reservation's wilderness area. "By the old trailhead sign."

Starr checked the sky. Two hours of daylight, maybe less, to get to the van, to get to the girl. It would be enough. She thought of the relief she'd see on Odeina's face when she delivered the news that her daughter was fine, just fine, after all.

Starr bolted into the old Bronco, which thankfully roared to life when she turned the key.

CHAPTER THIRTY-NINE

W hen Starr arrived at the trailhead, the Bronco rocking to a stop on its tired shocks, she threw the gearshift into park and grabbed the keys, ready to launch into action. But where?

There was not another vehicle in sight. From what Chak said the camper van should have been here, but all she saw was a faded placard marking a trail that led to an area she'd never ventured into.

Starr sat behind the wheel, listening to the engine tick as it cooled, watching the last of the autumn leaves clinging uselessly to their branches. A break in the waist-high underbrush, which she figured must be a trail, didn't look like it had been maintained, at least not for long after some government grant had paid for the installation of the marker that designated it.

This was where Chak said he had seen Chenoa's van. Starr didn't see anything—no van, not even tire tracks she could follow. Could Chak have been wrong?

She slammed her fist on the dash. Why did everything here have to be wrapped in mystery?

Starr drained the rest of the whiskey she kept stowed under the seat and tossed the bottle into the back, then pocketed the keys and felt for the steady weight of her Glock. She would walk a perimeter around the area, but it seemed unlikely that she'd find the van. She'd driven the only road that led to the trailhead.

After ten minutes of walking, Starr spotted the van, tipped into a steep ditch near an overgrown two-track that curled behind a hiking trail; its side was partially visible. Her breath caught. What if she hadn't come to look?

Another girl gone. Another life she would have let slip terribly into the ether.

Starr tried to shake the thickness from her mind, to quell the tingling running down her arms, the numbness in her hands. *Go to the van.* The driver's side was leaning into the ditch, so she ran to the front passenger door, climbed up on the tire and peered in the window, trying to take in the scene.

All the stuff that had been near the two front captain's seats had come to rest on the driver's-side door, which was nearly parallel to the ground. No one was inside that she could see.

Starr jumped down and tried to open the sliding door on the passenger side so she could check the back of the van, but gravity made it impossible to move the door. Tripping over vegetation and cursing, she ran back to the Bronco and got a tire iron so she could break out the passenger-door window. Once she'd cleared the glass from the edges of the doorframe, she hoisted herself up onto the door and climbed through. Everything in the van was in disarray, like it had been torn up even before the wreck. No Chenoa.

She peered into the back of the van, trying to figure out what to do. Chenoa wasn't here; that much was clear. Starr could make out an air mattress, now tipped against the ceiling, as well as books, tissues, some toiletries, an unopened bag of pretzels—all the detritus of a dorm room. There were two gray woven baskets that were now empty. The door had magnets clinging to its metal; Starr could see Yellowstone's Old Faithful, and more than one OU magnet, the crimson like that in the images of so many beetles in Chenoa's research.

She tugged at a corkboard overturned on the floor, then grabbed books, towels, anything she could get her hands on, and flung everything out of the way. She leaned back against the dash for a fresh look.

Was there a pattern underneath the chaos—an order? *Like Chenoa's room*, Starr thought, *layered*. Hadn't she thought that when she examined the room? First one layer, then another, until finally an excavation of the strata revealed the trajectory of Chenoa's plans. The movie posters, but also the research papers. The archaeology of a life.

Starr spied a set of binders—the three-ring kind, with hard covers—lying atop one another like they'd tumbled from a neat and orderly stack. Maps. Research. Plans.

Think.

She'd seen #vanlife photos with perfectly ordered interiors, vans' rear double doors swung open to scenic spots: beaches, mountainsides, deserts resplendent with sunset. This was not one of those vans. And it was not that life. This was a crime scene.

She thought again of Chenoa's girlhood bedroom, full of aspiration. She'd been a fool not to see it earlier. Too wrapped up in her own grief or anguished stupor to see it. This wasn't a miscalculated bid for freedom.

Chenoa wasn't leaving. She was coming home.

So where was Chenoa now?

Starr crawled out of the van through the broken window and rubbed her palms together for warmth. She looked from the chaos of the van to the woods around her. The wind bit into her neck, her cheeks, whipped itself under the hem of her heavy coat, her pant legs, relentless in its pursuit of raw skin. Tree branches shook overhead, remnants of sugar-rich leaves flung to earth like drops of blood. The storm had arrived.

But nature demanded order in chaos. She thought of one of the books she'd taken from Chenoa's room, and of the passages she'd read while thumbing through it—long paragraphs on trees, and in them, a new thought for Starr: evidence that trees communicate with one another, and all because a woman Chenoa's age had looked at a forest and seen community.

At twenty-two, the same age as Chenoa, the author had discovered how trees connect and care for one another, how they react to one another's pain. Central to the book was the discovery that within each network, each community, there was a mother tree that connected dozens of other trees. It was a network of support that academics had never previously stopped to study, or to notice—until the woman who wrote this book figured it out.

Starr hunched her shoulders against the mounting cold and thought of Chenoa, of Quinn, of all the daughters and mothers connected by invisible threads. If they could only see. If only *she* had seen. To seek Chenoa was to seek Quinn, to save them all. Even the ones who were gone. Didn't they deserve to be more than remembered—to be found, to matter?

The wind whipped harder, the energy bending branches low, stirring leaves into eddies, rocking the van farther onto its side, compelling Starr to pull her collar tight with both hands. *Take another look*, it seemed to say. *Really see this time.*

Starr stepped back, felt the first drop of cold rain on her cheek and clocked the scene like it was something new, taking in the terrain around her. She would have to search the thick woods for Chenoa, and beyond them—the grassland, the hills, the ravines. How in the hell was she going to find her?

CHAPTER FORTY

✳

Starr didn't know where to look. She didn't know which direction to turn, or even whether she would have to drive or walk to start her search for Chenoa.

She leaned into where the window had been in the passenger door of the van, her body a bulwark against the elements, as if she could stem the tide of this scene, stem the tide of missing and murdered Indigenous women. Leaves were blowing into the van—orange and red, beautiful and dead at the same time. *Red,* thought Starr. *There's something about the red.*

Red was . . . what? Another stack of binders dissolved in the back of the van, an imperceptible shift sending their slick covers crashing, papers and maps spilling out. *Red,* thought Starr. Red like the T-shirts at the Trading Post, with a painted handprint covering a woman's mouth, its red fingers ranging to the side of her face, a symbol of missing and murdered Indigenous women. Red like the American burying beetles Chenoa sought. Red like blood. Red like the marks Chenoa made on these maps.

Starr rose to her tiptoes, leaned farther into the van and carefully pulled a creased paper toward her. Greens, browns, a mass of lines. *A topographical map,* Starr thought, like the one she'd taken from Chenoa's room.

Someone, presumably Chenoa, had used a marker to indicate the likeliest locations of American burying beetle colonies, and the trails to reach them. There was an X on each of the places where Chenoa had looked for beetles and not found them, and a clear, open circle was around the one place that remained. Starr traced the thin red lines, all of them, ending with the only place left to explore. She recognized Chenoa's writing, something she'd scrawled in the margin. *Monday,* it read, *start here.* Starr tapped the paper.

Manitou.

Here was a map to Chenoa's world, one that literally translated the three-dimensional terrain into something flat, navigable. It was her only chance of locating Chenoa and making sure she wasn't injured or worse.

Starr tried to shield the map from the rain, which was falling steadily now. On it she studied the hills, rivers and valleys to orient herself. There was Crawl Canyon. She followed its route until she found the wide bend in Turkey Creek where the Awiakta girl had been found. Farther south was the wilderness area, challenging terrain with hills and ravines.

The Manitou caves were nearly too far to go on foot, but what other choice did she have? And even if she made it in this weather, would Chenoa be there? If she didn't find her, would someone else?

She already knew the answer.

Who would take action if she didn't? The Sisyphean role seemed hers alone. The women, so many missing and murdered Indigenous women, were all connected. To one another. *To me,* she thought, *to a mother tree.* They were all one. They were red.

Starr tried to refold the map but couldn't get it tamed, so she stuffed it inside her jacket. Then she leaned into the van to light the rest of her blunt, and smoked it while she checked her phone. No service. With Minkey gone, there was no one to call anyway.

Above her head leaves whirled and fell, and low, dark clouds roiled like a floodwater eddy, dirty and dangerous.

Starr went to the Bronco, opened a new bottle of whiskey and retrieved her backpack, then pulled on her gloves and followed a thin red line into the trees, which bent over her like grieving women.

CHAPTER FORTY-ONE

F or nearly an hour Starr had been heading down what might be a trail, hoping to make it to Chenoa before the weather intensified. It was growing colder by the second, and her mind was starting to wander in the kinds of big loops she knew spelled trouble.

Her last great act as a Chicago detective had been to pull every thread connected to her daughter's death until she finally cut one perp loose of his life entirely. After the shooting there'd been questions, but she'd eventually been cleared, with the condition that she leave not only the department but the state. It hadn't mattered at the time. Nothing had.

She would have gladly gone to prison in exchange for the life she took. And she'd taken it all right. What did she owe now? These thoughts were dangerous, and she kept them behind a veil of smoke and whiskey.

The buzz of her cell phone sent Starr's heart thumping.

"Winnie?" Starr answered.

"You can hear me?"

"Ten-two," said Starr, the officer code for *message received*. What she wanted to say was *ten-six: busy or out at call*.

"What? Where are you?"

"Never mind," said Starr. "I'm in the wilderness area, following a trail and looking for Chenoa. Found her van wrecked in a ditch."

"Oh my stars," said Winnie. "Should I call Minkey?"

"No, not Minkey. Definitely not. See what I find first."

Whatever Winnie said next didn't make sense to Starr, the signal cutting out every third word. Something about Minkey and middle school. She'd forgotten to tell Winnie that Minkey was fired, if she even had the power to fire a loaned officer. Either way, Minkey wasn't allowed near this investigation or into the marshal's office.

". . . game of the season," said Winnie, the call fading in and out. ". . . not as bad as I would have thought and—"

"Winnie," Starr said, louder.

"Then he took an elbow to the eye—"

"Winnie, I'm losing you. I . . ." She was shouting now.

Starr heard a click, and checked the service bars on her phone—one bar. She was trying to dial when it rang again.

"Can you hear me?" Winnie hollered down the line. "Can't hear you, but if you can hear me, I got a call from a Dr. Moore, out of . . ." Starr heard static, or maybe it was papers shuffling. She waited, running her hand across her forehead and then pinching the bridge of her nose. ". . . the medical examiner's office," Winnie said triumphantly. "Said you were waiting on some results from a sample you sent in?"

It was the blood she'd collected in an evidence vial when she was at the abandoned house after notifying Sherry Ann Awiakta's father of his daughter's death.

"She said the blood—" Static. ". . . not animal. The sample showed human DNA. Said to call her."

It could be one more clue in Sherry Ann's death. The abandoned house was remote, but near where Sherry Ann had lived—and where she'd been killed, by the creek. It could open new possibilities, new avenues of investigation. The abandoned house, Sherry Ann's location by the creek in Crawl Canyon, the Manitou caves noted in Chenoa's research. The locations were all within range of one another. They made up a hunting ground.

"One last thing, if you can hear me," Winnie said. "You asked me to keep an eye out for black trucks like the one Chak said he saw by the creek, and I have one more to add to the list. Somebody in a black truck's been coming onto the rez, might be a poacher. The tag came back with the name Horace-Wayne—"

More static, then the phone went dead.

"Holder," Starr said. "Ten-four. That's a big fucking ten-four."

Starr hiked to the top of a rise, leaving behind thick tree cover. She ducked behind an outcropping of rocks to get out of the wind. It took four tries to get a call to go through. As she listened to it ring the medical examiner's office in the basement of the hospital, she felt for the map in her coat pocket and pulled it free, wondering how far she had to go to reach the Manitou caves.

"Dr. Moore?" Starr shouted into the phone. "Bad reception. You got a match? An identity attached to the sample?"

Dr. Moore said something indecipherable.

"What?" Starr yelled into the wind. Winter had come on all at once, the temperature plummeting, the rain turning to sleet that stung her face in the biting wind. Starr watched pellets of ice fall onto the sleeves of her coat and build into drifts. "Who is it?"

"The sample had two separate profiles, actually. One matches Sherry Ann Awiakta. The other sample is unknown, but when I ran it against a few of your older cold cases, jackpot. Two more matches—" The line went dead.

The black truck. Holder's truck. Holder's sketchy behavior, coming onto the rez uninvited. She'd already cleared Minkey. And Junior. But that story about Holder stealing Junior's kill, then trussing and butchering the deer . . . And Winnie had found at least one eyewitness who'd gotten the license plate of his truck when it was parked on the rez. . . . Had Holder been the one to watch all along? She'd had a bad feeling about him from the start, and she should have trusted it. It was too late for Sherry Ann, but maybe not for Chenoa.

A gust ripped the map away and it was gone on the wind, along with the careful X's and the solitary O Chenoa had drawn. All the things Starr had studied from Chenoa's room began clicking into place. The news articles. The federal government would levy heavy fines if certain species were disturbed, and the new highway Dexter Springs was building to move oil off the rez would go right through the beetles' territory.

The deal everyone was banking on—Byrd, Blackstream Oil and the mayor—led right to the beetles. And the one woman who could prove they were there.

Chenoa. This was bad. Very bad.

Chenoa was missing. Gone. And thanks to Starr, she was twice gone too.

CHAPTER FORTY-TWO

At her vantage point on Holder's land, farther off the linear park trail than she'd yet ventured, Mayor Helen Taylor pulled the hood of her anorak over her head and squinted into the wind. The temperature was dropping and the skies were shedding sleet.

"Where did you say she found the beetles?"

"See that cut right there? The one that goes through the rocks?" Holder pointed into the distance, toward the wilderness area. "That turns into Crawl Canyon, but before it turns there, to the northeast"—he traced the ridgeline with his hand—"there's a series of hollers, some caves. Land that's not good for much."

"Except oil," she said.

"Yep, except oil," he agreed. "That's where the best yield should be, right under there."

"And that's where the beetles are?"

"Hate to tell ya," he said, dipping his chin and shaking his head, "but, yeah, them suckers are out there. Repopulated, so to speak. And that girl's got proof. I don't think she had any idea what she was onto, not at first, but you wanted me to keep this project problem-free. . . ."

"I got it, I got it," said the mayor, impatiently. She already knew what he'd gone over at least a half dozen times in the last few minutes. That he'd first been tracking the movements of this rez girl, for a lengthier time than he'd let on. And he'd somehow managed to talk to the girl's mother—without raising her suspicions, or so he said—and then he'd gone through the Cloud girl's van and torn it up so she'd be too afraid to continue her research.

What he'd found, though . . . that was the problem. There was so much proof.

Undeniably, there was an endangered species on the rez, right where the access road, the drill site and Helen's future was supposed to be. Everything—the oil deal, the return of the money she'd taken from the city, the lobbyist funding of her dark-horse senate campaign, the power grab that would put the rest of her life in motion—depended upon her ability to solve this one problem.

Holder parted two long strands of barbed wire stretched between fence posts and helped Helen duck between them and onto reservation land. It wasn't her normal Monday afternoon workout, but it would have to do.

She would have preferred to send Holder alone, but he'd managed to put everything in jeopardy despite all her careful planning. She was surrounded by idiots. Holder had let this happen. Minkey had not been a source of insider information like she'd hoped. They were both useless. Some things you just had to do yourself.

"You said there wouldn't be any screwups, but that's all you've managed to do."

"I figured it out, didn't I? What she was doing out here. Calm down, Lady Mayor. It's practically taken care of."

"It better be. I'm going to be there to make sure."

Holder half listened as the mayor rattled on about this possibility and that solution, even though he'd already tried to make it clear that he was as invested in the pipeline deal as she was. If Blackstream Oil didn't move forward on the rez, he'd end up holding the bag. He'd leveraged everything he owned to borrow enough to buy land abutting the rez.

"Ah, c'mon," Holder said. "You need me. Election's tomorrow, but it's not too late for me to talk to a reporter at the local station. Let folks here know what you're really up to."

"Who's going to believe you? You're more implicated than I am, so you better put a smile on your face and follow directions."

"And if I don't?"

"Ten to twenty with time off for good behavior, that's what. You're about to commit a felony, Holder. So, like I said, smile."

"If that's your defense, I'd start writing your concession speech now. When I'm through with you, you won't even be able to run for the library board."

"What happened to you?"

"Nothing happened to me, Lady Mayor." Holder looked her up and down. "I just learned from the best."

CHAPTER FORTY-THREE

✦

Starr started down the ridgeline, deeper into the wilderness area. The temperature, which had been dropping by the minute, was the only thing that kept her from crawling right out of her skin. If she could, she would unzip it and step out into the air as a new thing. But here she was, the weight of all that she carried wearing on her like concrete boots.

As she neared what looked like a game trail veering toward Manitou, she realized she was the only living creature not hunkered down. Every little thing knew the weather was bad.

She could see her breath, and she thought briefly about finding a place to take shelter, but from what? She couldn't hide from the storm that posed the real threat, the storm that enveloped her heart and mind and memories. It had been a mistake to come here, and a bigger mistake to think she could stay. It was time to move on to some other life. The expectation that she could make a difference was too much to bear.

She had waited too long to look—really look—for Chenoa. Was she too late? One more woman doubted, ignored. She was as bad as the rest. As bad as all of them. Worse, because she should have known better.

There was never enough time for both the job and Quinn. Starr had been so preoccupied, always preoccupied, with her work. Truth was, it had been wrong between them for a long time, like a door was being slowly pushed shut.

Quinn had been a wild girl with a big laugh and rowdy hair; then, little by little, she had begun to disappear in ways Starr didn't want to notice. If she came home late from working a case, Quinn would be in her bed in the dark, huddled over a dim screen. She stayed with friends more and more, but that was, in a way, a relief. It meant Starr was able to get the hours in.

They'd fought too. Loud shouting matches and long silences. There was an inevitability about it. *That's not to say I didn't check up on her,* thought Starr. But how does any parent ever really know? The little secrets move too fast, until one of them bumps against something big.

The game trail widened, taking Starr into a clearing where there wasn't shelter from the wind. It tore at her collar and burned her skin. From what she remembered of the map, she would reach a series of ravines that led into Manitou. The terrain was growing rougher and she'd need to watch her step. She was now miles from where she'd started.

That the blood from the abandoned house was human and not animal was a surprise, but she was relieved she'd had the foresight to collect it and have it analyzed. Even if she'd fallen under the detective's curse of not seeing what was right in front of her, at least her training had kicked in.

Starr pulled out her cell phone, checked for service. The line she'd cut through the grass, its seedy heads bent against the wind, closed behind her as she pulled a glove from one hand to dial.

Silence, then two beeps in quick succession. Dropped call. She redialed. Nothing. Redialed again. *Shit.* She'd stopped trying to reach Winnie and gone straight to 9-1-1, ready to rouse Dexter Springs police, the county sheriff, anyone.

Starr tapped the cell phone against the twill of her uniform pants while she looked at the game trail she'd traveled. If she went back to where she'd had reception she'd lose valuable time. Starr looked at the sky, where the roiling clouds were becoming lower and heavier by the moment. She thought of the weather alerts she'd ignored, thinking she'd find Chenoa at the van and be back at the marshal's office before the storm rolled in.

Bulletins had ticked through the old fax machine at the office, where they'd floated to the floor, drifting into a pile of warnings. A fax machine, of all things. She shook her head and tucked her hands in her armpits. Even with her insulated winter gloves, her fingers ached from the cold.

She'd been a fool to go out in this weather. But she'd been a fool to take this job in the first place. A fool to think she'd ever been a good mother, a fool to think she could make it right and, most of all, a fool to think she'd ever recover from losing her little girl.

Starr started to sob, hot tears searing across her freezing lashes. She would have done, would do, anything—literally anything—to change it. She was overwhelmed with thoughts of Quinn and revenge and killing, not anyone else but herself, in that slow suicide she crawled into every night.

Despite her years of training—and experience—she'd made a rookie mistake. She should have gone back and figured out a different way to traverse the miles into the hinterland, where the granite and shale rose harsh as the weather.

Starr imagined borrowing a four-wheeler, but she'd had to walk only a few feet into the woods to know the underbrush was too thick for anything on wheels. A horse, maybe. But where would she have gotten one? There were horses grazing on everything from front yards to pastureland, but to ride one? She'd only ever ridden the L train and the occasional city bus. And she couldn't have spared the time to wait anyway. She knew now, with certainty, that Chenoa faced death—or worse—and that every single second mattered in the bid to save her.

Holder.

She set one foot in front of the other, crunching through the frost glazing every dead and living thing around her.

She'd killed Quinn's killer. Overkilled. She'd never pretended that she'd track him down and only rough him up, never fooled herself in that way. She knew she'd kill him. Knew it from the beginning, as surely and steadily as she leaned into the sleet and wind now. When she pulled the trigger, when she felt the kick of the Glock again and again, she had been ready to get caught. She wouldn't even stand trial. They'd bring her in and she would confess everything. The confessional. A sacred telling of sins.

Starr didn't care who heard the shots that night. She was glad there was one less monster who could kill his prey in a thousand different ways, not all of them physical.

She'd tracked him to a long stretch between buildings, near the L's elevated tracks but remote enough that even the beat cops didn't care who took a piss against the bricks. It was a slim cut between tenements cleared of their working poor as part of an initiative to clean up the area by declaring it a PID—a public improvement district—which came with earmarked funds. Columnists called the initiative what it was, gentrification. She didn't give a shit either way. The building was stripped of anything useful and slated for demolition, but this created a cover for vermin—animal and human. An out-of-the-way place to get a fix, or sell a fix, sell anything, even oneself. To scratch the never-ending itch.

He'd been easy enough to tail. Easier to hate. The way he ran the girls, pulled new ones in, got them hooked or hooking, or both. It was a world away from her daughter's, or so she'd thought. A world away. A universe. A life her daughter would never see, save in a movie or maybe on the internet. Yet here she'd been, a little lamb like all those other girls. A victim.

A victim! If Starr had done one thing right, it had been to warn her daughter off sketchy situations, people, places. Never to be a victim. To know she had power. To listen to that small voice that said *Danger ahead*. Starr had coached her, educated her, shared with her how to avoid the things that could make her vulnerable: candy laced with drugs on playgrounds, some new scheme every few years; strangers good at grooming on social media, in real life; powders slipped into drinks; helpers who were wolves in sheep's clothing. *Trust the fear,* she'd told her. *It will save your life.*

Except it hadn't. Her daughter had gone and done it anyway. The parties, the lies, the friends her daughter ditched for a more exciting time. How had she failed her own daughter so deeply? So ultimately?

Starr wouldn't fail her that night, not with the man in her sights. Not with her daughter's precious little body, polish still on her toes, lying in the morgue, awaiting her turn for an autopsy. It didn't really matter to Starr what story it told. It was an ending, nothing more.

An ending.

And that's what she'd sought that night in Chicago. An ending. She was a raw nerve. She wanted to set herself on fire. To shave the hair off her head. To stick a knife into her belly, the blade so sharp she wouldn't feel the slice of skin and organ until the blood ran down to her softest places.

From her partner, Starr knew the circumstances, the who. She'd already discovered the terrible how. Discovered it like her own death when, after all that searching, and pinging of cell phones, she'd run down that alley in a panic. When she'd found Quinn lying against the building, she'd pulled her body to her, felt the weight of her only child slump against her chest. Starr had become a wild thing then, a howling creature; felt her eyeteeth elongate into fangs, her jaw pop and dislocate. She was venom and pain. She was a killer.

An autopsy confirmed the overdose, the damage behind the blood. When the bereavement cards piled up, when the funeral happened, when her daughter's little body was lowered into the dark grave—Starr still worrying that she'd be cold—she'd been on administrative leave. *Take some time,* department officials had said. They knew she wasn't normal anymore, could smell it on her.

Their instincts were right.

She was a predator—then and now. She wasn't going to let this happen again, not to Chenoa. She wouldn't be too late this time. Chenoa wasn't her daughter—but weren't they all her daughters after all?

Chenoa was alive, she was out here and Starr was going to find her. She felt the sleet hit her cheeks and decided to walk on, no matter the cost.

CHAPTER FORTY-FOUR

✳

Holder had trouble keeping up with Helen as she descended the ridge at a near run. She skipped lightly down a switchback trail of her own making, shale sliding at her feet.

She didn't look back, not even to see whether he was behind her. But he was making progress as best he could in cowboy boots. What did she think she was going to do, anyway, once they caught up with the rez girl? Get her own hands dirty? Fat chance of that happening.

The wind whipped mercilessly, and Holder was glad he'd traded his cowboy hat and denim jacket for a pair of coveralls and an insulated hunting cap with earflaps.

"Left," he said from behind her, and motioned with one long arm to the west. It pleased him that he was the only one who knew where to find the girl, that he'd tracked her so long and so well.

When they reached a plateau Helen stopped short, then jogged in place to stay warm.

The freezing rain was turning to snow. It drifted into piles set against clumps of bluestem and a nearby stand of red cedars and, miles from where they stood, a van tipped into a ditch that pointed like a finger toward Crawl Canyon.

Holder was sick of the mayor riding his ass, especially when he was the one doing the work. He was the one sticking his neck out, taking all the risk, and all she did was complain. Reminded him of his long-gone mother, she did, the anger spinning out from her like a heat wave. He'd been too powerless then, too young to get a city job and bring some money in. The bank seized the farm. His parents had stewed in their anger until it obliterated their family. It was an old wound, and the money he was about to make was going to heal it.

There was nothing he wouldn't do to change his fortune. All those years, he'd bided his time, knowing the right opportunity would come. Faith, that's how he thought of it. Faith.

He was going to own this town.

"Over there," he said.

They worked their way ever lower, looking for an easy path to slide into the ravine, Helen holding on to the sleeve of his coveralls to keep from falling.

"I'm not losing everything over a beetle," Helen said.

"Wouldn't matter whether it was a beetle or somethin' else," Holder said. "Could be a blind cave spider like the ones that jammed up that rancher in Texas. Hell, ever hear of the lesser prairie-chicken? Ask any rancher in western Kansas and they'll tell you, if you see one of these so-called endangered birds on your land, keep it quiet. Otherwise, Fish and Game will come around to have a look-see, and you won't have a say in what you do with your land anymore. The fines alone would—"

"And guess what will happen if this deal falls through," Helen interrupted. "You won't get a dime—that's what. Know what I should do? Find some other route to the oil on the reservation, let some other landowner make all that money."

Holder thought of his mother, the way she'd exploded or drifted into days-long silence. He knew what poverty could do.

"I can't believe I have to be out here to make sure you do your job. You think I have time for this? I have a city to run." She looked up at Holder. "And I put this complex project together, not you. You think Antell is easy to work with? You think Blackstream Oil goes around just handing out money? And the tribal council? It's a miracle we have an agreement at all."

They reached the bottom of the ravine.

"Not far now," he said, and held a gloved finger up to his mouth like a secret.

"After today I don't want any part of it," she whispered angrily. "After you take care of this problem we have out here"—she waved her arms—"I don't want you to contact me anymore. Get rid of the girl; then that's it. We're done."

"Quiet," said Holder, fighting to keep his voice low. "You need to stop pushing. You hear me?"

"You just make sure we find her," Helen said. "It should have been done already. I shouldn't have to micromanage every little thing you can't take care of on your own. You had one job. One job. And you can't even do that properly."

Holder's hand curled around a loose stone embedded in the wall of the ravine. He knew without even looking that he could palm it like a basketball, could feel the winning shot at his fingertips.

"Don't you forget, Holder, we're in this together. If the oil deal falls through with the rez because of you or some bug"—Helen spit the word *bug* into the wind shearing the rock with the mounting storm—"I'll bring you down with me. No, that's not true. I will make sure you go away for this instead of me."

Holder pulled the stone and swung for the side of her head. The last thing Helen heard was her own scream bouncing off stone walls.

CHAPTER FORTY-FIVE

✴

Over the wind, Starr heard coyotes in the distance, and the response of another, closer pack. The sleet had turned to snow and the footing had changed from undulating earth covered with prairie grass to a steady incline that slowed her pace with the slip of shale and granite.

Now the wind carried another sound. A scream.

Starr's entire body stiffened and she willed her ears to hear. She fumbled to pull her Glock from its holster with her frozen fingers and scrambled up the next incline, a game trail worn between outcroppings of rock that rose high on both sides. She kept her eyes upward as much as she could, but the lingering effects of so much weed and whiskey made her slow, lent soft edges to her perception, to the rocks, the trees. She hoped this new rush of adrenaline would override it.

Anything is possible, she thought. *An ambush, a person, a predator.* Then her feet no longer felt earth, and for one bewildering moment there was no gravity at all.

When reality kicked in, Starr was plummeting down a ravine.

Instinct forced her to grab wildly at anything solid, and, somehow, she managed to slow her descent by gripping onto roots that had tunneled into granite cracks and found life.

She heard her Glock clatter to the bottom of the ravine. *Fuck.* It was impossible to tell how much farther she had to fall before she hit the bottom.

Then Starr let go.

The fall should have knocked the drunk right out of her, cleared the whiskey she'd been sipping all day. Starr lay for a long while on the rocky ground at the bottom of the ravine, the snow riding great gusts to land everywhere around her. Her thoughts roamed to dangerous places now that she was penned in by the ravine's rocky walls on each side.

One hand went to her holster, and then she remembered. The Glock had fallen first. An image of the gun, the one she regularly took apart and polished with such care, bouncing down the ravine flashed in her mind. She felt a jolt of fear pulse through her abdomen, along with the heavy, painful squeeze of injury.

She moved her arms and then each leg, relieved when they responded, and took shallow breaths as the shock passed over her.

It was nearly dark now. She looked at the sky, then got on all fours, and, finally, to her feet. She left a shadow image in the snow, like she'd shed a layer of who she was.

It was okay, she decided, if it ended like this. She'd imagined her own death so many times but had ultimately been too . . . what? Scared? Lonely?

Maybe she'd been afraid that no one would care.

But the girl. She couldn't leave the girl out there, somewhere, could she, if there was a chance she was alive?

She could smell the sharp metallic scents of cold and fear coming off her body, and her mind went to an early memory. A sunny day fishing with her father. Had it been on the rez? They were putting a worm on a hook. She was the worm now. Bait and bated, waiting for a bite.

In any case, this was going to hurt.

Starr shivered and slipped out of her backpack. A part of her was grateful she'd had the instinct to curl into a ball, so that when she'd hit the bottom of the rocky gorge, the pack covering her center mass had taken the brunt of the impact.

Even with this distribution of force, Starr still winced when she took a breath. Her back burned along the arc of her left shoulder blade. And now her right ankle was a problem, since it had twisted in the fall.

The snow, falling heavier now, clung to her lashes as she tried to tamp down the panic that was rising from her gut. She forced herself to think of roomy spaces somewhere overhead, to help ease the feeling of being closed in, of not having enough air to breathe. *The ravine will eventually reveal a way up and out,* she thought. It had to.

Gun or no gun, she had to keep going. She had to find Chenoa and get out of this fucking chasm. Starr leaned against the cold, slick rock wall. She felt the surety slipping from her, dissipating like the heat of her body.

Starr thought of her training: She couldn't help anyone if she didn't help herself. It was the first thing she'd learned in law enforcement, their version of *you can't pour from an empty vessel,* and she'd stuck to it all these years. Well, not lately, but still.

Sometimes getting high fucked with her head. It had done more than that tonight, she thought, wincing as she stepped away from the wall and began picking her way over the rocky terrain.

It came to her suddenly that she'd heard a noise before she fell. It had been a wild sound, a scream. She thought of the nature shows her father had watched. There were creatures out here that could sound human. A bobcat? Mountain lion? Could it have been Chenoa?

Now that the adrenaline was wearing off, new aches were setting in that nearly overwhelmed her. Starr wished for her flask, somewhere in the pack she'd left behind. She couldn't carry it with her ankle hurting the way it was. If the girl was out here, could she reach her in time?

Don't count on it, she thought. It had been a stupid idea to look for Chenoa in this storm, and now she was in near darkness.

There was movement in front of her, and if she squinted, she could, barely, make out an outline. *No,* she thought, *it can't be.*

Starr went still with shock, the paralysis of fear undermining years of training.

The buzzing began at the back of her neck, and before long it crested, reverberating up into her brain and chasing out every thought. Ahead, she saw the silhouette of a beautiful woman atop whose graceful head was a crown of antlers.

They watched each other for a long moment, and then the woman . . . the deer . . . *Deer Woman,* thought Starr's deranged mind . . . Deer Woman slid an arm from her side, raised it and crooked a finger at Starr. *Come,* she motioned. *Come.*

Starr limped forward, so close that she could see the night sky reflected in Deer Woman's pupils, every constellation scattered across an endless indigo blanket. When the stamping of hooves rang in her ears, Starr looked down to see a pair of delicate, deadly prints in the snow. Then Deer Woman turned so that she was no longer blocking Starr's path, and took several steps away from her.

Deer Woman's delicate neck shifted so that one knowing eye looked Starr's way. The meaning was obvious.

Starr threw an exasperated look to the heavens and limped forward. She was going to follow Deer Woman, wherever she led.

There was no going back.

CHAPTER FORTY-SIX

✺

As Chenoa rose to murky consciousness, she felt only fear like a fist, its long fingers slipping into the space underneath her belly, tightening around the slick muscle of her intestines. She tried to press a hand to her stomach and realized she couldn't. Panic set in and she thrashed in the darkness, her head smacking against a hard wall of granite as she pushed and pulled, her wrists and ankles meeting resistance. She was bound. And she wasn't sure where. Or why.

The beetles. There was something about the beetles. She shook her head to clear the fog. Her tiny, scrabbling saviors, the ones that ensured her own escape. Where were the beetles now?

The only sound, once she went still, was the steady drip of condensation from somewhere overhead. She used her fingers to feel the ground where she was propped, the sandy grit moving over solid stone. It was too dark to see clearly, but the smell was . . . musty and dank, nothing at all like where she'd last been outside. Outside. In the ravine.

The beetles. She'd found a nest in a racoon carcass and had

been watching the movements of the beetles under the light of her headlamp. Then there was a man. The man . . .

"I see you're awake," came a voice from the darkness. "Took you long enough. I've been waiting for you to rouse yourself."

That voice. The last thing she remembered was watching the beetles as they emerged. Then she had heard that voice. She recalled it now, the man stepping into the circle of light cast by her headlamp. His outstretched arms, his splayed hands. "It's okay . . ." he'd said. "I didn't mean to spook you. . . ."

Now her head pounded, and her legs ached from being bunched beneath her. *Waiting,* he'd said. How long had she been out? She tasted cloth, stretched tight across her mouth. Would anyone hear if she screamed?

"I've been so patient. Since our unexpected meeting, I've been waiting for you to wake up. Sleepyhead."

Chenoa scrabbled away from the sound of his voice.

She heard a click, and the space illuminated. She was in a room, of sorts, with camping supplies. It looked, and smelled, like it was underground. She traced the ceiling, a faint line of moisture seeping to its surface, and thought of the caves she'd marked on her map. Manitou, where porous substrate had been worn down by centuries of dripping spring water and hollowed into a series of caves that ran like veins through the wilderness area. If she was in the Manitou caves, she was still on the reserve, maybe within ten or fifteen miles of her camper van. But who would know to come look for her?

"It's a pleasure to formally meet you," said the voice. "Welcome to my home away from home."

CHAPTER FORTY-SEVEN

The snow continued to fall. Large flakes built up along the bottom of the ravine, layering over ice, making each step treacherous.

But Deer Woman propelled Starr forward.

I've really fucked up now, Starr thought. *I must be dead, and maybe this is the spirit world.*

She squared her shoulders against the wind, the pain. She was not going to leave this world fully without finding the girl. *Find the girl.* It echoed in her head with every footfall that crunched on the frozen shale.

Deer Woman was a dark shape ahead and to her right, where the walls of the ravine shifted to some new direction Starr couldn't identify in the moonlight. Instinct kept her reaching for her gun; then she remembered she no longer had it. She was cycling through her own personal version of hell.

Starr continued her slow and aching progress. Steady, measured. She was living out a predetermined ending, a life heading toward this destination all along. Starr could see it clearly now, the trajectory that had brought her here.

She concentrated on each step. And when she looked up again, the antlers were gone.

Deer Woman was gone.

Maybe she'd only imagined her. It was getting harder and harder to know what was real; it had been since the moment she set foot on the rez.

She thought she heard voices on the wind that whipped and tore at her ears. Low and certain. Had she found Holder? Was she hearing Chenoa negotiating for mercy?

Starr was half-frozen. When had she fallen into this crevice, lost her gun, lost her mind?

Deer Woman appeared before her once again, and Starr reached out a slow hand to caress the fur of her cheek. Her hand went right through, touched the coarse surface of rock behind where Deer Woman stood. Starr peered more closely, just to the left of her hand, and into the blackest pitch she'd ever seen. Darker, somehow, than the night that had closed in around her.

A cave, she realized. She was standing at an opening in the rock wall. Where did she know this from? Red lines, ranging apart and knotting together, looping into circles and cascading across paper, swam through her mind. Red. Women with raven hair, their mouths blocked with red handprints. Red. Beetles that raised their young.

Manitou.

Deer Woman had led her to the spot circled on Chenoa's map, to the final place where Chenoa planned to look for a beetle colony, to the woman determined to preserve them for the future. Would Starr be able to preserve her?

The knife. She carried a knife in her boot. Starr caught the edge of her glove between her teeth and pulled it off her freezing hand so she could feel for the folded blade. The voices from inside the cave were becoming clearer, closer. She got low, put her weight on her haunches, ignoring the burning in her ankle. She listened, trying to gauge the distance. No telling how deep the cave might be. She might be dead, but that didn't mean she couldn't be smart about confronting Holder. For the girl's sake.

After several shivering minutes, Starr could not make out what the voices were saying, could not tell whose they were.

She put a hand down for balance, concentrating on the snatches of conversation she could pull from the wind. She inched closer.

"Sherry Ann, oh, Sherry Ann," came a man's voice in an oddly lilting singsong. "When I met you at the creek bonfire, I knew you were the one. But now I have a new love. See this?"

Silence.

"Do you see this?" the man screamed. Then he laughed. "Oh my my, you can't really answer me now, can you? Here. Let me loosen that naughty ol' gag in your mouth, poor dear."

Starr heard muffled, panicked sounds, then a woman's voice.

"Please, just let me go. I won't say anything. Please."

"Pay attention! What is this?"

"I don't know. A plastic baggie?"

"And? What's in it?"

"I don't know. Powder?"

"Stupid girl. This white soil is how I protect myself from their spirits when I'm done. I fill their mouths with this, which I gather right here, in this very cave."

There was the stamping of hooves behind Starr, a warning. She tried to rise and felt the hot burn of a blow to the head.

CHAPTER FORTY-EIGHT

I hate everything about you. Why do I love you?" It was an old, angry song and it played on the Bronco's radio as Starr . . .

No, that's not right at all, Starr thought. I'm not driving.

Where was she? She forced her eyes open, hoping the spinning would stop, but pain overtook her thoughts instead. She was fucked over, fucked in the head. Ooh, her head. It ached like a motherfucker. Where was she, again? "Today seems like a good day to burn a bridge or two." New song, same anger.

"My oh my, what a time I'm having! And just think, we're in here warm and cozy while out there . . ."

The man's voice again. Who? Starr wondered. She tried to get up, but the spinning was too intense. And her hands. She couldn't move them from behind her back. She breathed in deeply to quell the panic.

"Out there, I'll make sure no one will ever find you."

"For crying out loud, it's the middle of the night. Can you put the crazy in park for a minute?" Starr heard a second man's voice. This one she knew: Holder's.

"I saved your bacon," Holder went on. "You're just lucky I found that marshal out there, 'bout to come in and bust your ass. I think the words you're lookin' for are *thank you.*"

"You believe in fate?" said the other man. "The odds that we'd be tracking this same girl, they've got to be . . ."

A deep laugh echoed around the dark space, and Starr heard the crunch of footfalls on grit as a pair of cowboy boots emerged from the shadows. "Astronomical," Holder said. "Seems like, anyway. But that's just small-town luck; that's just everybody's paths crossing again and again." He squatted. "Like you and me being on the same side of this oil deal, me making sure the access roads are built on my land and that Blackstream Oil promises enough money to keep those Indians from asking too many questions. And you . . . I'm guessing there's no way you want an oil camp coming anywhere near your . . . recreational activities. Must have really stuck in your craw to help the mayor."

Starr squinted against the dizziness. Holder's back was toward her. She still couldn't see the man Holder had been talking to, but she could hear him humming contentedly.

"Well, Little Miss College Girl, you thought it would be so easy, didn't you?" Holder said.

Starr's entire body jerked into alertness. *College* . . . He had to mean Chenoa. Where was Chenoa? She'd been following Chenoa. . . . Her head set to spinning again and forced her eyes closed.

Holder let out a mocking laugh, hard-edged. "Hell, ain't nothing easy around here. I'm living proof of that. The 1980s—you don't remember those, do you? They were tough on farmers. Called it the 'farm crisis,' banks calling in loans, families torn from their livelihoods. And you know what was behind it?" He didn't wait for an answer. "Oil. Yep, the price of Oklahoma's black gold plummeted; then savings and loans failed; then banks seized land, equipment, whole herds of cattle."

Holder stood and started to pace, the low stone ceiling curving his lanky frame into a question mark.

"Now I'm making it right." He leaned down, talking into the shadows. "Get it? Nobody is gonna know a thing about those beetles you found. There is a hell of a lot more at stake here than endangered bugs. More than you could ever imagine, little girl."

"I didn't know, I promise. I really didn't. We can just forget about all of it. I'll destroy my research. Never speak of it again."

Starr listened to the woman she now knew was Chenoa and she waited for the revolutions to slow. She squinted until her eyes adjusted to the light of the lantern that cast shadows against the rock walls of the cave. She could feel the aching in her hands and feet, the cold leaching into every cell.

"Beetles," said the man in the shadows, bemused. "If I'd only known. They're endangered, you say?"

"Rare enough to bring in the feds," Holder said. "That happens, and they'll seize the land for a preserve. Huge fines for disturbing habitat. A fucking mess."

"The beetles would have stopped it all?" the other man said. Starr could hear the slap of his palms on his knees. "No construction crews? No oil workers? I could leave Loxie where she is? It would have been perfect."

"Perfect?" Holder said, turning sharply. "The beetles would have wrecked it all."

"Au contraire," the man said. "I have a big secret buried out here—which, by the way, I came to dig up. And then I found this girl. Can you believe my luck? She was right here, in the dark, right outside my cave like she was meant for me. I couldn't help myself."

"You didn't know about the beetles?"

"Not until now." The man laughed. "Isn't it ironic? If I'd left her alone, I guess she could have saved me a lot of work."

There was a long silence between the men. Holder removed his cap, rubbed a palm over his hair and let out a long breath.

And Bernard stepped into the light.

CHAPTER FORTY-NINE

Bernard, Starr thought, recalling in a flash the tribal meeting at which he'd presented, and her brief meeting with him in city hall. And afterward, when she'd seen him at the library.

Bernard was responsible for Chenoa being held captive in this cave? Starr tried to notch all the pieces into place. Bernard had taken Chenoa. If he hadn't, Holder would have.

The men began talking again, but Starr didn't care. *Chenoa.* Starr could make out the shape of her now, huddled along the same stone wall of the cave. *I'm here.* She wanted to comfort Chenoa, to let her know she would take her out of here, take her away from this place, these men, this terrifying moment. The most important thing—the *only* thing—was that Chenoa was alive. Not twice gone, like the other rez girls. Like Quinn.

Starr shifted her back against the stone and inched closer to Chenoa, counting on the argument that was building between Holder and Bernard to distract them. Chenoa was subdued, her body listing away from Starr. She'd carry her out of here if she needed to, but first she had to get her bearings. Make a plan.

Starr looked around. On the opposite wall was a weak semi-circle of light from a lantern that hung on a hook jutting from the rock. The ceiling was low, she thought, and she felt the panic of tight spaces. Antlers were strewn here and there, casting strange shadows. Wooden crates were stacked in a tower near the lantern, a silk scarf spilling out of one, and on the floor of the cave below it there was a woman's boot.

"You in this with the mayor?" Holder said. "I know you helped her present the drilling agreement, that you were—how did she put it?—the logistics guy, the finance guy."

"True, so true," Bernard said. "But I'm in this for myself. What I had, see, was access. To budget information. Information that could come in handy to, for example, stop a project like this. Problem was that it came together faster than I expected, and what I needed was time. Time to reveal the mayor's financial crimes so I could continue with my hobbies. I'm quite a mineralogist."

Starr watched Bernard's hands reach into the light, where he grabbed a metal coffee can, peeled back its plastic lid and pushed his fingers into it. He let a handful of white chalky soil fall from his hand into the can, a puff of dust churning above it.

"How well do you know the mayor?" Bernard said, and when Holder didn't answer, he shrugged and kept going. "I see. Not as well as you probably think. Hired you to smooth the way, did she? Keep this girl from sharing news of these endangered whatever they are. No matter now. I've just made public the proof that she's been embezzling funds from the city. Can't have her digging up my past. You can see my history for yourself, there in the crate. The one on top."

Holder reached into the box, then held up a stack of Polaroids. He shuffled through them, winced and dropped them. "Well, how 'bout that?" he said. "These pictures. They your doin'?"

"Well, a man can have more than one hobby. And now"—he motioned toward Chenoa—"you and I have a secret."

Starr shuddered, knowing too well what the images must be. She turned her attention to Chenoa. Whatever had happened before Starr arrived, at least Chenoa was alive. She could see Chenoa's tears sparkle in the lantern light.

Starr wanted to sprout antlers, feel them tear through her scalp, rise out of her tangled hair. She wanted to turn her feet into hooves, turn her life into one final strike of vengeance. But there she stayed. Able to do nothing.

In the end, it was her fault, wasn't it? Her failings, her daughter dead and gone. And the one thing she'd never told anyone about that night.

Starr had told Quinn to go. Screamed it at her, in fact.

They'd fought that night, in the hours before Quinn's murder, cabinets slamming in the kitchen, Quinn relentless with her pushing. Starr had hung tight for so long, such an exhaustingly long time, but it was just her alone to withstand the constant buffeting of rules and wants and requests and demands and slights and sass. It had been an achingly arduous day; she'd come off a seventy-two-hour investigation that hadn't amounted to much, despite all her efforts. And still she had to go back to the station. The victim's family was coming in . . . the family . . . anxious for answers and she had none. She knew she wouldn't have any, no matter how well she followed every thread.

And here was Quinn, a volley of demands. In the end Starr had told her to go, when what Quinn needed was the demand that she stay. Instantly Starr regretted it, but she'd been so vigilant for the girl's entire life. The bicycle helmets, the seat belts, the stranger warnings; every little thing she'd watched and managed; everything she'd cajoled and commanded the girl to do for her own safety; the endless calls and texts to other parents to confirm plans.

In the end, just that one time, she'd told her: *Go*.

Starr's shoulders wracked with sudden pain, a seizure of sobs without sound, her face frozen in horror at her own shortcomings. Who did she think she was, that she could come out here and save this girl? She was angry. She wanted justice for fucking once. But she wasn't Deer Woman. As much as she had wanted to be, it was something out of reach.

She knew the grief had turned her mean. There was a snake inside her, its lean, taut muscles curling around her organs, gripping her heart and squeezing her lungs. She could feel fangs erupting through her gums, knew that if she opened her mouth wide her jaw would unhinge and she could sink her teeth into flesh and swallow someone whole. What was she without a child, without her child? She was carrying a betrayal heavy as a life she couldn't lay down.

"Knew I'd never stop," Starr heard Bernard say. "Knew it would get the best of me someday, even though I was careful. Buried the first one out here. I was still in high school. Did the next one in college. A few after that. And now her."

Rage warmed Starr like a fire that had been lit a long time ago. The old frustration came back. A thousand interruptions. A hundred small cuts. A knife in the sternum. An arrow in the back. A scream in her mind. It built until she was the frustration itself, a whirling dervish with a maw like a cave at high tide, pulling in all the water and everything that came with it—boats, shells, sailors—and pummeling it all to fine grains of white sand, so violent the color changed into one sparkling hue.

CHAPTER FIFTY

✳

There were a lot of things Bernard had planned to do, but this had become a two-birds, one-stone situation. He'd planned to move Loxie's body from where he'd buried her in a natural divot he'd covered with soil and rock so many years ago, but then he'd discovered a delightful bonus. A real live girl. Alone. In the dark. Near the mouth of his cave.

Still, he couldn't believe the wasted effort. If only he'd come across Chenoa and been able to leave her alone, then he could have figured out what she was up to, let her take the evidence of the endangered beetles with her; she could have stopped the project for him. He wouldn't have had to spend so much time uncovering the mayor's financial fraud. He wouldn't have needed to release the budget files to Mitzie so she could tell everyone what the mayor was hiding. He'd been looking forward to seeing the mayor led away in handcuffs before Blackstream could drill the first well.

It was all coalescing in an unavoidable way, his past and his future. Sure, Holder was a complication, and the marshal was a problem he'd need to solve.

"Let her go," Starr said, "and I won't kill you."

"Yeah, okay. C'mon, then. Activate your superpowers. Get me." Bernard laughed as he walked closer to the marshal. "You think you know what I am? You don't." He wheeled around in the cavern, balancing on one foot, swinging his arms wide. He thought of Loxie with the long dark hair. He'd had a few classes with her, even though he was a senior to her sophomore. She was smart, accelerated. Different. "The first one was an accident."

"Her name was Loxie," Starr said. "She had a big smile and she liked to wear small starfish earrings. She read books about the ocean. She dreamed of seeing it for the first time. Her father said it was the only thing she wanted for graduation. Is that where you met? High school?"

Bernard stilled. Even Holder, pacing near the entrance of the cave, stopped to listen.

"I tried to help her," said Bernard, his voice almost reverent. "It was after a JV football game."

Through the windshield of his old car, he'd watched Loxie argue with her boyfriend and then storm away, so he'd pulled up beside her to issue an invitation over the rough idle of the engine.

"I didn't think she should try to walk home, so I offered her a ride."

He'd wanted to bring her here, to this underground haven, his own personal refuge where he'd spent hours going over his rock collection—he'd always liked to collect things.

"She broke up with him right there in the parking lot, you know? So she gets in. But she doesn't want to go home yet. She couldn't give a damn who she's with or how late she stays out.

We have to stop at Junior's, she says, but then she tells me to stay in the car. I would've done anything she wanted me to, just to be with her, so I wait until she comes back. Then we drive around the rez, go to the creek to drink the beer she's gotten from Junior. She's cold, and I give her my coat. I want to show her something, a surprise."

Only now he was missing curfew and Mother was going to be worried. He hoped this would be worth it, showing her the cave, his rock-and-mineral collection. And he hoped that she could keep a secret. He was trespassing, after all.

"So I make her walk with me, but when we are almost here, she stops. Yells at me to take her home, that she's too cold, that it's too late."

When Loxie spit at him it landed like a slap, hot and wet on his face.

"Now she's looking at me with those eyes and I know she's going to tell. She is going to ruin everything. High school graduation. College. My life. Everything I wanted. I don't remember much after that."

Except that this first death wasn't an accident, exactly. It just happened so quickly. He'd wanted time with her, but he went too far.

"It was so quiet."

"What was?"

"Afterward, I mean."

And during. After the first shot of pain, after she'd moved past the pure animal terror, Loxie didn't cry. She didn't scream. She looked into his eyes.

"It was like nothing else I'd ever known."

He thought of all the girls. Girls like Loxie, who were too good to give him their time, to offer their undivided attention. Until he made them. He remembered the pain as he gathered handful after handful of white chalk from beneath Loxie and filled her mouth with it; they were both keeping secrets now.

"I buried her right out there." He would visit her, he thought. Yes. On college breaks and, later, when he took vacations from his lucrative job.

"You're a monster."

"Maybe," Bernard said slowly. "Maybe I am."

Chenoa whimpered. Bernard's head jerked toward her and he retreated to the darkness. He liked to watch.

"Quiet," he said in a singsong voice. "Quiet, or I'll make you quiet."

The marshal stirred, in a rage of pent-up energy, and he was relieved to see that her ties held.

"Right out there," Bernard said again, "so I could come back to her, whenever I wanted."

But he hadn't come back. At first he'd been scared, plagued by a fear that his life would dissolve around him. He'd kept his head down. Behaved. Until the rotating sickness thrummed within him, whirling from fascination to fear and back again. New girls crowded into his mind, pressing him forward, urging him to leave Loxie behind.

"The oil project threatened everything." He couldn't let them rip a roadway right through the wilderness area. Right through Loxie's final resting place.

"You stupid bastard," Starr said, laughing. "She's not out there."

"What did you say?" He eyed Holder as he spoke. They both turned to Starr.

"I said, she's not out there. Her body's been in a BIA evidence locker for years."

"Shut. Up!" Bernard roared.

She wasn't there? What did it matter? It was Loxie who had changed him, and now he was someone new. Jobs and oil towns, public funds and perfect performance. How could any of that matter anymore? This was what he lived for, what everything was building toward.

In three steps he was upon Starr, his fists raining against her body.

CHAPTER FIFTY-ONE

✺

Outside in the cut that ran through the reservation's wilderness area, snow fell and a gibbous moon began to cast a strange light over the landscape. Inside the cave, Chenoa had been trying to get a better look at the woman hunched next to her.

"Bet this is strange, huh?" said Bernard as he sat down beside Chenoa. After a few seconds, he reached over and put his hand under her chin to make her look at him. She gagged at the feel of his hand, clammy in the frigid cave, and shrank away from him. He was so close she could smell his sour breath.

Holder pointed to Bernard and addressed Starr, who was slipping in and out of lucidity. "Hell, Marshal, you've been here a whole week. Think you would have found him out eventually? Enough girls go missing, even you could piece this together, I'll bet."

Bernard leaned into Chenoa, peering around her at the marshal, then at Holder.

"Don't say anything," said Holder before Bernard had a chance to speak. "Let me think."

"You bet, big guy," Bernard said, and then he whispered in Chenoa's ear, "Give us a chance to get to know each other."

Maybe Holder would be her way out, Chenoa thought. Maybe he was the better of the two men. Maybe greedy was better than psychotic. Maybe the marshal would have helped, but it sure didn't look like she could now. Chenoa scooted along the stone wall, away from Bernard and closer to the marshal, whose head had dropped onto her chest.

"So . . . college, huh?" said Bernard. "I did that. College, I mean. Everything that made me weird here was interesting there. This girl down the hall from me, she thought I was so fascinating." Bernard closed the distance between himself and Chenoa and leaned on her shoulder, his musty hair tickling her nose. "I was a spider calling to a fly, *Come in, come in.* She knew what she was doing, egged me on until I wrapped my hands around her neck. I still think of her dark hair dangling over the side of the mattress. Do you know what it's like to watch a soul leave a body?"

Chenoa didn't move, though the weight of his head on her shoulder made her want to vomit. She thought of the story her grandmother had told about how to survive the brutality of men: *It feels wrong to accept your circumstances, but you must. Otherwise you'll be paralyzed with shock. Your survival will depend on your ability to fight or flee, or both. You do whatever it takes.* Her grandmother had watched the mask of the Deer Woman as she spoke, curling her fingers under until her hands looked remarkably like hooves.

"It's not sad," Bernard continued, "not at all. It's beautiful, better than a drug. The only way I could get some relief was to do it again. So I did. There have been so many now. One just last week, in fact, not too far from here. There is nothing like being able to relax after the girls have gone quiet. That's the best part, the *after*. I didn't know that with Loxie; I was too scared of what I'd done."

Bernard took his head off her shoulder and turned his mouth toward her, close enough to brush his lips across her cheek. She wanted to bash his skull, gore his belly, kick his teeth in. She steadied her breathing over the thumping of her heart. She'd find a way out.

Holder, who had been steadily pacing and muttering, stopped to stare at Bernard, mouth agape.

"Get outta town," Holder said, training his eyes on Bernard. "That dead girl by the creek was you? Damn, boy. You get around."

Starr, who had come to, listened intently. She could feel Chenoa beside her, practically vibrating with fear or anger or white-hot hatred. *Good.* Whatever the girl felt, it was fuel.

Beside the crates, the dull gleam of a bent golf club caught Starr's eye. Holder reached for it, as if her thoughts had sent him to it. He regarded the club for a moment, then held it in a putting stance.

"You golf?" Holder took a few strokes with the club.

"Stole that from the mayor. Thought I might use it to make her look guilty, sabotage the road construction before Blackstream started to drill out here." Bernard stood and walked to Holder. "Had it the night I presented the city's offer to the tribal council. Didn't think I would use it yet, but when I left the community building the parking lot was still crowded with people watching the fight, so I drove around the rez. A little celebration, if you will. Somehow, I found myself alone at Junior's—like I'd gotten there on autopilot—and I suddenly knew exactly what I needed. I had to go into the house. Surely it was still there, that necklace Loxie had woven and hung on the gun rack, but the dog would not shut up. And I was running out of time. I didn't want to be caught out there when Junior came back. The racket that dog made, so ridiculous. Surely by now you know how I like things quiet."

Bernard shrugged and bent over one of the wooden crates, looking for something.

"Used it on the girl next, by the creek. That was twofold. It scratched that itch for me, and then I thought I'd plant the murder weapon later. You know, return it to the mayor, where it belonged. It might not stick, sure, but it could be enough to halt the project while I waited for word of her embezzlement to get around."

Starr considered the slender wounds made on Sherry Ann's skull. Junior's Yella dog, beaten to death. Loxie. Now Chenoa. All the others Bernard had harmed or would harm.

Holder held the club at arm's length, disgusted.

"Hell's bells. Seeing as how you don't want the Blackstream Oil deal to come together, I think we're gonna have a problem." Holder shook his head and laughed. "You don't know what I've done to get this far. And I gotta tell you, son, you ain't stopping this roadway." He stood behind Bernard, holding the golf club. Bernard was pulling something from a crate. "And I'm about to be the hero."

Holder didn't look like he played golf, but the swing he leveled at Bernard's head would have sent a ball two hundred yards—if it had made contact. Instead, Bernard turned as Holder put the golf club in motion, and it hit the crate instead. The gun Bernard had been reaching for in the crate went skittering across stone and slid out of the mouth of the cave.

Chenoa felt an ancient power course like static across her skin, like when the quality of air suddenly changed, grew heavy or light, or when the clouds, whisked away by wind, were replaced by a too-bright sky. It was electric. She'd been built for this moment all along.

CHAPTER FIFTY-TWO

✸

Starr's head still throbbed from the blows Bernard had delivered. A new line of blood made its way through her hair and onto her neck. Before the attack, what had she been doing? The knife in her boot. Was it still there? Starr drew her feet under her, closer to her hands.

She could hear Holder and Bernard outside the cave, their voices raised. It sounded like they were scrabbling over rocks, both searching for the gun. She might have time.

"*We* ain't going to do nothing!" Holder shouted. "You're the answer to my problem here. I kill you because you killed them. Self-defense. That's what I'll tell the cops, and—how 'bout that?— my problems with those damn beetles, with the mayor, with these two gals, all of it will be solved."

Starr cranked her shoulder, grimaced at the pain and used two fingers to pull the knife from her boot, where it clattered uselessly to the stone floor. She leaned and strained, and finally felt her fingers close around steel. She pulled it to her and used both hands to work open the blade.

"'The melancholy moonlight, sweet and lone, / that makes to dream the birds upon the tree,'" came Bernard's lyrical reply, "'and in their polished basins of white stone, / the fountains tall to sob with ecstasy.' Paul Verlaine. You know—French poet?"

Starr could hear Holder say something, unclear even though the night had grown still.

Starr locked eyes with Chenoa. She'd seen the blade. Chenoa scooted closer to Starr, who worked the blade through the tie on Chenoa's wrists.

"Now take the knife. Do mine." Starr shook her wrists, and in a moment the knife was out of her hand. Chenoa sawed through the ties on her own ankles instead.

"Okay," Starr said. "Okay. That's fine. Now my wrists." She could be patient. Chenoa was probably in shock, and Starr knew from her experiences with crime victims that panic made it nearly impossible for them to follow complicated directions. "Now my wrists. Cut through the ties on my wrists."

Starr willed herself to stay calm, meter out simple instructions.

"Chenoa," she said. "Take the knife. And cut the ties on my wrists."

Starr watched as Chenoa held the knife in one hand and massaged her blood-starved feet.

Over the roar of blood in her ears Starr could hear Bernard outside the cave, and a new sound: the knife clattering onto the cave floor beside her. Chenoa was gone.

"Fuck," Starr said, throwing her body toward the knife and wrangling it into her hands. The blade sliced her fingers, which became slick with blood, making it difficult to work the knife up and across her palm. Once she felt the solid surface of the handle, Starr pressed the sharp end against the ties binding her hands.

Outside, Holder's voice was a running stream of promises

punctuated by threats. Starr ignored him entirely, her fingers cramping on the bloody grip of the knife. Finally, her wrists sprang free.

Starr wiped her wet hands on her pants and ripped at her ankle ties, then bent low to work the blood back into her legs. When she stood, vertigo set in and she stumbled, cursing at the way her body let her down. She looked toward the exit, where Chenoa had gone, where she had followed Bernard and Holder. She had to get to Chenoa before—

A muzzle flash singed her vision, instantly blinding her in the low light of the cave. The report followed, the sound cracking in her ears. Starr clutched at her head and felt her way out of the cave, her eyes still sightless.

The nearby sound of something large clambering over the rocks that lined the bottom of the ravine made her senses come alive. Starr moved quickly toward the sound, but the slick and uneven surface of the rocks sent her spilling onto them, the knife slipping from her hand.

She froze when she heard the unmistakable click of a gun. But no shot. Silence. She allowed herself a moment of pure relief. The gun had jammed. She scrambled to her feet, launching forward to find anything solid to put between her body and the shooter.

She was too late. Someone knocked Starr to the substrate. Bernard. And he had something sharp. Her knife.

Starr tried to deflect Bernard's swinging hands and the biting blade by pulling her knees up to her belly and bracing them under her attacker. She could feel the knife rake across her shins, and hoped she had created enough distance to give her a split second to grab his wrists and stop the onslaught of strikes.

For a moment their faces were so close that they locked eyes in the light of the moon. Bernard ran the blade into her left side, again and again.

Then he stopped, stood and calmly walked back toward the mouth of the cave.

Starr pressed the damaged fingers of her right hand to the sting under her left armpit, where she knew the blade had found its mark. *I'll be okay,* she thought, *once I find Chenoa.* Starr stood as best she could, then faltered. She could hear the hollow clank of hoof on stone. She leaned on the rock wall, its pearly face soaking in moonlight.

There was a new, keen-edged pain in her left side, above her beltline, only now reaching her consciousness. She touched the wound with her hand. As soon as she felt the slick liquid, viscous like motor oil, she knew she was in trouble.

CHAPTER FIFTY-THREE

TUESDAY

Starr was trapped in a nightmare—in a small, dark space where she couldn't move her arms. She launched herself upright but was stopped by a surface that was hard and damp. It felt like she was underground.

"Quinn," Starr said, the word a small hope in the darkness.

"Whoa, whoa, stay down," Chenoa said. "You're hurt."

"Get me out, get me out," Starr said, low and distinct to keep the fear at bay. *Don't panic,* she thought. *Find Quinn.* "Get me out."

"You stay in here. We have to stay warm," Chenoa said. "I'm trying to start a fire. To keep us . . ."

Starr began pulling herself toward the light of an opening by pressing the heels of her boots on the ground. It was a strategy of desperate inches. Her side burned, and the heat rose each time she moved.

"Wait," Chenoa said. "I've about got it."

The dim interior brightened. *A cave,* Starr thought, *not a grave.* It all came rushing back to her, the gunshot, the knife fight, Chenoa leaving her in the cave . . . Bernard. He was still out there, a threat.

"Okay, that should do it, and then we'll . . ." Chenoa stopped talking. Starr was still working her body toward the mouth of the cave.

"Fine," Chenoa said, exasperated. "Have it your way."

Starr felt hands on her ankles and the scratch of gravel on her back as Chenoa pulled her outside. *Thank God.* Outside.

Starr slouched against a cold rock wall beside the cave's opening, a fire crackling pleasantly inside, the heat beginning to radiate from the mouth of the cave. She fought to keep her eyes open. In the ravine, the first light of dawn illuminated a body— Holder's. That meant she still had to watch for Bernard, to stay vigilant.

Looking back into the cave she'd just escaped, Starr could see that the light would never fully reach into its depths.

Chenoa's form took shape as Starr's eyes adjusted to the lifting of the darkness, but the idiocy of her own sludgy mind held her down.

Chenoa was here. Starr had found her.

But Quinn? Still gone.

The weight of her confusion made her want to weep. A shiny black beetle with orange-red bands on its back scurried along the rocks at Starr's feet, its movements quick and purposeful.

"See those antennae?" Chenoa said, crouching next to Starr, pointing to the beetle and then pulling a thick coat around herself.

Where had she gotten that coat? Starr wondered. Had Bernard been wearing it?

It had stopped snowing sometime during the night, and every surface around them sparkled as if the spirits had strewn glitter.

"Those antennae"—Chenoa pointed to the beetle again— "contain special chemical receptors to detect dead meat. They're so sensitive that they can detect a carcass from a long distance, and very quickly—usually within an hour of the animal's death."

The beetle crawled up Starr's boot and onto the leg of her uniform pants. Chenoa set a knife on Starr's lap. It was the one they'd used to free themselves, the one Bernard had attacked her with outside the cave, the one responsible for the red stain blooming on her left side.

"After I cut my ties with the knife," Chenoa said, "I saw red. I thought that was just a saying, but I'm not kidding. I literally saw red, I was so angry. I wasn't thinking about you at all when I left the cave. I was thinking about them, those men. Not just Bernard, but every man who's made women afraid to walk after dark or caused us to check the backseat of a car when we get in or had us looking over our shoulders. What right did they have to interrupt my life, any woman's life? They thought they could hurt me, hurt any woman they chose. I remembered what Grandmother told me, how to survive. I thought of Loxie, of every girl, every woman, whose life had ended at the hands of a man, whether she was dead and buried or just dead inside. What if every woman met violence with violence? What if we made sure the men who tried to harm us could never do it again, not to anyone . . . ?"

"There'd be a lot fewer men fucking around, that's what."

"I needed to stop them. Then . . ." She hesitated. "I saw Bernard shoot Holder." Starr looked at Holder's body.

"After the gunshot, I couldn't hear anything, couldn't see"— Chenoa pointed to another form, lifeless on the rocks, then looked down at her feet—"until my senses rushed back to me, but not just my senses, something larger than myself. Ancient. Everywhere. My head filled with the sound of hooves beating like drums."

Chenoa went silent. Starr felt her eyelids slipping down, down.

"I don't know how to describe it. No one will ever believe me, but I don't care. I know how it felt. The sound was inside me and all around me. Part of every rock, each tree, every cell, every fiber of my skin, my fur. I stomped and kicked, but it wasn't until . . ."

Chenoa looked at Starr for a long moment.

"It was the antlers," she said. "That's what took care of him."

"Justice," Starr said, and smiled grimly.

Starr looked again at the bodies, first at Holder's and then at the smaller one lying a few feet farther away. She couldn't tell it was Bernard's, but she was willing to take Chenoa's word for it. Bernard's head was a bloody mass, swollen beyond recognition, and beyond him, there was something else.

Starr's teeth began to chatter as she squinted into the distance. She wondered if this was the end, if she had crossed a barrier, if a veil had been lifted between worlds. She could clearly see the silhouette of a beautiful woman turned to the rising sun, her crown of antlers glorious and deadly.

"You were her," Starr said. From far away, she heard the slur in her speech. Had she said that aloud?

"What?"

"You'll always carry her with you," said Starr. "Don't you see? You'll be okay."

Starr curled her fingers around the handle of the knife in her lap as Chenoa settled beside her.

This young woman was smart. Once, Starr had known every little thing about a girl like that: how it felt to brush her hair, watch her pick onions out of every casserole, burrow into the tenderness of a hug.

Starr grieved—would always grieve—the promise of that girl's future. There were so many ways it could have turned out, and in her mind she'd traveled every one of them.

A string of pink drool slipped from Starr's mouth and onto the knife. It was difficult to control the bobbing of her head, the intense need to close her eyes. And what about her own future? Maybe if she'd been raised here, been part of the rez, part of an extended family tree whose broken branches remained inextricably tied to one another, she would know about caves, about ghosts, about half lives and how to cure them.

Chenoa made a small sound and shifted closer, and Starr could feel the memory of Quinn's warm frame pressing against her like a gift.

She thought of the old woman and of Odeina, of daughters lost and found, of Deer Woman. Cautious. Powerful. Imbued with the strength to avenge, whether by hoof or by old magic descended through the ages.

Starr and Chenoa stared at the bodies, heard in the distance a round of cries. Help had come for them.

"Put it all on me," Starr said to the girl. "The bodies. This is on me."

Starr wanted to pat Chenoa's hand, to pull her into a protective embrace. Instead, she used the last of her strength to fumble open the snap on the front pocket of her uniform shirt, then light an awkwardly bent joint. As the flame flashed and the paper burned, she watched a pool of crimson spread beside her, flowing from her body and onto the rocks that had seen a million lives, large and small, pass over them. The burying beetle marched on.

Maybe this was the place of her salvation.

Maybe she finally understood where she belonged in the world.

Half in. Half out. A stranger between nations.

EPILOGUE

Carrie Starr didn't have many visitors during her hospital stay—not when she was in that nearly pleasant state of suspension like a cloud above her pain, her problems; and not when the care transitioned to something worse: walking the halls, lifting her arm overhead, feeling the pain of muscle knitting itself back together all along her side. There was Minkey, who, summoned by Winnie, had ignored his termination and led a search team to Starr's location. And there was Byrd, of course, which was how she'd learned that the recovering mayor was putting the blame for her financial misdeeds and Chenoa's trauma on Holder and Bernard. Starr told him that one of the BIA cold cases labeled a Jane Doe had been his daughter—not missing but dead all those long years—and he rose from the bedside chair and left without saying a word. A pair of tight-lipped investigators sent by the BIA spent several long hours trying to draw details from Starr, which she made sure never to change. *Yes, it was me. No, Chenoa was only a victim here, nothing more.*

The administrative leave hung like a fog over everything she did: sleep, ask for pain meds, walk, move, think.

It was the thinking that got her, caused her the most trouble; ran like a current under her skin, worries wired directly into her brain. She was alive. And maybe she wasn't meant to be.

Death stalked her body, showed up like a knife in every electric twinge. Deer Woman walked her memories, traversed them like a game trail, some familiar, hidden route. Starr kept death and the Deer Woman at bay by concentrating on looking out the window like it was a film, some immersive performance that captured all her attention. But it was the birds, finally, that saved her.

Not that she'd ever paid attention to birds. Hadn't really given them a second thought. But the view from her bed was nothing but treetop and sky, the action nothing but flight. The witnesses to her slow recovery had wings.

When Starr left the hospital, wheeled by an aide over the bump of an industrial doormat and out into the world, the only thing she had that she wasn't wearing was *The Sibley Guide to Birds*. In the too-bright sky, a murmuration of *Sturnus vulgaris* shifted from shape to shape. "Starlings," she said, her voice sounding strange in her ears, like she was leaving as a different person.

The aide, who was kneeling in front of her, busy releasing the footrests of the wheelchair, looked skyward. "Pests," she said. "Farmers hate those things. Must be a feedlot over there."

She might as well have said to take the bus to Times Square and have lunch with the Dalai Lama. Starr had no idea what she meant.

"You know, cattle?" The aide stood and surveyed the cracked and pitted parking lot. "They feed up the steers, then send 'em to the processing plant. All them birds come along and eat dropped grain, pick through manure for it even, then poop everywhere. Real nuisance."

Thousands of black birds were changing direction as one, signing out a message Starr couldn't understand. So beautiful she might stand suddenly from this chair, throw off the chains she carried and run. *What it must feel like to be free,* she thought.

"All right, let me give you a hand here." The aide grabbed under her elbow, offering steady pressure to help her rise, and when she did, Starr felt all the heaviness of gravity. Not hers, not this earth's, but some other planet's gravity that would crush such a ridiculously fragile thing: the human body. "Got it? You're doing great. Just take a minute and make sure you're stable. There you go. That's the way."

Starr laid a hand on the aide's shoulder to stop her stream of encouragement but knew it would be taken as a sign of gratitude. She had woken to discover that her mask had slipped, that all the raw edges of her were exposed to air, and, inch by inch, she was pulling the mask back on. She would remember how to be a person. She would take on human form.

Starr thought of Chenoa, safe and back on campus, then pulled the keys from a pocket with her good arm, moving the side of her body that hadn't been shredded and forced to mend, and shook them in a wave as she walked away. She wasn't looking back.

"You don't have someone to drive you?"

She kept moving.

"Wait. You need someone to drive you."

Farther.

"But hospital policy . . ."

Key in lock, door cranking open, groan of broken bench seat. Then ignition. The old girl sputtered, fired. Starr leaned her forehead against the cracked vinyl of the steering wheel in relief. The

Ford Bronco, that BIA castoff, smelled of Febreze and weed and, as always, oily exhaust. *Byrd, thank God.* Byrd said he'd drop her service vehicle in the parking lot. She'd never had a horse, never even ridden one, but she thought of cowboys and the trusty steeds that offered them comfort on the dry Oklahoma plains.

Starr turned the Bronco toward the rez, toward Junior and Odeina, toward the old woman with the wild inside. Toward home.

"Better get out of here before they take me back in."

Beside Starr, at the far end of the bench seat, her daughter nodded.

"You better," Quinn said. "I'm sick of that place. Hospitals only make you sicker. Everybody knows that. I know that. And look at me. I'm already dead."

AUTHOR'S NOTE

Sometime in the 1970s, my parents received a call from an agency inquiring whether they would be interested in adopting a baby of Indigenous descent. A few hours later I became part of an extended family, and I spent the rest of my childhood on a working farm. I was welcomed by my dear parents, brothers, grandparents, aunts, uncles and cousins, and by the entirety of the Mennonite church we attended.

One of my earliest memories is of riding a horse with my father, a passion we would share for a lifetime. My mother made sure I had stacks of books by visiting the library every time she drove to town for supplies. I often read under a willow tree, with farm dogs panting contentedly beside me in the summer heat: endless books about horses, about gray wolves trotting across frozen landscapes, about sisters growing up in restrictive societies, about mysteries at sea, about dolphins and islands and about determined Indigenous women who made their own way.

My adoptive family never made a secret of how I'd joined them and they also ensured I was aware of my Indigenous heritage; it was beautiful to grow up with this openness. Later, as an adult, when I sought to learn more about my birth family, I realized there were some aspects of my history that might remain unknown to me.

While *Mask of the Deer Woman* is purely fictional, writing it allowed me to explore the what-ifs of my personal history. What if my birth family had a clearly established connection with an Indigenous community? How would this community receive me as an outsider, a stranger? Questions such as these prompted me to become an engaged listener, taking in the lived experiences of people who were born into and raised in Indigenous communities. My understanding continues to evolve as I respectfully learn more about a collective heritage haunted by a traumatic past.

Writing *Mask of the Deer Woman* was a cathartic process in which I also grappled with my fears as a woman whose confident daughters were launching their own lives into the Big, Wide World. What I have written in this book is in no way a reflection of them—or their decisions or experiences—either past or present. One of my daughters allowed me to borrow her name for a fictional character. Her generosity let me breathe life and love into a character who became the vessel for all the worst-case scenarios that existed only in my worried maternal mind.

Ultimately, this novel—and those novels to come—is a love letter to myself, to my daughters, to every woman. We are all children of the same mother in the end.

ACKNOWLEDGMENTS

The first thing I realized about writing this acknowledgments section is that it will inevitably be incomplete. There are so many people over the years who have influenced my life as a writer, and who have impacted this book, that I will never be able to thank them all in the way they deserve. Your insightful comments, thoughtful conversations and continual encouragement fill me with an appreciation that means these two words will never be enough: thank you.

My unmatched gratitude to the many talented people at Berkley and Penguin Random House, but especially to Tracy Bernstein and Carly James. For the rest of my life, I will remain grateful to you, and thankful for the talents you've shared with me and with the wider literary world. One of the greatest pleasures of my life has been the opportunity to work on this manuscript with you.

To my agent, Sharon Pelletier of Dystel, Goderich & Bourret LLC, for our great first discussion, and for becoming my intelligent and trusted guide. There are so many more books to come.

ACKNOWLEDGMENTS

To my husband, with whom I have lived many lives, I would choose you again. Every time. And I promise I won't ask you to read the next manuscript as many times as you read this one. Your enthusiasm for and encouragement of my writing career is unmatched—and so is my love for you.

To my daughters, half-wild and whip-smart women all, it began with you. Becoming your mother created in me love and fear, admiration and wonder, a complicated stratum that I will spend a lifetime mining for meaning.

To my sons-in-law. Thank you for becoming my sons too. And to my especially and delightfully clever grandchildren, with whom I continue to take in the world with wonder. To my parents-in-law, whom I consider to be my parents as well, I appreciate the gift of your love. For Annette, who left us too soon.

For Oakley, obviously. May we all have the confidence of a spoiled Shih Tzu who has turned into a Real Boy, which he "does and does not appreciate, You Lady."

To my parents, for teaching me the joy and work and determination of farm life. Saying "Thank you" seems wildly insufficient, and I hope you know I carry your love and support with me always.

For my dear and lifelong friend Erica, my trusted first reader, who knew this dream of mine would come true. For Ann, who has made such a difference in my life, thank you. You are both amazing and I know my life is better for having you in it.

For my birth mother, for sending me into the world with love.

To my Harvard writing group: Christine Boyer, Jennifer Byrd, Beth Killion, Eileen O'Neill-Connors. I'm grateful for our years together, for our weekly sessions and annual retreats. Your creativity is a joy to witness. You are the literary community of which dreams are made.

ACKNOWLEDGMENTS

To the Harvard Wellwrites—Emily Lord-Kambitsch, Maureen Rostad, Charles Saini, Ash Sparks and Rachael Quisel—and our critique group that emerged right at the time I needed it most.

To Bryan Brewer, my Harvard friend, a prolific and multifaceted writer. If you haven't read his books yet, you should. I'm so glad our families met that beautiful day on campus.

For my Harvard professors and advisers from the Extension School and beyond: Collier Brown, Talaya Adrienne Delaney, William Holinger, Daphne Kalotay, Katie B. Kohn, Elizabeth Sharp McKetta, Chris Mooney, Mary Sullivan Walsh, William Weitzel and many others, I only wish I could do it all over again. Thank you especially to Chris Mooney, an author to admire, whose early encouragement made an immeasurable difference.

Thank you to the board members of the 2020 Amy Kellogg Memorial Residency, for selecting me as an inaugural artist-in-residence, and to the late Susan Wesselowski, whose tomato bisque is still famous at Watermark Books & Café—a place you should definitely visit if you come to Wichita, Kansas.